The Rival's Obsession

The Black Ledger Billionaires

Rebekah Sinclair

This novel contains **mature themes, explicit content, and dark romance elements** that may be **disturbing or triggering** for some readers.

This book is **intended for adult audiences** and **reader discretion is strongly advised.** If any of these topics are sensitive for you, please proceed with caution.

- Sex Work / Escorting
- Sexual Power Dynamics & BDSM Undertones
- Toxic Relationships & Power Imbalances
- Obsession & Emotional Manipulation
- Stalking & Surveillance
- Physical Violence, and Threats
- Blackmail & Coercion
- Explicit Sexual Content (M/F, M/M, Voyeurism, Group)
- Derogatory / Degrading & Explicit Language

- Past Child Sexual Abuse (referenced)
- Past Sexual Assault (referenced)
- Past Attempted Suicide (referenced)
- Mental Illness & Dissociation (referenced)
- Parental Death / Loss (referenced)
- Implied Suicide by Firearm (off-page)

The Black Ledger

Welcome to The Black Ledger

An elite, highly exclusive escort service where billionaires strike discreet deals, and escorts set their own terms.

~ No complications.
~ No attachments.
~ Just business.

But desire is never that simple.

Here, control turns into obsession, rules are meant to be broken, and the one risk no one dares take—falling in love—may be the most dangerous deal of all.

Because at The Black Ledger, contracts are final...

But hearts were never meant to be part of the deal.

Each book is a **standalone** with interconnected characters. ***No cheating***, ***no cliffhangers***—just powerful men, the women who bring them to their knees, and spice that will leave you breathless.

Thank you for choosing The Black Ledger and we hope you enjoy your contract.

Lucian Vale

To Gnome—

My plotting therapist.
My lube logistics advisor.
My ride-or-die through
bi-awakenings, billionaire brawls,
and how many rim-jobs are too many?
(Spoiler: The limit does not exist.)

This unholy book wouldn't exist without you.

May your kink be specific,
your smut abundant,
and your lube always generously applied.

To the reader who thought their fantasies were confusing—

They're not. They're just real.

This is for the ones who wanted her and him.
Who craved more, even when the world told you to pick a side.

Now, you don't have to choose.
You can have everything.

Chapter 1
Dante

There are worse ways to end a day.

My cock down his throat.

Her pussy on my tongue.

And me, flat on my back with nothing to do but enjoy the view.

Vegas is still burning behind my eyes—exhausting convention, press scandal, and one very public punch that's already making headlines.

But right now?

Right now, she's using me to come, and he's swallowing me down like he doesn't care if he breathes again.

It's quiet here.

Wet. Warm.

Obedient.

Exactly how I like it.

And until morning, I don't give a single fuck about the empire I might lose—

as long as I get to come with one hand fisted in her hair and the other forcing him deeper.

My phone rings.

A very specific ring.

The one I set for my personal assistant.

Fuck.

Fourth time since the jet probably took off. I say probably because I wasn't on it.

I was supposed to be. Five hours of flying beside Grant Harrow—my business partner and all-around pain-in-the-ass—while he iced his busted lip and seethed in silence?

Yeah, no thanks.

Instead, I called the Black Ledger's Vegas office and requested something far more therapeutic.

Sam. Kris. A custom order in silk and sin.

And right now, Sam's pushing my cock to the back of his throat like he wants to live there.

I let the call go to voicemail.

His mouth sucks harder. His throat clenches around me, that warm, tight slide making my eyes roll back.

Goddamn.

My grip tightens on Kris's thighs, dragging her closer until she's trembling above me. My tongue circles her clit—slow, then fast, then brutal. Relentless.

She gasps—high and breathy—and grinds down like she can't get close enough.

Marble walls bounce every sound back at us. Her mewls. My low groan. The wet, slick sounds of her cunt on my tongue and Sam's mouth sucking my cock like it's a fucking reward.

I shift just enough to suck as I tongue her—tight, rhythmic, coaxing. She falls apart with a strangled cry, fingers threading through my hair and pulling as she rides it out, hips stuttering in that desperate, helpless way I love.

She tastes like luxury and power and everything I've earned.

Her orgasm ebbs in soft tremors across my tongue, thighs twitching around my head.

Perfect and spent.

My phone rings. Again.

This time, it's paired with the sharp ping of a text.

Frankie is a persistent little thing. I'll give her that.

I chuckle against Kris's thigh, licking up the last of her cum—slow, savoring every drop—while Sam settles back into his rhythm. Up, down, wet and eager.

Such a good fucking boy.

Kris lifts herself off me, just enough to check that I'm still breathing. Barely. Her lips curve in a lazy grin, and I seize the pause to turn the night in a new direction.

"Champagne," I say, voice rough. "Make it cold."

She rises without question, those long legs carrying her toward the minibar while I slide my fingers through Sam's hair.

He hums, deep and needy, and I lean up on one elbow to watch—really watch—his lips stretch around my cock.

So fucking pretty.

Spit slips from his mouth, sliding down my shaft.

It helps his hand glide with him, stroke for stroke.

Christ almighty.

Kris returns, slow and unhurried, a glass in one hand

and the bottle in the other. She sips, eyes locked on the show between my legs, licking a stray drop off her bottom lip like she's the one being satisfied.

Sam pauses, mouth parting, tongue barely out. He looks up at her with those deep brown eyes—pleading.

My cock twitches at the sight.

He's fucking beautiful when he begs.

Kris smiles—always generous—and tilts the bottle.

Champagne pours over her breast, golden and cold.

It rolls down her skin, catching on her nipple, then sliding right into Sam's waiting mouth as he laps it up like it's the only thing he's been allowed to taste all night.

Fuck.

I want to bend him over the nearest table and ruin him.

His mouth returns to my cock just as the chilled champagne hits the heated skin of my shaft, and I hiss—back arching off the bed.

"Shit."

The contrast is electric. Sharp and decadent.

Sam hums again, clearly pleased with himself.

And I decide—he's earned a reward.

I cup Sam's face with both hands, holding him steady as I thrust up into his mouth.

Slow at first. Then deeper. Harder.

"Yeah, take it," I murmur, watching the way his lips stretch around me, spit-slick and shining. "Just like that. Fucking perfect."

His throat tenses, face flushed red as he fights the urge to gag around my cock.

But he doesn't stop.

He's obedient and mine—for tonight.

I pull out, cock glistening, and run my thumb across his soaked bottom lip.

"Look at you," I praise, voice low. "Taking so much of me like you were made for it."

His eyes flutter, and I tug him up—pulling him into a kiss that starts with tongues, swirling and teasing, until our lips finally collide.

The moan we share is filthy and raw.

Behind us, the mattress dips—Kris shifting.

"Lie back," I say, barely pulling from Sam's mouth, still tasting him. "Head at the foot of the bed. Legs apart. You know how I want you."

She obeys without a word—always the picture of grace and filth.

I kiss Sam again—deeper, slower this time—before turning and crawling down Kris's body.

The angle's awkward, upside down, but I make it work.

My mouth latches to her breast, teeth catching her nipple while I squeeze the soft weight of her other tit in my palm.

She sighs, arching beneath me.

Sam moves behind me, his strong hand wrapping around my cock, gripping hard.

"Fuck," I hiss as he strokes, lips brushing my shoulder. His mouth follows the movement of his hand—kissing, teasing, leaving warmth and promise in his wake.

We're both standing now, side by side.

I turn to him, grip the back of his neck, and pull him into another kiss—rough and eager, heat flaring between us.

My hand finds his cock—thick and hard—and I stroke him as our mouths clash again.

"Lie on top of her," I growl, breaking the kiss just enough to speak against his lips. "Fuck her throat while you eat her pussy. I've got a feeling I'll be getting another—"

Rrring.

We both laugh—dark and breathless.

Of course.

I kiss him once more, then release him, trading the weight of his body for the chill of the champagne glass.

The fizz tickles my skin as I bring it to my lips—

then I swipe to answer.

"Frankie Lane!" I greet, too damn pleased with myself. "To what do I owe the pleasure?"

"You didn't get on the fucking jet."

I smirk, swirling the champagne in my glass with one hand while the other strokes lazily over my cock.

Across the room, Sam lowers himself over Kris—forearms braced on either side of her hips as he dives between her legs.

His mouth meets her pussy with focused hunger, and Kris arches off the bed with a sound that makes my cock twitch.

She doesn't waste time, either.

Her hand wraps around his length, guiding him to her mouth.

There's something poetic about it—her on her back,

throat full, moaning around him as he eats her like it's his last meal.

Filthy and fucking perfect.

Frankie's still talking.

"Punching your oldest friend. Becoming a trending topic for all the wrong reasons. And now? Skipping your flight home like some jilted prom queen?"

"Hmm," I hum, keeping my eyes on the show, hand working my cock—slow and steady. "I did promise myself a productive evening."

"Dante." Her voice cuts sharp, like a blade across silk.

I sigh, releasing my cock to snag a condom.

"Yes, Frankie?" I mutter around the wrapper as I rip off the corner with my teeth.

"You've got a charming little two a.m. flight now, courtesy of my ability to clean up your goddamn messes. You and Grant are expected in front of the board at eight a.m. sharp. In suits. With answers."

I glance at the wall clock.

Eleven-oh-two p.m.

My toys are booked until sunrise.

"Plenty of time," I murmur. "Tell the new jet I'll be fashionably late. Or fashionably satisfied."

Pinching the tip of the condom, I get it started over the head of my cock. Sam cuts his eyes—watching—before looking up at me, mouth still suctioned on Kris's pussy for dear life.

Yes, pretty boy. I'm about to fuck the shit out of you.

"Try fashionably employed," she snaps. "You miss this

meeting, they'll crucify both of you. And I'll hand them the nails myself."

My laugh is low, indulgent. "Noted."

I roll the condom down the rest of my shaft's length and stroke a few times, eyes fused on Sam.

"Anything else?" she deadpans.

"Yes, actually. I just had a lovely idea involving Sam, a mirror, and about three feet of silk."

"Dante—"

"Goodnight, Frankie."

I hang up before she can threaten my bloodline.

Downing the rest of the champagne, the glass clinks as I set it back down.

My gaze catches on the mirror across the room.

There I am—naked, cock hard, lips swollen from someone else's mouth, about to fuck away everything I don't want to feel.

Again.

Why do I always do this to myself?

I blink once.

Jaw tense and eyes narrowing at today's memory.

The words out of Grant's mouth—when he didn't know his mic was on.

"Dante's nothing but dead weight. Has been for years."

Yeah, fuck that.

This one's on Grant. His fault I'm here, spiraling in silk and moans instead of handling shit like a civilized business partner.

His fault I'm drowning what I should be dealing with— buried so deep in pleasure I forget how fucking empty I am.

But fuck it. That's tomorrow's problem.

Tonight?

Time to make the most of the next few hours.

And right now, it's Sam's turn.

"Lie back," I say, voice low but firm.

He obeys without hesitation, stretching out across the bed. Kris moves with a feline grace, straddling him in reverse—pussy poised just above his mouth, but her eyes on me.

She knows who's really in charge here.

One knee on the mattress, then the other, I move between Sam's legs. One hand wraps around my cock, the other around his. I stroke them both—slow, firm. His hips jerk in response, and Kris lowers onto his mouth with a satisfied sigh.

He moans. It vibrates through her.

"Has he been practicing?" I ask, eyes locked on Kris as I thumb the slick head of Sam's cock. "Like a good boy?"

She smiles, breath already coming fast. "He has. Every night this week."

"Mm," I hum, pleased. "Good."

Sam and Kris—they're the real deal. A couple. Devoted to each other in their love.

The Ledger doesn't usually allow emotional entanglements between Companions, but some pairs work so well, it's worth bending the rules.

They know each other's bodies like second nature.

And they know how to perform like fucking art.

Sam's been training. Working on his stamina. Trying to edge himself, strengthen control, learn how to orgasm without release—just tension and pleasure rolled tight without the crash.

It's impressive.

And useful in their line of work.

I stroke my cock tighter now, then guide it down between his cheeks, teasing his ass with the thick, leaking head.

He gasps against Kris's pussy, and she lets out a shuddering breath, already close.

"I want you to focus, Sam," I murmur, voice gravel and heat. "Here's what's going to happen . . ."

Kris begins to rock her hips—small, desperate motions. Riding his mouth like she needs it to breathe.

"You're going to make her come," I continue, watching the flush spread across her chest. "Then I'm going to fuck your ass. Deep. Hard."

Sam's throat vibrates with a moan. His fingers dig into her thighs.

"And when I do?" I grip his cock harder, fingers tightening. "You're going to be a good boy and hold it. No coming. Not unless I say."

Kris cries out, her hands flat on his chest as she grinds down harder.

He moans again, lost in her, and I fucking love it.

Because once she breaks, it's his turn.

And I'm going to make sure he feels it.

Kris comes hard.

A shudder, a cry, her body trembling above him as she rides it out.

Then she climbs off, legs shaking slightly, her mouth curved in a satisfied smile.

My turn.

I settle fully between his spread thighs, placing a kiss on the inside of his knee.

He props his hips up on a folded pillow, just enough to tilt his pelvis and give me a better angle—he's so fucking eager.

I slick my cock with lube—slow and deliberate. Watch his eyes follow every stroke.

Then I grip his thigh and press in.

His gasp is sharp—his chest rising with it.

I groan, low and guttural, as that tight heat stretches around me.

"Fuck, that's good," I mutter, my voice wrecked.

He clenches instinctively, and I still—one hand bracing on the mattress beside his head, the other firm on his thigh.

Our mouths drift together, not quite kissing yet, just close—breath mingling, heat radiating between us.

"So big," he whispers, voice trembling but full of desire. "Fuck, you feel so good, Dante."

I smile against his lips. "I know."

I start to move—slow, steady thrusts as I let him feel the full length of me.

We kiss then. Hot, open-mouthed. Messy.

His moans feed mine.

"Just like that," I murmur, lips brushing his. "Taking me so fucking well."

His legs wrap tighter around me as I build him higher.

I keep moving, thrusting deeper with each pass, watching his face as he starts to lose himself in it.

"You close, baby?" I breathe against his ear.

He nods. Desperate. Sweating. Eyes blown wide with need.

"You gonna hold it for me?" I ask, voice darker now. "Gonna be a good boy and feel it all without making a mess?"

He nods again, breath hitching. "Yes—yes, I'll try—"

"That's not good enough," I growl, looking down at his hard cock pressed between us. "You will."

I grip his hips and drag him closer—my other hand braced on the mattress, flanking his head now—as I drive into him hard.

Sucking on his full bottom lip, I nip him and tug.

His answer: unsatisfactory.

Each thrust forces a broken sound from his throat.

"Fucking gorgeous like this," I grit out. "Laid out and begging. Mouth open, cock twitching, hole so fucking tight it's like you're made for me."

He moans—loud, desperate.

"You don't come," I snarl, slamming into him harder. "Not till I say. You understand me?"

"Yes—Dante—yes—"

"Good."

My thrusts turn brutal. Controlled. Designed to destroy him in the best fucking way.

His eyes roll back, fingers digging into the sheets, and then—

He crests.

"Hold it," I growl, fucking him through it. "Squeeze. Don't let it go."

His body trembles violently beneath me, his lips parting in a ragged cry. His eyes flutter closed—just for a second.

"Eyes on me."

His gaze snaps back to mine, glassy and wide, barely hanging on—but he's doing it. He's not ejaculating while he rides the waves of his pleasure.

Good boy.

I keep thrusting—deep and hard—grinding against that spot that has him gasping like he's drowning in it.

And it keeps going.

Longer. Higher. The kind of orgasm that isn't cut short by release but stretches out—sharp and shimmering—cresting again and again like waves dragging him under.

"That's it," I murmur, voice thick with praise and hunger. "Just like that. My good fucking boy."

He moans louder, shaking now, and from across the room, Kris lets out a sharp whimper.

I glance over.

Her fingers are between her thighs—slick and glistening.

"Naughty girl," I call out, not stopping my thrusts. "Coming without permission."

She just moans in response, too wrecked by the scene to form words.

I slow my pace, easing Sam back down from the high. Letting him breathe again.

Every motion still deep. Still deliberate.

His hands clutch my arms like he needs the anchor.

I lower myself over him, our chests brushing.

His mouth finds mine again—hungry and grateful.

We kiss through the aftershocks—soft and deep this time.

And when I finally pull back—his lips swollen, eyes blown wide, chest heaving—I drag my knuckles down the side of his face and smirk.

"You were so fucking good for me," I murmur against his mouth. "And you're gonna take so much more tonight."

Chapter 2

It's eight ten a.m., and Dante still hasn't shown.

I shouldn't be surprised. In fact, I'd be more shocked if he had walked in on time, freshly pressed and pretending not to be the human disaster currently burning a hole through the company's reputation.

I've been pacing the hallway outside for the past twenty minutes, waiting for the inevitable—trying to keep my breathing steady while my phone does its best to destroy me.

The trending hashtag—#DeadWeightVegas—is a car crash I can't stop watching.

Every time I scroll, there's a new video. A different angle. A different slow-motion replay of the exact moment everything imploded.

Dante's fist. My jaw.

The mic still hot as the crowd gasped, every eye in that cavernous convention center turning on us.

We were supposed to be the keynote—the headliners for

the biggest architecture convention in the country. Months of planning, of PR, of perfectly controlled messaging—wiped out in twelve seconds of live humiliation.

I don't even remember saying it.

The words were meant for one person, offstage, off record. But somehow, the sound team caught it, crystal clear:

"Dante's nothing but dead weight. Has been for years."

The punch came less than thirty seconds later.

Now it's everywhere.

I tap a video—a TikTok this time. Someone slowed it down, added dramatic music, bold font that reads Corporate Breakup of the Year?

Christ.

I lower the phone and press my fingers to the bridge of my nose, trying to stave off the headache clawing at the back of my skull.

The board's waiting. No one's said it out loud, but we all know this is a reckoning.

And I already know how it ends.

What I don't know is how the hell I'm supposed to tell my father.

My phone buzzes again, a text lighting up the screen.

CORRINE: Deep breath. You've survived worse.

She nods at me from her seat at the table—subtle, supportive—like she's been my entire life, even when I didn't deserve it. None of that changed when she took the CFO position at the firm.

If anything, she's been more of a rock than ever before.

I nod once. She catches it, and her eyes meet mine for a beat—calm and steady—before leaving me alone with my thoughts and the slow churn of anxiety rising in my chest.

This isn't how the legacy was supposed to unfold.

Marchesi & Harrow was never just a firm. It was a dynasty.

Built by our fathers in the late eighties, it grew from a shared vision—sketched on bar napkins and blueprints—into the most respected architecture firm in Manhattan. Award-winning. Influential. A name that opened doors.

We were raised inside it.

Dante Marchesi and I were expected to inherit the empire.

The sons of visionaries.

The next generation.

When we were sixteen, everything shifted.

Dante's parents sent him to the UK—a boarding school outside London, followed by Cambridge.

I stayed in New York, immersed in the bones and breath of this city. Interned early. Shadowed my father. I knew every corridor of this firm before I was old enough to legally sign a contract.

When Dante came back, it was like someone had dropped a lion into a room of well-mannered wolves.

The boy I'd once known—my childhood best friend—had grown into something sharp-edged and impossible to predict.

He returned with charm that could dismantle a room, an ego that didn't ask for permission, and a disdain for authority that grated against everything I'd spent years learning to navigate.

But none of that mattered because the plan was already in motion.

We were hired straight out of college—two golden boys stepping into their fathers' shoes. Equal partners.

On paper, it should have worked.

But it's been chaos since day one.

Clashing visions. Competing egos. Personal history weaponized in every argument.

There's a reason the board installed a clause when we took over. They saw the fault lines even before we did.

Five years. That was the deal.

Five years of shared leadership. Of oversight.

Until then, the company's controlling shares—one-third me, one-third Dante, and one-third the board—would hold each of us in check.

At the end of that term, the final controlling shares—held in escrow since the transition—would be released to us jointly.

We'd be untouchable.

And we almost fucking made it.

Five years is up in two weeks.

Fourteen days, and the board would have had no power left to stop us.

But now?

Now they have video footage of a meltdown at the largest architecture convention in the country.

A hot mic and my voice calling Dante dead weight.

Let's not forget the perfectly captured moment when he

punched me onstage in front of hundreds of witnesses—and every major press outlet we invited.

Now they have cause.

And if they want to push us out—both of us—they can.

I exhale slowly, then rub my jaw out of habit. Not because it hurts—he didn't hit that hard.

But because this morning, the weight of it is starting to feel permanent.

If Dante doesn't show up soon, I'll be walking into that room alone.

And I'll be the one explaining to the board how everything we've worked for—everything our fathers built—came undone over one mic, a fist, and five years of slow, silent sabotage.

My mind is stewing over every possible scenario, trying to craft a plan for each and file them away so that no matter what the board says, I can be ready.

But I can't stop fucking seeing his face when he heard the words come out of my mouth.

He lashed out with his fist—but it was pain I saw there.

A part of me knows I should apologize. The other part is satisfied he finally showed some fucking emotion toward this firm.

He walks in fifteen minutes late like time's a suggestion and this meeting is some minor inconvenience. Just that usual air of detached arrogance—like he's operating on a schedule no one else has access to.

Same suit from yesterday. Wrinkled. Charcoal gray. Still perfect on him.

He probably came straight from Vegas. Probably spent

the flight getting his dick sucked by one of his favorite rotations, thinking he'd stroll in, flash a grin, and spin the whole thing into a joke.

I don't bother hiding my irritation. "Nice of you to join us."

He doesn't even look at me.

Just shrugs off his jacket and drapes it over the back of his chair. Then he starts rolling up his sleeves, slow and unbothered.

His forearms are tan, dusted with dark hair, the muscle taut and easy to notice.

But it's the ink that draws my eye—because it always does.

Ti aspetterò.

XXI•VI•MMIX

I only know the date—June 21, 2009—was the day he was sent to boarding school.

I remember it because it was the day after my mother's accident.

That day still lives in my bones.

The curve of her legs at a wrong angle. The way her neck looked broken before I could even make sense of it. Those eyes—bright blue—wide, stunned, staring up at me, ready to tell my secret.

That image is burned into me so deep I still dream about it.

Even now, all these years later, it takes everything in me not to flinch.

I blink a little too long and force the memory away.

Dante sits, forearms now bare, posture loose and arrogant.

He doesn't seem rattled. He never does.

Corrine gives him the briefest nod, and he ignores her—as always.

I follow her lead, settling in beside him like I haven't spent the last twelve hours preparing for this exact moment.

One of the board members leans forward, expression lined with something between disappointment and finality.

"We've reviewed the footage from yesterday's incident," he begins, "as well as the ongoing record of internal conflict over the past five years."

My stomach knots.

I don't have to hear the rest to know where it's going.

"We believe it's time to explore a transition in leadership."

Silence.

"The firm will begin evaluating external candidates to assume the roles of co-CEOs."

It lands with all the subtlety of a wrecking ball.

There's no shouting. No protest. Not yet.

But the floor just dropped beneath us.

And we both know it.

I clear my throat and lean forward slightly, the practiced calm in my voice doing everything my pulse refuses to.

"If the board feels strongly about a leadership transition," I begin carefully, "then perhaps the solution isn't replacement but revision. We could extend the escrow period—another quarter, even six months. Give the firm time to stabilize and allow us to rebuild your confidence."

A few of the board members glance toward each other—thoughtful, but unreadable.

Before anyone can respond, Dante moves.

He stands, grabs his jacket from the chair, and slings it over his shoulder like we've just finished lunch and not been handed our professional execution.

"Transition in leadership." He mutters. "That's cute."

I turn toward him, already tense. "Dante—"

He ignores me. His gaze is fixed on the board now, posture loose but loaded.

"You have anyone in mind?" he asks, voice smooth but sharp.

There's a beat of silence. A few board members exchange a glance—irritated, clearly—but no one answers.

"Didn't think so," Dante says, already half-turned toward the door.

I lower my voice, trying to cut him off at the knees before he does more damage. "Dante, don't—"

But he doesn't care. He never fucking does.

"Why waste our time if you don't have someone set?" he goes on, louder now. "And good fucking luck finding someone who can run this place better than we have."

It isn't bravado. Not exactly.

It's conviction. That quiet, reckless certainty that's always made him dangerous.

He starts toward the exit.

The room stiffens.

"We're assessing options," one of the board members calls after him.

He doesn't stop walking.

And that—that silence—says everything.

They don't have someone. Not yet.

Which means this isn't done. Not completely.

But then the board member keeps going:

"Regardless of that outcome, the board will not be transferring the controlling shares in two weeks' time."

A direct blow, but Dante doesn't even flinch.

He reaches the door, one hand already on the handle.

"Then we have two weeks," he says without turning around.

And just like that, he's gone.

No rebuttal. No negotiation. Just a declaration.

Two weeks.

It's a line in the sand, and it's exactly what I feared.

Because if we couldn't figure out how to run this firm together in five years, there's no fucking way we'll do it in fourteen days.

Hell, at this rate?

Two weeks may as well be two minutes.

It still won't be enough.

The SUV hums through midtown, a quiet bubble of leather seats and tinted windows between me and the rest of Manhattan's chaos.

Across from me, Frankie Lane is dressed like a retro ad for heartbreak and vengeance—red lips, winged liner sharp enough to slice a man open, and a pinstriped pencil skirt that somehow makes her fury more efficient.

She's swiping through slides on her tablet like each one has personally offended her.

"This is a multibillion-dollar contract," she says without looking up. "With the richest man in Manhattan. I swear to God, if you freelanced anything without telling Grant—"

"Relax."

Her gaze snaps to me. "Dante."

I lean my head back, eyes half-closed behind my sunglasses. "You say my name like it's a warning. It's not working."

"This is Damien Wolfe," she bites. "Not some bored

developer with a vanity project. He's ruthless. Brilliant. The man built his empire from scaffolding and steel and zero family favors. He could buy and level half this city before lunch."

"Which is why I made a few adjustments," I say, stretching out my legs.

Frankie stills. "What adjustments?"

"I just reorganized the pitch deck," I say. "Financials are tucked toward the back—where his investors will still get their fix. I expanded the sustainability section. Brought in some new renderings—off-grid cooling systems, solar-integrated glass, water reclamation. Wolfe's going to love it."

She narrows her eyes. "Did Grant approve the changes?"

I give her the kind of shrug that says *not exactly*.

"I'm sorry," she says, deadpan. "Was that a yes, or was that one of your classic 'fuck it, I know better' shrugs?"

"It was a 'Wolfe will see the value and no one else matters' shrug."

She groans, pinching the bridge of her nose with manicured fingers.

Before she can launch into another lecture, my phone buzzes.

I glance down.

A text.

> KRIS: Thanks for this weekend. Still can't feel my legs.
>
> Come back to Vegas soon. 💋

There's a blurry photo attached. Kris's tongue running up a hard, veined cock that I recognize as Sam's. She's got a crooked grin, looking far too satisfied for a Monday morning.

I smirk to myself. Type a quick reply: *Next time I'm in town, we're getting the weekend.*

"Unbelievable," Frankie mutters, yanking me back to the moment. "You're sexting your weekend romp before the biggest pitch of your career."

"It wasn't a sext," I reply, slipping the phone into my jacket. "It was a thank-you."

"God, you're infuriating."

"I'm appreciated."

Wolfe isn't some silver-spoon legacy baby. He's our age—early thirties—but he built his name the hard way. Construction. Development. Scale. Influence. Now he's the city's apex predator, and every firm in the country wants a seat at his table.

He's been with Marchesi & Harrow for a decade. Back when our fathers still ran things and Wolfe was a rising name with a sharp mind and no patience for bullshit.

Now he *is* the table.

And this skyscraper—the one we're pitching today— isn't just another high-rise. It's a fucking monument. A vertical legacy in the heart of Manhattan. Whoever designs it becomes a permanent part of the skyline.

I darken my phone and slide it into my jacket pocket. Finally meet Frankie's stare head-on.

"We'll land it," I say quietly.

She crosses her arms. "You better hope so."

The SUV slows, curbside just outside Wolfe Tower.

Time to find out.

Frankie drops me at the curb, and I walk for-fucking-ever to reach the entrance. Wolfe doesn't do anything half-ass—especially not his own complex.

The building is sleek—an all-black design and a statement to the city that Wolfe Industries is here to stay.

It was the first project Grant and I ever worked on together.

First.

And last.

Still, it's one of my favorites.

The elevator climbs too quickly. Smooth. You can barely feel the motion, save for the faint mechanical whirl as each floor races past.

Dead.

Weight.

Dead.

Weight.

Grant's words from Friday echo in my head on a loop, and I squeeze my fist. Fucking asshole.

I know he didn't realize his mic was on, but that doesn't change what he said.

The truth.

The way Grant really sees me.

Bullshit. But I swallow it down like it doesn't fucking destroy me inside.

The doors open with a soft ping—and speak of the fucking devil.

Grant's standing there like he's been waiting for me, the sun behind him casting a halo around his dirty-blond hair.

His light-gray suit and dark-blue shirt sharpen the storm in his eyes, and they land right on me.

He's only out here to make it look like we arrived together.

Like we're still a team.

It's a goddamn joke.

"Let's not fuck this up," he says, putting his phone away, chin up, matching my pace.

I slip my hands into my pockets—cool, unbothered.

"You say the sweetest things, Bug."

His jaw clenches—just enough to make it worth saying.

He's never liked the nickname. Never asked why I call him that, and he never will.

Which only makes it better.

Damien Wolfe greets us just outside the glass doors, all effortless charm and quiet authority. He's in his usual all-black suit—sharp, clean, tailored like sin—and flanked by his business partner, Marcus, who's more smiles and hand-shakes, less looming-billionaire presence.

Damien gives Grant a brief nod before turning to me. "Big pitch. But you already know that."

His tone is casual, but there's steel beneath it.

"This one isn't for me," he adds, walking us toward the boardroom. "It's for the investors. You want my vote? Show me you can sell it to them."

We step inside, the room already filling with murmured conversation and glossy portfolios. Floor-to-ceiling windows frame the skyline like we're already inside the tower we haven't built yet.

"Got my notes?" Damien whispers to Grant.

"Reviewed and integrated," Grant replies, crisp and sure. "They made it into the final deck."

A flicker of doubt scratches at the edge of my mind—unsure if that was before or after my contributions.

Grant takes the lead as we begin. Damien and Marcus sit at the head of the table, flanked by five investors and two advisors. The click of the remote is the only sound as the first few slides go up.

Overview. Legacy. Vision.

But then he stumbles—right on the first change I made.

Grant pauses for a beat too long. Clears his throat as he looks over the slide.

I step in before the moment stretches any further.

"The next phase of the structure will incorporate a solar-integrated glass façade. Each panel is custom-engineered for passive light harvesting—no compromise to the aesthetic."

One of the investors—O'Connor, I think, the one with the oil-refinery empire in Houston—leans forward, brow creased.

"Wait. You're saying the façade itself is energy-generating? That's... ambitious."

He doesn't sound impressed. He sounds threatened.

Of course he does. The man made his fortune off fossil fuels and political lobbying. Passive solar makes his portfolio nervous.

I open my mouth to respond, but Grant steps in first.

"It's one of several options on the table," he says smoothly. "We're still evaluating which features will be most strategic for investor alignment."

It's a nice way of saying *don't worry, your outdated bullshit is safe.*

He clicks forward. Supposed to be financials next.

Instead—my section.

I nod toward the screen and take the floor again.

"This is where we're pushing the boundaries. The building will feature an off-grid cooling system—zero reliance on municipal electric—and we'll recycle ninety percent of water on-site through our reclamation circuit. It's sustainable, yes. But more than that—it's resilient."

Eyes track to the screen. I see the investors trying to do math in their heads, trying to reconcile the beauty of the tower with the systems beneath it.

Finally, Grant steps in again. "Let's move to the numbers."

He runs through the financials—sharp and efficient—but I can feel the shift in the room. The questions at the end are fine. Mostly surface level. Timeline. Budget. Tax credits.

But I can see it in their faces. They wanted the numbers first.

We buried the lede.

When the meeting adjourns, there's a round of handshakes and polite nods. No fireworks. No buzz of excitement.

Not a disaster.

But not the home run it should've been.

They asked about ROI and bottom lines, not the systems that make this complex a showpiece.

They're looking at the price tag.

Not the fucking crown jewel.

Damien doesn't say a word as he walks out of the boardroom. He doesn't have to. The tension in his shoulders says plenty.

We follow, and I trail behind the group, jaw tight.

His office is sleek and dark like the rest of Wolfe Industries, but the whiskey cart by the windows is the only thing I care about right now. Four crystal tumblers sit waiting—because Damien knew this wasn't going to be a toast.

He pours without ceremony. No ice.

"Shut the door," he says.

Grant does. And just like that, we're locked in with one of the most powerful men in Manhattan—and I already know he's about to hand us our asses.

Damien passes around the drinks, then leans a hip against his desk, arms crossed.

"So…" He takes a slow sip. "What the fuck happened in there?"

He's not angry. Not loud. But disappointment from Damien Wolfe lands harder than most men's rage.

Marcus stands beside him—quiet but alert. Watching us like we're two boys who brought home a failing report card.

"There's no synergy," Damien says, voice even. "You're not working like partners. And don't tell me it's just a bad day."

Grant clears his throat. "We had a few last-minute changes—some crossed wires, that's all. It won't happen again."

"Next time," Damien says mildly, "might be too late." His eyes flick to mine. "This was supposed to be the jewel of the skyline. A legacy project. And you had them counting pennies over concept renderings."

I feel the fire stir in my chest.

"And yet no one asked how those concepts are redefining sustainable vertical design. They asked about costs because that's all they know how to measure."

"They measure what matters to them," Damien says, calm as ever. "And like it or not, that part matters too."

We fall quiet.

I don't look at Grant. I keep my gaze locked on the glass in my hand, then shift to the window—the skyline stretching wide and brilliant, just waiting for its next crown.

Then Damien sighs. "So." He lets the word hang in the air. "Is this about Friday?"

My jaw clenches. I don't look away from the view, but I feel both of their eyes on me.

Grant jumps in before I can answer. "I'm not going to lie. That was a trainwreck. I'll give you that. But it's over. And we're not making excuses. The board made a few… comments. Nothing we can't fix."

Bullshit. He's not telling him the whole truth.

Not that it matters.

Damien lifts a brow. "I already heard about the threat to pull the firm. And I'm not asking as your client. I'm asking as your friend." He glances at Marcus, who nods once—quiet affirmation.

"We don't always agree," Damien continues. "Hell, we argue like bastards behind closed doors. But out there?" He gestures toward the conference room. "We're a team. Always. And we sure as shit don't bring our fights to the table."

Grant exhales. "We're working on it."

Marcus huffs a laugh. "Yeah. That's cute. But you two have been 'working on it' for what—three years? Four?"

"Five." I saw too quickly. Too quietly.

The silence stretches. Tighter. Heavier.

"You need more than *working on it*," Marcus says, direct.

Damien doesn't argue. He just reaches into his jacket pocket and pulls out a sleek, matte-black card holder, taking a card from the back.

He slides it across the desk like a challenge.

Grant doesn't touch it. Doesn't even look at it.

I do.

Of course I do. Because I'd know that logo anywhere—three words in gold foil that, in some circles, can open any door you need. Even one that leads straight to Hell.

The Black Ledger.

"Ask for Eve Sterling," Damien says. "She's not just a Companion. She fixes things—relationships, reputations, business disasters... whatever the fuck this is." He motions between Grant and me.

Grant laughs under his breath—dry, cold—then finally looks at the card. "I know this is an elite escort agency to the rich and filthy rich. You want us to screw our problems away?"

"No," Damien says. "I want you to stop dragging them into my boardroom. How you get there is your business. And if anyone can handle you two assholes, it's her."

Marcus leans back, arms folded. "You're not the only firm in Manhattan. Just the one with the longest history with Wolfe. Don't make it the shortest future."

Grant rubs a hand over his face and mutters, "We'll handle it."

But I catch the flick of his eyes down to his phone screen. He reads a message. Doesn't reply. Just locks it and slides it back into his pocket.

Corrine again.

Always fucking Corrine.

She's a constant stick up his ass, and if it weren't for Frankie, she'd try to pull her same shit on me. That's one of the reasons I'll never let Frankie work for anyone else but me.

She doesn't just bust my balls—she busts Corrine's too.

I turn slowly, taking my time. The card stays on the table. Untouched. Daring.

I give Damien a nod—polite enough to pass. "Thanks for the drink."

Damien watches me with that sharp, knowing edge. "You know where to find her."

I do.

And I will.

Because if the only way to beat Grant is to get him to stop playing by the rules—

Then maybe it's time I flip the goddamn board.

Chapter 4

Grant

I've been staring out the window for hours.

The city keeps moving like it always does—horns, sirens, the occasional helicopter slicing through the June haze—but I don't really see any of it. Just a smear of noise and glass. Distraction pretending to be focus.

Dante left Wolfe Tower in some dramatic storm-out. Didn't say where he was going. Typical. Theatrics over substance. He'll probably show back up whenever it suits him with that smug, untouchable air like none of this matters.

It matters.

It all fucking matters.

And he keeps treating it like a game.

I pinch the bridge of my nose, trying to ease the pressure building behind my eyes. The headache's been creeping in since we left Damien's office. I haven't even opened my laptop since we got back. Haven't returned a single call. Because I don't know how the fuck we fix this.

Two knocks on my door make me inhale deeply.

I don't have to look. Only one person knocks like that—like she belongs here, but she's still polite enough to ask.

"Come in," I say, already softening.

Corrine steps inside, holding two foam cups with plastic lids and striped straws. She gives me a faint smile and sets one on the edge of my coffee table without waiting for an invitation. Banana milkshakes. She always brings them after visiting her mom, despite the fact that I've told her a hundred times I hate bananas.

She still forgets. Or maybe she doesn't. Maybe she just likes the ritual of it.

"How was she today?" I ask, stepping away from the windows.

Corrine pauses mid-sip, then shrugs. "She blinked."

"Yeah?"

"Maybe it was the light. Maybe it was me being hopeful."

I nod, even though I don't know what to say. Corrine never expects comforting words. She's been through too much for anything I could offer to make a dent.

Her story is tragic—objectively so. And I know people say that about all trauma. That pain is pain. But hers?

Hers carved trenches.

A murder-suicide. Well—attempted suicide.

We were fifteen when she stumbled over to our house. I remember the blood first. Then the way her hair stuck to her cheek. The gash above her eyebrow. She didn't cry. Just stood there, shell-shocked and silent. It was my mom who coaxed a few words out of her.

I remember the way my mom went still. The way she sent my dad sprinting across the lawn without another word.

Corrine's mother had caved in her husband's skull with a riding trophy—one of the dozens that lined the shelves in Corrine's room. Beautiful, heavy things she used to polish after school.

Corrine was dropped off early when her riding lesson was canceled, and her mother came after her too—but whatever drugs she had taken kicked in, and all she managed was the gash.

Took five stitches.

Her father died. Her mother lived.

If you can call her current condition living.

Now she sits in a psychiatric center uptown. Catatonic. No speech, no eye contact. Just a slow, rhythmic tap of one finger against the armrest of her wheelchair. Over and over. Like she's stuck in a loop no one can break her out of.

The doctors say she's aware. That somewhere in there, behind the slack face and unblinking eyes, she knows what's happening.

Corrine visits her every week, like clockwork.

And then she comes here, drinks milkshakes with me, and pretends it doesn't gut her.

I pick mine up and swirl it, if only to give my hands something to do. It's already melting, so I put it back down.

"How'd it go with Wolfe?" she asks.

I shake my head. "Dante fucked it up, and he's off licking his ego somewhere."

She lifts a brow. "Want me to key his car?"

That gets a smile out of me. "Not yet."

But maybe.

We sit in silence for a minute. The city hums outside. Her straw squeaks as she takes another drink, and I lean back in my chair, suddenly tired.

Not physically. Not even emotionally, really.

Just tired of carrying the weight of a partnership that feels more and more like a war.

She keeps holding her breath like she wants to say something but doesn't.

Halfway through her milkshake, she changes the subject —but I know this is not what she really wants to talk about.

"Hey... do you know what those recurring charges under Dante's codes are? Started showing up again this quarter— small line item but steady. Something about educational disbursement?"

"Yeah. That's legitimate." I set my cup down. "It's for that intern, Collins, from last summer."

Corrine looks off, as if remembering. "The one from the scholarship program?"

"Yeah." I lean forward, elbows on my knees. "Kid was sharp. Showed up every day, outworked half the team, and never asked for a damn thing. Dante's been covering his tuition ever since. We tried to set up a board-managed trust, but they shot it down."

Corrine nods slowly. "So, Dante just... paid for it himself."

"Yeah. Quietly."

She doesn't say anything for a second. "Alright. I'll bury

it under consulting services. If the auditors ask, we loop it in with diversity initiatives and mentorship. No one needs to raise eyebrows."

I meet her eyes. "Thanks."

She offers a little shrug like it's nothing, but her fingers tighten slightly around the foam cup. A few more deep breaths that pause at the beginning of a word she never says.

"Just spit it out, Corrine. What do you keep stalling to bring up?"

She snorts a laugh, looking at her straw like it'll say the words for her. "You always could read me."

"Yeah, which is why I know you've got something running through your mind—so spit it out."

"Fine," she says, dragging the word out a little too long. "I've been wanting to talk to you about something. Sort of... personal. But also... not."

Corrine shifts in the chair, drawing a soft pop from the leather cushion. She plays with the milkshake's straw, giving herself more time.

"The board's two-week mandate. That clock's ticking."

I nod, dragging a hand down my face. "Yeah. I'm aware."

"You know as well as I do that Dante is not going to help you fix this," she says—not unkindly, just matter-of-fact.

She thins her lips, looking at me like she's still debating this next part.

"Just spit it out."

There is only one more second's hesitation before she rushes through, "Maybe you don't need him to."

"What are you getting at?" Something in her tone makes me lean forward, brows pinched.

"You know the escrow clause. But there are also shares reserved for legal spouses."

My breath hitches, and I close my eyes. I know exactly where she's going as soon as she says the words.

She lays it out cleanly, like a business proposal. "A marriage gives you the swing vote. You'd have majority control. You could vote him out. Salvage what's left."

I stare at her, trying to read the fine print on her expression.

"A contract. No romance," she adds. "No sex. Just strategy."

I look away, toward the glass coffee table in front of us and the worn silver frame sitting on it. It holds a photo of us as teenagers at one of my mom's charity galas. Corrine had just moved in with us. Her head was still bandaged, and her smile was too small, but she held on to me like I was the only stable thing in the room.

Corrine picks up the frame, brushing a thumb over the glass.

"She always said we were a good match."

I exhale through my nose, and she hands me the frame.

I hesitate, then take it.

"I just..." I pause, turning the photo over in my hands like it might give me a different answer. "I never thought it would come to this."

Corrine sets her cup down and gives me that *I feel sorry for you* smile people give. "I know this is the farthest thing from what you wanted."

"I spent years building this thing with him—even when he made it hell. And now I might have to burn it down to save it."

That's all I can say. But she's looking at me like she's expecting me to pull a fake engagement ring out right here and say, *Let's do it.*

"There's got to be options. Some loophole we can use to force the board. Draw out the time frame."

"Grant, I've already looked into every possibility. Short of a miracle—which would be Dante suddenly becoming a new person—this is your best choice. Quick and effective."

Corrine watches me for a moment, then looks at her watch and offers a soft smile.

"I've got to run to my next meeting, but... think about it." She stands, putting my untouched milkshake closer to me. "You don't have to decide anything right now. Just... if it comes to that, you're not alone."

She squeezes my shoulder gently as she passes. Then she's gone, leaving the door half closed and the weight of what she's offered sitting squarely in my palm.

I'm still turning it over in my mind as I walk to the bookshelf behind my desk.

Sixteen years. That's how long it's been. The same age I was when she died. The day I swallowed down more than just grief. The day I learned how to bury secrets deep enough they stopped clawing at the surface.

I slide the photo of Corrine and me behind the one of my mother—just as the door opens behind me.

"Miss me, Glowbug?"

Christ. Dante's voice carries like smoke—smooth, self-satisfied, and always a little flammable.

It rolls down my back like fire, and though I wanted to ignore him, I turn anyway.

And there he is. All long legs and swagger, like he owns the oxygen in the room.

But it's the woman on his arm who stops everything.

Red dress. Perfectly tailored. Poised. Confident. Unreadable.

She doesn't smile. Doesn't fidget. Just takes in the room like she's already figured it out.

Ledger Companion. I know it the second I see her.

Not just because of the way she carries herself—like a secret with legs—but because I've seen the uniform before. Red dress, sleek and unmistakable. Worn like armor by the women who work for *The Black Ledger*.

Dante's had plenty of them. Paraded through events, meetings, after-hours functions like they're accessories. Men too, in their all-black ensembles—every one of them polished, trained, contract-bound.

This isn't new.

What *is* new is him bringing one here.

To our office.

To me.

Dante's grin widens like he's been waiting for me to put it together.

"Grant," he says, tone overly polite and fucking annoying, "this is Eve Sterling."

She extends a hand with effortless grace. "It's a pleasure, Mr. Harrow. I understand you're the rational one."

Of course he did it. Of course he went around me, took Wolfe's advice, and made a move while I sat here doing nothing but thinking.

He's got a plan.

And I have nothing.

Chapter 5

Eve

I've never been one to rush foreplay.

And make no mistake—what's happening in this office? It's foreplay.

Two men. Two egos. One ticking clock. And me, dropped into the middle like a match to dry kindling.

I cross one leg over the other, lean back in the leather chair, and watch the two men argue in the world's loudest whisper.

It's not subtle.

It's not productive.

It is, however, entertaining as hell.

I was interested the second Dante Marchesi sat down in the Ledger's lobby this afternoon. Wolfe had already sent word to Lucian—something about a last-resort referral. Two executives. Two weeks. Fix the tension or lose the company. No details, no history—just the kind of vague urgency that usually means someone's already made a mess of things.

I was about to input Dante's info into the system, rush-approval flagged and ready, when his name lit up green.

Already a member.

Even easier.

I was looking over his bio and profile picture—Italian heritage, likely speaks it fluently, six feet and change, espresso eyes, tan skin, black hair that curls just slightly when it's long enough—when he strolled in like he owned the damn place.

A toothpick dangled from the corner of his smirking mouth—casual to most, but I know a displacement tactic when I see one. He needs something to take his frustration out on.

Something—or someone.

And now, here we are.

Two weeks to save a company. No personal background. No therapy-style deep dives. Just a mandate: get them back on the same side of the table.

Even if Wolfe hadn't tossed my name in the ring, I would've taken this contract the second I saw Dante Marchesi walk through the door. Not just because of the smirk or the swagger or the tailored suit hugging his shoulders.

But because of the way he looked at me.

Like he already knew I'd be a problem.

Like he wanted to know how much of a problem I'd let him be in return.

Now I just have to get the other half of this dynamic duo to look me in the eye instead of trying to incinerate Dante with his glare. Grant hasn't said much—not to me, anyway —but the tension between them is... impressive.

I wonder how much of it is sexual.

Hell, maybe none. Maybe they just hate each other. Or maybe that's the problem.

They don't hate each other—and that's the issue. Which is where I'm placing my bets.

I smile, fold my hands neatly in my lap, and wait for them to remember I'm still in the room.

It doesn't take long.

Grant Harrow is the first to glance my way. Brief, controlled. A flick of his storm-gray eyes over me like a scan, not a greeting.

I've watched enough high-powered men to know when I'm being cataloged. He's not checking me out—he's assessing risk. And that makes me like him just a little bit more.

He's not a Ledger client. I checked. No history in our database, no contract preferences, no kinks filed under an alias. Which means I get to dive in the old-fashioned way— research, surveillance, inference.

It's practically a PI job, and I have to admit... I'm excited.

The man is layered like cold steel. Five eleven, broad-chested with a cut that says discipline, not vanity. Dirty-blond hair, neatly styled—though I've seen the strands at his temple twitch toward disorder every time Dante opens his mouth.

His suits whisper money. Tailored with intention. Not a single accessory out of place.

His voice is the most telling. Cool and low. Measured.

Enunciated with a precision that says he doesn't need to shout to command a room. It's the kind of voice men listen to and women try to impress.

And still... he's a mystery. A locked vault.

For the last fifteen minutes, I've watched him stand just stiff enough to suggest he's never fully at ease. Not with Dante. Maybe not even with himself.

He's playing his cards so close to his chest, I'm not convinced he knows what they are.

Dante, on the other hand?

Oh, Dante's going to be difficult just because he can be. He'll emote, posture, grandstand, distract—and every bit of it will be performative. The trick with him isn't drawing him out.

It's figuring out what's real.

Grant's reality is buried beneath a lifetime of control. Dante's is buried under layers of charm and chaos.

Well, enough of this. It's time to leash the dogs.

I rise from my chair and glide between them, heels silent on the polished floor as I insert myself into the no-man's-land like I've owned it all along. They part just enough to let me in. Like instinct. Like gravity.

"If I get stabbed walking between you two, I'm charging hazard pay," I murmur, voice light and laced with something wry. "But since I like my heels blood-free, how about we stop posturing and get to work?"

Dante's grin blooms instantly, all teeth and heat.

"I don't know," he drawls, eyes dragging down my frame like a slow caress. "Depends where you want the blood, sweetheart. I can think of a few places that—"

"Jesus Christ," Grant snaps, throwing his hands up as he stalks to the windows. "This isn't a fucking game, Dante. This is our legacy. Our company. Not a goddamn locker room."

"I was just having a little fun," Dante replies, smirking—but it tightens around the edges, like he's getting tired of being the one always blamed for making things worse.

I sigh, loud enough to interrupt whatever verbal grenade Grant's about to lob next.

"Right now," I say coolly, "neither of you are fuckable. You're liabilities."

That gets their attention. Dante blinks. Grant turns slightly from the window, his jaw tight.

"If you keep measuring your dicks in boardrooms, neither of you will have one left. Let me fix that."

Grant's gaze flicks to Dante. Not with rage. Not with that same sharp bitterness he's been throwing around like knives. It's something quieter. Deeper. Not desire. Not quite.

Just . . . memory.

I let that settle before I step back, businesslike now. "Here's how this works. Two weeks. Full access. No lies. I'm not your therapist—I'm your mirror. You don't like what you see? Fix it."

Dante lifts a brow, arms folding lazily across his chest. "Does this mirror include sex?"

I tilt my head, lips curving. "Only if you earn it."

He smirks. "Darling, I always do."

I glance at Grant. "He's going to be exhausting, isn't he?"

Grant doesn't answer right away—too busy letting his

eyes drag over my legs. He catches himself a second too late and clears his throat. "He already is."

Dante leans in just enough to drop his voice. "I'd be happy to show you how exhausted I can help you get."

Grant can't hold back anymore and snaps. "Fucking Christ, Dante. This is completely—"

"Oh my God," Dante groans, rolling his eyes and cutting him off. "Would you stop? Just for once, stop fucking fighting everything. At least I'm doing something, Grant. At least I'm showing up. To fix this. Can you fucking admit that? It's a start. Which is more than we've had in years."

That lands.

Grant doesn't respond or look at him.

Just goes back to the skyline—brooding and quiet.

I let the silence settle. Let the weight of Dante's words and Grant's reaction fill the room like smoke—thick, choking, unresolved.

Then I cut through it.

"I don't need you two to hold hands and sing campfire songs," I say, voice calm but firm. "But if you didn't want this to work, you wouldn't be here."

Grant doesn't look at me, but he's listening now. I can see it in the way his jaw ticks, in the way his hand curls against the edge of the window frame like it's the only thing holding him up.

"You don't owe me anything, Grant," I continue, stepping closer. "But you owe it to yourself to try. One hour. If it's a waste of your time, I'll walk."

Still nothing. No answer.

So I lean in, just slightly, and drop my voice.

"But something tells me this matters more than you're letting on."

Grant finally turns—just enough to meet my gaze.

"Fine," he says. Low. Gritted. But it's a yes.

I smile, already pivoting to Dante. "Great. That means you can go."

Dante laughs, not offended in the slightest. "Kicking me out already? That's cold, baby."

"You'll survive," I shoot back. "I want to talk to Grant without a backseat driver, thank you."

Dante moves to the door, pausing just long enough to toss Grant a look over his shoulder. "Try not to be too charming without me, *Lucciolina*[*]."

Then to me: "Don't get too comfortable, sweetheart. You're not the only one who knows how to play games."

He leaves with a grin that says *checkmate*.

And somehow . . . I think he means it.

Hm. We'll see about that—*sweetheart*.

---

[*] Little glowbug / firefly

Chapter 6

The executive lounge is quiet—too quiet for midafternoon and empty.

Glass walls, leather chairs, some overpriced art on loan from a gallery in Tribeca. The whole place looks like money, but not comfort. Designed for efficiency, not reflection. The kind of space where no one lingers longer than they need to.

"Coffee?" I ask, already moving to the machine by the liquor cabinet.

"Espresso," she answers without hesitation.

Hm, not a drip-kind-of-girl. Not sweetened. Just— espresso. Direct. No room to hide.

The answer hits with a quiet precision, like everything else about her.

Sharp. Uncompromising. Unexpectedly attractive.

I slot the capsule and press the button, watching it hiss into the small porcelain cup. I always pay attention to how people take their coffee. It tells me what I need to know.

Whether they want to be soothed or jolted. Whether they're used to waiting—or used to getting what they want immediately.

I hand it to her. She nods with a polite smile.

Her fingers graze mine.

It shouldn't register. But it does.

Warm. Steady. Not flirtation. Just presence. And somehow, that's worse.

I take the seat across from her, posture straight. Not stiff, but not casual either. Calculated.

She crosses one leg over the other and asks, "Tell me how we got here."

There's nothing overt in the motion—no seduction, no signal. But my eyes catch anyway.

Noticing the way she fits this space like she owns it.

How smooth her legs look. How soft they must be.

I've always been attracted to women—that part's never been hard to admit. It's just been a while.

And this woman bargains sex like a commodity and according to Wolfe, she's one of the best the Ledger has to offer. That must be why I'm cataloging each small move and subtle expression.

I lean back slightly, arms resting on the chair's edges, and swallow. "You'll have to be more specific. 'Here' could mean a dozen things."

"You know what I mean."

Yes. I do.

But I'm not about to hand her the match and point her toward the fuse.

I glance toward the skyline instead, give a low exhale.

"You run a company long enough, you accumulate cracks. Some visible. Some... structural."

"Which kind are you?"

The corner of my mouth lifts. "I suppose that's what you're here to figure out."

She doesn't blink. Just watches me like she's already peeling back the layers.

I hate that I'm wondering who's calling the shots here. Technically, she's contracted. But it was Dante who brought her in.

And Dante...

Dante thrives on chaos. Always has. If he thinks breaking something will expose the rot underneath, he'll strike the match himself just to watch it burn.

Maybe Eve's here to push me into the flames.

Corrine just left, floating a plan to cut Dante out—for good. I didn't say yes. But I didn't say no, either.

So now I'm wondering...

What if this isn't a coup?

What if it's a trap?

What if they're working together—and I'm the one being cornered?

I give Eve an answer that looks honest on the surface. But underneath it says nothing and reveals less. Because until I know who's playing whom, I'm not putting my cards on the table.

"People change. Priorities shift. Eventually, even partners start pulling in different directions." I meet her gaze head-on. "This is nothing more than that."

A lie. Polished. Practiced. Delivered with enough

distance to keep her from getting closer.

But I know her type.

She won't stop until she finds a crack.

And if she keeps looking too long...

She's going to find the truth.

The kind you can't bury—no matter how deep you dig.

Eve leans forward slightly, fingertips grazing the rim of her demitasse. Her espresso sits untouched. She's letting it cool. Watching me instead.

"Tell me about you and Dante."

I give a soft huff through my nose. "You'll need to narrow that down. We've got decades of dysfunction to unpack."

She smiles faintly, like she's heard that before from other clients—but it doesn't reach her eyes.

"Start wherever the silence is loudest."

I pause, fingers flexing along my own coffee cup.

Clever.

But I can't give her silence.

The silence I feel is a small tug in my chest. A pull toward something I haven't looked at in years.

Something heavy. Still festering.

And then it's there—uninvited.

The silence of a gasp. A door slamming. The deep thud.

Blood on white porcelain. The way it had pooled with such impossible calm.

I blink.

The room rights itself and Eve is still watching me.

I bury the memory beneath concrete. Reinforce the vault.

Not now. Not with her sitting right in front of me.

She shifts gears like it's nothing. "How long have you known Corrine?"

I blink, not expecting Corrine to surface as a focus. "Our families go back a long time."

She hums. "So… not since prep school, then?"

I narrow my eyes. "Why the interest in Corrine?"

"She's the CFO," Eve says casually, though her gaze is anything but. "But something in her bio made me think your history goes back farther. More personal."

I study her a beat longer. She's sharper than I gave her credit for.

Eve leans back, crossing one leg over the other. And yes, I look. "Men and women aren't often just friends. Not without an attraction somewhere in the mix."

The shift in tone is deliberate. She's circling something.

"Did you two date?"

"No."

"Ever want to?"

I keep my face still. "No."

"Fuck?"

"No."

"Never?" Her head tilts. "Not once?"

She's relentless. And not just for the sake of curiosity. She's testing me.

"I don't sleep with coworkers," I say coolly.

"Do you fuck women?"

"Yes."

"Men?"

I say nothing.

The corner of her mouth quirks, like that's an answer all its own.

"Has Dante ever fucked her?"

The question is thrown so plainly I nearly miss the land mine beneath it.

And yet—my chest tightens. Blood spikes.

The idea of it... something vicious coils in my gut.

I don't understand why it bothers me. Not really. But it does.

"They've despised each other for years," I answer. Clipped. Controlled. "Since we were kids."

She doesn't look convinced. But she doesn't press, either.

Just glances at the clock on the wall, then downs the last sip of her espresso and places the cup carefully between us on the table.

Then she levels her gaze on me—sharp, calm, and cutting. "Hour's up."

My mouth curves, but there's no humor in it. "And just like that, you think you've got it?"

"Yup." She stands. "See, I'd bet this entire contract—whatever happened between you and Dante, whatever you're lying about... Corrine was there. Right in the middle of it."

We stare at each other. Long enough for the silence to grow teeth.

"If I'm wrong, let Dante know he can cancel the contract."

She starts to walk off, heels clicking on the polished tile, but just before the door, she glances back.

"But I have a feeling I'll be seeing you tomorrow."

And then she's gone.

Leaving me alone with a cold cup, a dozen dead memories twitching beneath the surface—

and the echo of her knowing smile.

And beneath it all... that silence again. The one that started everything.

Chapter 7
Dante

"I have to admit... I'm impressed." Eve hums as she sets her wineglass down, the crystal ringing softly against the marble.

I arch a brow as I walk back into the dining area with a second bottle. "That I opened a bottle of Barolo without spilling it on the rug?"

"That you didn't order in," she says, grinning as she sinks a little deeper into the chair, like we're old friends. "You don't exactly give off homemade-risotto energy."

I chuckle and move behind her, reaching over her shoulder to top off her glass. "What kind of energy do I give off?"

"Wearing the fuck out of an Armani suit. Power lunches. Sex-on-a-desk kind of energy," she says without hesitation, and the heat behind her tone makes me pause.

I lean in closer, lips brushing the shell of her ear. "For the record, I'm excellent at all three."

Today was her first official day under contract—her first

conversation with Grant, her first step into the powder keg I handed her with a smile and no warning. And she handled it.

Well enough that Grant actually texted me.

Just me.

Not in a board-wide group thread. Not through an assistant. Not as some thinly veiled jab buried in a press release.

It was three words.

"I'll do it."

We haven't texted directly in nearly a year, and prior to that, it was nothing but the occasional low jab and arguments.

And now... here we are. The two of us agreeing to face this. The spark of possibility between us, crackling hotter than the flame I cooked with.

"I figured you were too self-centered to cook," she replies, and smiles like she expects me to be offended.

I am.

But only a little.

I lean back in my seat, fingers toying with the stem of my glass. "There's a lot about me you don't know."

"Oh, I'm counting on it." Her gaze flicks up. "That's what makes this job interesting."

I should keep this professional.

But she's not making it easy when every move she makes gets the attention of my hardening cock.

"You're not curious?" she asks, breaking the silence. "About what Grant and I talked about?"

"I already know what matters." I trace the rim of my glass. "He said yes."

"True," she concedes. "But what I really want to know is how you two fell out. I mean, I'm supposed to fix it. Seems a little unfair you left that part blank."

I watch her. "I didn't want to bias you."

"You mean you didn't want to be the villain up front."

"Same thing."

Her eyes narrow like she's trying to read me. And she is. Smart, strategic. She's not just beautiful, not just sharp—she's trained. Every word I say, she files away like evidence.

I slide my chair back, letting the tension stretch between us like a drawn wire. One leg crosses over my knee as I settle deeper, slower, needing more distance and less of it all at once.

She gets up, and my eyes trail down.

The temperature in the room spikes in a second.

That red dress hugs her body like it was stitched directly onto her skin. Tight, short, indecently elegant. It shifts with her every step, clinging to her hips and ass like it wants to make me suffer. She brings her wineglass with her—never breaks eye contact—as she crosses the room with the kind of grace that makes my cock twitch beneath the table.

When she reaches my side, she doesn't ask for permission.

She slides onto the table beside me, smooth and unbothered, her thighs flexing as she settles on the polished mahogany like she belongs there.

She fucking does.

My mouth waters watching the fabric inch up as she crosses her legs—slow, sensual, elegant. Her calves rub together, the movement so deliberate I know she's doing it for my benefit.

And it's working.

My hands ache to reach between them, to slide beneath that dress, grab that perfect round ass she's clearly sculpted with hours in the gym—and maybe a personal trainer or two. I want her on her knees. I want her on all fours. I want her bent over this table with my hands digging into her hips so hard she bruises.

But she's talking. And I want that too.

"What do you know so far?" I ask, voice low and steady.

She lets the question settle as she takes another sip of wine. Then she starts her assessment like she's peeling a label off a fine bottle—slow, deliberate, ready to see what's underneath.

"You speak Italian," she says. "But only in two situations. When you're furious and when you're fucking."

She smirks when my brow twitches—just barely.

"You have extraordinary taste in men and women," she continues, "but you lean toward men."

I smile at that, slow and dark. "Molto brava, bellissima."*

I lift the wine to my mouth and swallow its rich flavor. She watches when I run my tongue along my bottom lip like she wants it on her pussy.

Anch'io, piccola†. Me too.

---

* "Very good, beautiful."

† Me too, baby.

"Don't tell me what's in my Ledger profile," I say, voice deepening just enough to catch her attention. "I want to know what you've found out today."

She sets her wineglass down with a soft click, flips her hair off her shoulder, and leans back on her hands—chest lifted, neck long, body stretched and offered like temptation personified.

The scent of her perfume hits me—subtle, floral, with just enough spice to make it feel sinful. I inhale slowly and feel it in my spine.

She's shifting the tone now. Guiding the conversation exactly where she wants it. And I let her—because watching her work is half the fun.

Her voice dips lower. "The key to fixing this will be Grant."

I nod once, silent.

"You're part of it, of course. But he's the one with the armor on top of armor, and not nearly enough time to dismantle it all. Not in two weeks."

She glances at me, waiting for me to push back, but I don't.

"And then there's Corrine," she adds casually, like she's dropping a match in a puddle of gasoline.

The name hits like a shot to the ribs.

I feel it before I can stop it—the hard pull of muscle across my jaw, the way my grip tightens on the stem of my glass. I say nothing.

But Eve saw it.

Her lashes lower, lips curling like she's just confirmed a theory.

"Not sure what role she plays yet," she says lightly. "But you do. That much is obvious."

I keep my mouth shut. No good can come from giving her a reaction.

"What I can't figure out," she says, shifting her weight just enough to draw my eyes back to her thighs, "is the catalyst. Something changed. Something snapped. And for everything else I've studied—body language, speech patterns, boardroom dynamics..."

Her eyes meet mine again, sharp and hungry.

"...none of it tells me this."

She leans forward slightly, her voice a blade wrapped in silk.

"What changed between you two—was it personal or professional?"

I smirk.

She's bold, I'll give her that. But she should know by now—I don't give away information for free. Not when everything in this contract has a cost. And not when the truth she's after is worth far more than a glass of wine and a well-cut dress.

"There's a price for that answer," I say smoothly, sipping from my glass.

Eve tilts her head, intrigued. "I thought I was the one charging you a fee, Mr. Marchesi."

I push up from my chair and walk into the kitchen. I feel her watching me, tracking my every move like a predator waiting to pounce—or maybe a thief watching the vault, wondering how many steps until it opens.

From the drawer beneath the wine fridge, I pull out a

deck of playing cards. The box is matte black, worn at the corners. I toss it in my palm once before returning to her.

"Simple rules," I say, placing the deck on the table near her thigh. "We each draw a card. Highest one wins."

She raises a brow. "And if I win?"

"You can ask a question. Any question."

Her eyes flick down to the deck, then up again, sharp and glinting with interest. "What do you get if you win?"

I take a slow sip of wine, letting the moment stretch until she shifts on the table—just enough to betray her anticipation.

"If I win," I murmur, "you follow directions."

As if on cue, the lights above dim to a soft golden glow. Romantic music hums to life beneath the quiet tension— slow jazz, sultry, threaded with the kind of bass that moves through your bones. In the living room, a fire roars to life in the inset fireplace, shadows flickering up the slate wall.

Eve laughs, the sound warm and indulgent. "Smooth."

I shrug. "It's on a timer."

"Hm. I bet it is."

"I like ambiance," I say, expression unreadable. "Helps me relax."

She toys with the corner of the deck but doesn't touch it yet. "And when does this game end?"

My answer is as dark as my hair and twice as dangerous.

"When one of us refuses the other."

Her eyes narrow—assessing, calculating—but the corner of her mouth tugs upward as she brings her glass to her lips. She takes a sip and nods.

"I'm in," she says. "Let's play."

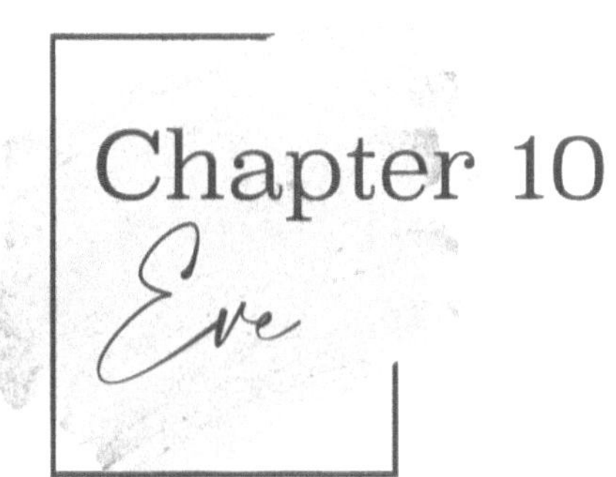

He picks up the deck of cards like it's an old friend, sliding the box open with one hand and pulling the cards out in one practiced motion. There's something effortlessly masculine about it—controlled and casual. Like everything he touches obeys him eventually.

Dante begins to shuffle. Slow. Measured.

The sound of cards slipping over each other is the only thing in the room besides the low jazz and the soft crackle of the fire.

"Any boundaries I should know about?" he asks, glancing up at me.

Cute.

I tilt my head, holding his gaze. "There are very few boundaries I have, Dante. And I'm confident you won't come close to crossing them in your harmless little game."

He grins.

The deck stills in his hands. He sets it between us on the table.

"Ladies first."

I draw. Seven of hearts.

He flips his—nine of spades.

I exhale through my nose, more amused than disappointed.

Dante offers his hand, helping me slide off the table. He doesn't look at my face now—his eyes have dipped lower, drawn to the sway of my hips and the hem of my dress clinging to the tops of my thighs.

I'm already guessing what direction we're headed. And I'm right.

"Clothes off," he murmurs. "Heels stay on."

Of course.

I smirk, turning around in front of him with an exaggerated arch of my back as I take a seat on his lap, deep and slow. I feel his cock—already hard—pressing up into me through his slacks.

Ooh. Big boy.

His hands go straight to my hips, fingers tightening in a grip that promises he's been thinking about this since I first perched on the table.

"Having a hard time, Mr. Moretti?" I tease, voice brushing the shell of his ear as I lean back and whisper.

His grip tightens.

"I was," he mutters, low and rough. "Still am."

"Mind helping with my zipper?"

I move my hair to one side, exposing my bare back to him.

His hands slide up—deliberate, reverent. Palms dragging up the curve of my spine, fingers brushing bare skin until they find the zipper. He takes his time, lowering it inch by inch until the dress loosens around me, held only by gravity and posture.

I rise from his lap and turn around slowly, catching his eye as I push the dress off my shoulders and let it fall. The fabric slips down my body, pooling at my feet like silk spilled from a secret. I step out of it with one heel, nudging it aside with the other as I stand there, bare and unapologetic.

His eyes move.

They start at my feet—my tall, black heels he told me to keep on—then slowly, hungrily, they climb. He drinks in my legs, the slick heat between them. He lingers there. His gaze sharpens.

Then it moves higher.

My breasts lift with each slow breath. Nipples pebbling under his heated gaze.

They're high, bouncy, natural—just the right size for attention but not too much to be mistaken for an offering.

One of the best surgeons in the world is a longtime Ledger client, and mine are some of his best work.

Dante licks his mouth. Doesn't even try to hide it.

I watch his throat bob with a swallow, his fingers flexing against his thighs like he's holding himself back.

His eyes are locked on my chest now, and I know exactly what he's thinking about.

Sucking.

Biting.

Teasing them until I'm gasping under his mouth.

His voice drops, velvet-dry. "Are you often without your panties?"

I grin, unabashed. "Usually."

It's the truth. Confidence isn't just a costume I wear— it's the skin I live in.

He shuffles the cards again and places the deck back between us. We draw.

He wins.

Again.

Smug confidence settles across his face like it belongs there. The fire paints him in bronze and shadow, his dark hair gleaming at the temples, his mouth curled into something self-satisfied—and fucking dangerous.

A new song spills into the room, slower and deeper. Something sultry and bass-heavy. The kind of beat you feel first in your chest—then lower.

It seems to inspire him.

His eyes flick lazily over me, then he leans back in his chair with a single word etched into the heat between us.

"Dance."

God, that smile. That smirk. That challenge.

I start slow.

Just a sway of my hips, a ripple of my spine. My hands glide over my own skin, circling my breasts, down my sides, between my thighs. I drag a finger through the slick of my pussy—hot and soaked from nothing but tension—and lift it to my mouth, parting my lips to taste myself.

The moment I suck my finger clean, his jaw tightens.

It looks like it physically pains him not to touch me.

So I straddle him, slow and fluid. His hands smooth up to my ass the moment I settle. He squeezes—hard. His cock strains against his slacks, thick and ready beneath me, and I grind to the rhythm of the music, rolling my hips until we're moving together like the beat is our pulse.

He's enjoying my ass immensely.

He should. I've worked hard on it. No shots. No surgery. Just hours of effort and the occasional good fuck for inspiration.

I lean in, lips barely brushing his ear. "Is it okay if I make a mess on your pants?"

He groans under his breath. His grip tightens.

"I mean . . ." I purr, rocking a little harder now, dragging my pussy along his clothed length, "you've got me soaked, Dante. I think you've earned the cleanup."

His reply is immediate. Low. Hungry.

"I want you to make a mess of me."

That earns him a moan, just soft enough to pass for breath. It's like getting a Christmas bonus when my clients are good at fucking.

And I can tell Dante is a goddman pro.

I keep my hips moving, circling. I don't stop as we draw again.

The cards flip.

I win.

A slow smile spreads across my lips, and I don't bother hiding the pleasure that comes with it. Not just the sensual kind—but the strategic one. The kind that sinks its teeth in deep and knows it's earned.

I keep grinding, slower now. A tease.

Then I ask—voice close to his ear, warm and wicked:

"How long has it been since you and Grant got along without tearing each other apart?"

Dante's voice is husky with desire when he answers, his breath brushing warm across my skin.

"Five years."

He leans in, his mouth heading toward my breast—and fuck, I want it. I want his tongue. I want the scrape of his teeth, the possessive pull of his mouth around me. I can already feel the phantom heat of it and the way my body would melt for him.

But I want to win.

And I'm enjoying the game far too much to give him an edge.

So, I slide off him instead, turning my back to him like a teasing punishment. I sit again, this time with my back against his chest, and begin to roll my hips—slow, sinful circles over his cock that's still straining against his slacks.

He groans low. His hands find my ass again, rough and greedy. Fingers splayed wide, squeezing and spreading me like he's imagining what it'd feel like to push inside and watch himself disappear into my ass.

"Not long after you both became CEOs," I murmur, letting it click into place.

But before I can follow it up with another question—because I absolutely want to—his voice cuts in, smoother than the wine and twice as dangerous.

"Time to draw," he says, and I can hear the smirk on his lips.

Technically, he's right. A second question would be cheating.

I wonder if there's a punishment for cheating.

If there is . . . I'd almost certainly try for it.

We draw.

He wins.

Again.

His hands slide to my hips and hold me in place, guiding me into one more slow grind before he stills me with a possessive squeeze. Like he's trying to memorize the feel of me—slick, hot, relentless—before I slip away again.

Then comes the direction, murmured like a command sealed in silk.

"On your knees. Take out my cock and stroke it."

A pulse goes through me. Every nerve awake. Aroused. Ready.

I get up slowly, turning to face him with the kind of deliberate movement that tells him I'm not just going to obey—I'm going to put on a fucking show.

I lower myself to my knees, parting them wide as I go. My pussy is on full display—glistening and flushed from the grind of his cock through his clothes—and when his eyes drop to look, he curses under his breath.

"Fuck."

First, I unbutton his crisp white shirt, pulling the tails tucked into his slacks. His olive skin and sculpted body are perfect.

He would be living art fully naked.

Next, I reach for his belt.

I slide the leather through the buckle and pull it free

with one slow, satisfying tug. Then I slip it over my head and let it fall around my neck like a collar, tightening it just enough to feel the bite but not enough to bruise.

Dante's head tips back.

His control is starting to fray.

I unbutton him. Lower his zipper and let my eyes follow the trail of short, dark curls where they disappear beneath the band of his fitted boxers.

He lifts his hips slightly to help as I slide his slacks down just enough to free him.

And fuck... he's big.

Thick. Heavy. Hard.

I look at it the way a starving woman looks at a feast, and when my gaze flicks up to his, he's wearing that proud, cocky smile that tells me he saw the moment I became impressed.

"I fucking love it," I murmur, licking my lips, "when my clients have big cocks."

He groans again, low and deep, as I wrap one hand around him.

My fingers don't touch on the other side.

So I bring in a second hand—one stacked above the other, moving together, squeezing and stroking in a rhythm that's smooth and slow.

His groan travels straight to my clit, and it throbs in response—desperate for pressure. For anything. For everything.

God, I'd love to sit on his face.

But if I do that... he can't answer my questions with his mouth full of my pussy. And I have questions.

So we draw again.

I keep one hand moving up and down his length, stroking him with purpose, just long enough to flip my card.

Ace of diamonds.

Finally.

My voice is steady, sweet, and sharp as a blade.

"Whatever happened… is that the reason you use sex like a shield?"

For a moment, there's only the crackle of the fire and the soft sound of jazz wrapping around us like smoke. His jaw tightens. His eyes narrow—but not with anger. With precision.

He doesn't flinch. Doesn't try to deflect.

Instead, he leans back just slightly, his voice rough with restraint, low like a secret.

"Let's just say… it's easier to fuck than to feel."

The words roll out with perfect control—measured, detached—but I catch the muscle twitch in his jaw, the flicker of something raw behind his eyes.

It's not an admission, but it's not a denial either.

Because denying it would be a lie.

And we both know it.

It's exactly the answer I wanted—crafted like armor but heavy with truth.

My smile deepens. My hand never stops moving on his cock.

And the game continues.

It's Dante's win.

His voice is low and sharp, smooth as black silk.

"Get your mouth on my cock and suck. Deep."

God. The way he says it.

Commanding. Controlled. No hesitation.

A fresh gush of arousal slicks between my thighs at the sheer authority in his voice. That rough edge. That tension he never loses.

I fist him in one hand, holding him still as I look up at him. I want him to see it—the way I obey, the way I enjoy it.

Then I lower my mouth.

My tongue circles his head first—slow and teasing—flicking around the ridge, collecting the bead of arousal already gathered at the tip. I hold his gaze as I lick it up, making sure he sees every second.

He curses, the word a whisper ripped from his throat.

I work him for a moment, lips wrapped tight, cheeks hollowing, tongue dancing beneath the head and down his shaft. I can feel how much he loves this. How he's losing pieces of himself in the feel of my mouth.

This man—so powerful, so put-together, so utterly in control—groaning because of me.

I pull off with a wet pop, keeping my fist tight around the base of his cock as I reach for the deck and draw.

I win.

But I don't ask my question yet because I know this will end the game.

And I want another moment with his cock in my mouth.

I lick up his shaft again, watching him the entire time. I finally look down while I take him deep, inch by inch. My hand squeezes, guiding him as I slide lower.

He groans. Fists my hair. The sound he makes is feral—deep and primal.

Then he growls, voice wrecked and full of need:

"Così brava per me, piccola... così perfetta con la bocca piena del mio cazzo."*

And fuck, I throb at the praise. I don't know everything he said, but enough to know he fucking loves my mouth on him.

Every filthy word vibrates through me like permission.

Like reward.

And I don't want the game to end—but I've earned my question.

"Does he know you love him?"

I punctuate my question by taking him deep into my mouth once more—slow, unrelenting, sucking hard until his thighs tense beneath my hands. Then I release him with a wet pop, licking my lips as I look up.

"Grant. Does he know?"

I wait and watch.

But I already know the answer.

This thing between him and Grant—it's not about a woman. It's not about money. It's not some petty power play in a boardroom, no matter how convincing their performance might be.

It's deeper.

More intimate.

A denial. One so complete it created a canyon between them—wide, brutal, and burning. A fire that's raged for five years without cooling, without softening, without healing.

The deep pools of Dante's eyes bore into mine.

---

*   *"So good for me, baby... so perfect with your mouth full of my cock."*

And my answer is right there. Just like I knew it would be.

He reaches down and gently takes my chin between his thumb and forefinger. His touch is soft—unexpectedly so—and the pad of his thumb brushes over my bottom lip.

The command is quiet. Intimate.

"Game's over, piccola*."

There's a reverence in his tone I don't miss. A kind of ending that feels like a beginning.

He helps me to my feet as he tucks himself back into his pants, the moment slipping between us like silk drawn through fingers.

I bend to pick up my dress from the marble floor—slowly, deliberately. His hand drags over the globe of my ass—one last squeeze, a silent confession.

He loves it.

I know he does.

I straighten and glance over my shoulder, returning his belt from my neck. "See you tomorrow."

His eyes are molten.

I take a final look at the hard plane of his abs, still partially exposed from where his shirt has come untucked. Then I turn, my dress clutched in my hand, heels clicking softly as I walk toward the elevator wearing only them.

And the heat of his stare burning into every step I take.

The doors close behind me, sealing the night with a soft chime.

And I don't smile until I'm alone.

---

* *Baby*

The limo pulls through the gates of the Silverleaf Invitational—a charity golf tournament so drenched in old money and sports legacy it practically smells like polished wood and generational privilege.

It's hosted annually at the Wexley Club, a *country-club-meets-five-star-resort* with rolling green hills, manicured fairways, and a press line long enough to make my jaw clench.

Flashbulbs go off before we've even parked. I can already see retired pros, billionaire donors, and influencers pretending they understand anything about golf—as long as there's champagne.

"Fucking white carpet," I mutter.

"Of course," Eve replies smoothly from beside me. "This is Manhattan's elite. They'll wear white after Labor Day if there's a camera involved."

She's calm. Relaxed. Like this is just another Tuesday—which it might be, for her.

I was surprised to see her at my penthouse this morning.

I'd just finished shaving when my housekeeper let her in. Wearing wide-leg cream slacks and a black halter-neck blouse that managed to be chic, commanding, and just androgynous enough to make it feel like she could seduce both the room and the boardroom at once.

She wanted to review the plan for today. Check my outfit. Adjust my tie. Make sure I didn't look like I wanted to throw a driver at Dante's head the minute we stepped onto the course.

She wanted me to switch to a navy suit, so I let her.

I may not disclose every secret of my past, but I also have no intention of sabotaging this.

But when she mentioned she'd already prepped Dante last night—that they'd talked strategy over dinner—I felt something shift in me.

Not jealousy.

Not irritation.

Just... something.

And I don't have time to unpack what the hell it was.

The limo slows to a stop, and Eve turns toward me, all business now.

"This is our first joint appearance since the slap heard round Vegas," she says. "The press is hungry for blood. Or unity. Either one will sell."

I grunt. "So, let's not give them the first one."

"Exactly."

She straightens the cuff of my blazer. Her fingers brush my wrist, cool and efficient, like it means nothing.

"You'll be paired with him for the photo call," she continues. "There's a group moment on the green with the charity ambassador, and I've lined up a quick quote for *Socials Magazine*—feel-good PR about rivals putting the past behind them for a cause."

I nod once, jaw tight.

She watches me a beat longer.

"I'll be nearby if you need me," she says. "Consulting in a professional capacity, of course. If anyone asks." Her voice dips just slightly—mocking, warm, edged in mischief.

"Professional capacity?"

"It's not a lie," she adds, lips twitching. "I *am* consulting in a professional capacity."

I glance at her—an unimpressed stare that does absolutely nothing to her.

So much so she actually winks at me.

"They just don't know that part of that capacity could involve a blowjob."

I snort, biting back a smirk. "Jesus, Eve."

"What?" she says innocently, her hand resting on my thigh like we've already fucked each other. "It's called multitasking."

Eve's parting comment still lingers when the limo eases to a stop.

It was calculated. Timed.

A not-so-subtle jab wrapped in a velvet glove—all to make sure I didn't step out of this car looking like I was ready to put someone through a hedge.

The door opens. Her hand slides off me, and cameras flash before I'm fully upright.

I take my time, looking around as I button my suit jacket.

No rush. No grandstanding.

A simple nod to the first bank of press, then I turn back to the car—and stop.

Eve's still seated inside, one leg crossed, her hand resting lightly beside her. The cream slacks, the black halter. The tailored elegance. It's not just put together—it's intentional. Every inch of her curated with the ease of someone who understands how to make people look twice.

And that smile.

Not the Ledger Companion smile.

This one's relaxed. Alive. Real.

Like she's saying, *You've got this.*

I reach out without thinking, and when she takes my hand, her skin is cool and certain. She lets me help her rise, like this is what people do for her. And of course they do. They pay well for her company... fuck. *We're* paying well for her company.

And I'm starting to see why.

"Thanks," I say under my breath. "For thinking ahead."

She only nods, lips curving like she knew I'd say it eventually. "It's what I'm here for."

We walk the carpet together, smooth as glass.

I don't speak unless prompted, and she doesn't over-direct. Just a soft glance here, a light brush of her fingers on my sleeve there.

At one stop, she greets a publicist by name and offers a polite kiss on each cheek. Says something I can't hear. Then gestures toward me, her smile professional, but her body language reading *watch this one.*

The press does as they're told. Cameras click.

She's not just easing the tension—she's shaping the story.

And for once, I don't feel the need to plot out every next step or align things into order. I let her lead.

As we move forward again, a tall woman in a white suit glides past us—broad, athletic shoulders, cropped hair, unmistakable presence. WNBA. I recognize her from a sports equity panel last fall.

She gives Eve a nod and a quiet, knowing smile. Familiar. Intimate.

My brow lifts. I lean in just enough so only she hears me. "Client of yours?"

Eve doesn't miss a beat. Doesn't confirm. Doesn't deny.

Just murmurs back, low and smooth, "I never kiss and tell."

Then she glances at me, then my lips.

And for just a second... I wonder if that was more than a witty reply.

A promise, maybe.

Or an invitation.

Should I ever want to test it—it would be our secret.

My gaze lingers a second too long, like I'm already answering her back.

It's been five years since I've even *thought* about sex in any real way. Not in passing. Not in the quiet of night. Not even during those rare stretches of boredom or loneliness that might tempt lesser men.

Desire is a distraction. And I've had more important things to rebuild.

But now—here she is.

Eve, in her tailored pants and wicked mouth, smoothing down my lapel like she owns the right. Tossing glances that feel like they're testing the temperature.

And Dante's question yesterday—if sex was on the table—

It shouldn't matter.

Except it does.

Because now, I can't stop wondering if it *is*.

The crowd gathers under the main event tent—one of those massive temporary structures lined with fresh florals, chilled champagne, and enough money to make it feel casual.

Laughter hums like background music. Crystal glasses clink against manicured nails. People greet each other with air kisses and firm handshakes, dressed in designer golfwear they'll likely never sweat in.

I know most of them.

Not well.

Old acquaintances. Business associates. Friends of my father's who see me and offer the same strained smile that says, *I remember you in short pants.*

No one here is real. No one here is safe.

Just sharks circling until someone bleeds.

Eve hangs back, close enough to be noticed but far enough not to intrude. She's perfected the art of proximity —close enough to be accessible, detached enough to be mysterious.

It works.

She checks her phone discreetly, then steps forward and lightly tugs at the crook of my arm. Barely a touch, but enough to cut through the senator's latest pitch about the tech corridor bill and—more irritatingly—his daughter.

"Grant," she says quietly, so only I hear. "Dante's arriving."

I nod once.

She'd already briefed me on how we're to play this. Not too far, not too close. A visual dance. Partners orbiting each other. Space to breathe, to watch. A slow thaw the press can track over the course of the day.

It's smart.

I take a slow inhale through my nose.

Can't tell if it's to ease the pressure building in my chest —or if it's the way her perfume drifts between us. Cool. Subtle. Clean. It doesn't announce itself. It lingers.

Probably both.

There's a commotion at the edge of the carpet. Not loud. Just a hum of attention sharpening. Cameras click before they even see him.

Dante always did know how to arrive.

He steps into the tent like he belongs on a goddamn movie poster—light gray suit tailored to his frame, top two buttons of his shirt undone like he's allergic to formality. The sun cuts a glint off the compass tattoo inked on his chest, just barely visible as he lifts a hand in a wave to someone behind me.

His smile is wide. Bright. Performative.

I've seen that smile used to charm CEOs, disarm investors, and publicly pretend he didn't just verbally anni-hilate someone ten seconds earlier.

But then his eyes find mine and there's a shift.

So slight most people wouldn't notice it.

But I do.

His mouth doesn't falter. But something in his gaze—adjusts. A knowing behind the façade.

I look away before I feel it too deeply. Back to the senator, who's now talking about the second of his daughters, conveniently also single.

I nod politely.

A familiar burst of warm, melodic Italian curls behind me like cigar smoke—comforting if I weren't choking on it.

"Ciao, come stai, vecchio amico?"

*Dante's voice. Effortlessly smooth. Directed at some silver-haired relic from Florence who beams like he's been waiting all year to hear it.

Give them a few moments and they'll be trading secrets over wine and stories no one else remembers.

I force my attention back to the senator, whose pitch remains on the accomplishments of his very eligible daughters. But the words are filtered through static. I hear him, but my brain's refusing to absorb it.

Because Dante's voice is too close. His scent—some expensive blend of bergamot and something darker—threads almost too perfectly with Eve's perfume. Together, it's an intoxicating blend. Clean. Sharp. Slightly sweet.

Distracting as hell.

I sense a shift the second Dante leaves the old man's side.

---

* "Hello, how are you, old friend?"

His voice dips—not in volume, but in intent. A private register meant for one person.

"You look lovely today," he says, low and warm. "*Piccola*."

Piccola.

Eve.

The familiarity grates more than I expect. A name spoken like a habit. Like history.

I remind myself—this is a professional engagement. A staged partnership. A game with real stakes. She's here under contract, and Dante flirting with her in public—at this event—is reckless.

Unprofessional.

And that's the reason it bothers me.

Of course it is.

I don't have time to dwell on it. Not when Corrine steps into the tent from the side entrance, moving like she owns the breeze itself.

Her eyes sweep the crowd as a hand reaches for a passing platter of champagne flutes.

She's looking for me.

Always does. She's not a fan of these kinds of things and usually sticks close to me. But today, a chill prickles down my back.

I don't need to turn around to know she's spotted me and is making a move to join me.

I square my shoulders and offer the senator a tighter smile, letting him drone on, while each of Corrine's steps feels like a drum against my chest.

I glance sideways at Eve—still tucked just behind me—because in this moment, it hits me.

Corrine has no idea Dante brought in someone from the outside.

But she's about to.

And when she does, she won't take it lightly.

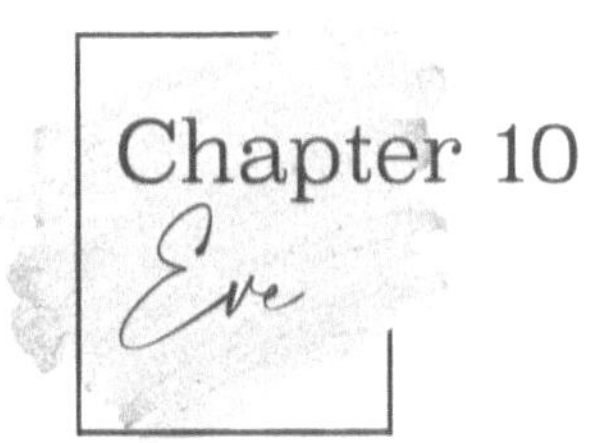

Chapter 10

Eve

I stand between them—Grant on my left, Dante on my right—just far enough apart to keep the space neutral. To anyone else, we look polished. Strategic. Like a unit with a plan.

Which we are.

Because they're doing exactly what I told them.

No bickering. No distance.

Just proximity with purpose.

Still, something shifts.

Grant's posture tightens almost imperceptibly. A subtle clench at the jaw. A stiffening of his spine that sends a silent alarm straight down my ribs.

I follow his gaze—and find the source of the disturbance.

Platinum-blonde bob. Crisp cream blazer. Confident stride.

Corrine.

She strikes me as the type who has *can I speak to the manager* down pat.

She doesn't announce herself when she slips in beside Grant, doesn't greet Dante, doesn't acknowledge me at all until she absolutely has to.

"Corrine Ashwood," she says smoothly, offering her hand without smile or warmth. "Chief financial officer at Marchezi and Harrow."

Her tone adds: *And who the hell are you?*

"Eve Sterling." I return the handshake, calm and pleasant. "Consultant."

That catches her off guard. It flickers, barely—a millisecond stutter behind her eyes—but then she recovers, recalibrating with a grace honed by years of boardrooms and bloodsport.

"Oh, I didn't realize we has a project in the consulting phase," she says, turning to Grant, lowering her voice to a near whisper. "You brought on a consultant and didn't tell me?"

He avoids Dante's eyes and mine. Which is saying something—because Dante's looking anywhere but here. His gaze is fixed on the far side of the tent like it contains the meaning of life.

Grant offers Corrine a tight-lipped smile. "I meant to fill you in."

Dante talks over him at the same time. "I hired Eve."

He looks at Grant, his stare holding a moment before moving back to Corrine. "Unlike my partner, I don't need to run every decision through the finance office."

"I see." She turns her head back toward Grant, tone dropping again as if we aren't supposed to hear. "I thought we were in this together."

Ah. There it is.

Not a protest.

Not even an accusation.

Just a well-wrapped gift of guilt, sealed with professional concern. *I thought we were in this together.*

It lands with precision—soft enough not to raise suspicion, sharp enough to cut.

I see it for exactly what it is. A control tactic. But still, I want to know what '*this*' is.

I don't know the full story between these three, but I'm not naïve enough to believe this is just about financials or internal communication. Whatever happened between Grant and Dante fractured something bigger, and Corrine— well, she seems very interested in keeping them exactly where they are.

Which means I have to move.

Literally.

I step forward—just half a foot—into the little circle she was trying to form with Grant. It forces everyone to adjust their angles. Forces Corrine to step back—or get boxed out. The shift is subtle but deliberate.

She hates it.

I love it.

Her smile doesn't budge, but her jaw ticks once, and I know there's something brewing beneath the surface.

I want to see what's underneath that mask.

"I've actually had quite a bit of success with corporate pairings," I say easily, now addressing the group. "Two partners at odds, high-stakes positions. Like a walk in the park. These boys are in good hands with me." I throw in a wink and let my hand rest comfortably on Grant's shoulder.

Dante smothers a cough. Grant's cheeks burn a subtle pink, but he doesn't move away.

Corrine takes a long, slow look at me.

Down.

Then up.

Unapologetically. Dismissively.

She doesn't even try to hide her disdain now.

Which is fine.

I'm used to the insecurities of other women. Comes with the job.

When it's a client, they're paying me to tear those insecurities down.

Then build them up. Reassure. Make them feel like the most beautiful person in the room.

But Corrine isn't a client.

She's just some bitch trying to wedge herself between the contract I'm here to protect.

And I don't need her to like me.

I just need her to know she's not the only one with sharp teeth.

Corrine pivots back to Grant with the kind of ease that only comes from years of emotional proximity.

She doesn't touch him—but she doesn't need to.

Her tone tilts just enough to imply closeness. Her body angles in like they've done this a hundred times.

She tries to re-center his attention—reestablish her orbit.

I catch it instantly, and I'm already moving to shut it down.

I slide my arm through the crook of Grant's elbow, anchoring myself to his side. His posture shifts just slightly —shoulders squaring, chin lifting.

Dante tips back the last of his champagne, but he doesn't look at me when I press a soft, intentional squeeze to his bicep.

I keep my eyes on Corrine.

My touch is measured. My expression, unreadable.

But my body language?

A clean, quiet claim on both of them.

"Pardon us," I say smoothly. "We've been asked for a quick interview."

Corrine's brows lift. "No one mentioned that to me."

I smile—warm, professional, untouchable. "No need. It's exclusive. A favor from an old contact of mine."

Should I let her know this contact pays me handsomely to peg him once a month?

Mmm, probably not.

Before she can find footing in the conversation again, I guide the men away with polite efficiency.

Grant moves with me without hesitation, my hand still on his arm, his other settling neatly into his pocket like we've walked this path before.

Behind us, Dante shifts fluidly to my other side.

When the crowd thickens and we're forced to narrow our path, his hand drifts low across my back—steadying, sure.

I release Grant's arm and slip my fingers into his instead.

He doesn't hesitate to close his hand over mine.

And it doesn't feel like it's for the act or the press.

But because, for whatever reason, in this moment—it feels better than not holding it.

We step forward together.

And behind us, Dante lingers just a breath.

His hand still at my spine.

His smirk unreadable.

And for the first time since stepping into this political circus, I feel... good.

Like maybe these two men might not destroy each other after all.

Maybe they'll let me be the gravity that holds them steady.

We nailed the interview.

I didn't even prep them. My contact won't publish a piece without me okaying it, and I wanted to see how they'd do on their own.

So I stood to the side like some glorified bookend while years of history snapped back into place. Reflexive. Effortless.

And now I'm watching it all unravel across manicured green.

Everyone's changed into their golf attire—collared shirts and curated smiles. The tournament's in full swing, with a handpicked rotation of players meant to stack the odds in Grant and Dante's favor.

But one off-script question sent things sideways. Dante fielded it fine. The problem came when Grant overreached with a joke that fell flat—more rust than rhythm.

That reflex between them? Gone.

I pulled them aside to regroup by the golf cart. Gave

them space, adjusted my blouse, made a mental list of talking points for the next round. Grant was just heading back to the greens when Corrine arrived.

Correction—when Corrine was delivered.

A club-branded golf cart dropped her and her plus-one at our feet, then peeled off like a yellow cab.

The man beside her is a press leech. Tabloids, by the look of him—smug expression, mirrored sunglasses, tan like he paid for it. Which he probably did.

"Mind if we ride with you for the next round, Grant?" Corrine asks sweetly, gesturing between her and the blood-sucker before she looks between Dante and me. "I'm sure you two can catch another cart?"

Translation: *You two—go fuck off somewhere else.*

My smile is all teeth. "Afraid not."

I loop my arm through Grant's like we've been paired this way from birth. "I've been the good-luck charm all day. Boys are up on strokes. Can't risk shaking up the energy now."

I toss a look toward one of the other players, a high-ranking city official—flirty, but clean. "Especially since I've got ten grand riding on this."

He chuckles, tipping his hat. "Then here's hoping they do lose their luck charm. I'm not looking to cough up ten K."

We move on before she can recover, Dante and Grant flanking me again as we head toward the next tee.

Dante leans in, voice low and silk-smooth against my ear.

"If you keep handling her like that, *piccolo*, I'm going to need a cold shower before the next hole."

Grant doesn't look at him—just keeps his eyes on the path ahead as he mutters under his breath, "Let's just focus on the game."

Calm. Controlled. But I hear the edge beneath it.

And I'm not the only one.

Dante chuckles low, clearly entertained.

"Relax, *bug*, no need to get jealous. I'm only admiring the strategy."

Grant's jaw ticks, but he says nothing.

I slide a step between them, voice light but firm.

"Boys."

I give them a look—sharp enough to slice tension but smooth enough to pass for charm.

"You're both pretty. Now let's not blow the lead just because our egos can't share a golf cart."

That earns a smirk from Dante. Even Grant's mouth twitches—almost a smile—but he covers it with an eye roll.

And I've got my boys back on track.

At least—I did.

Corrine hasn't shut up since we teed off.

She's holding court with the press leech like he's Pulitzer-adjacent, hanging on his every word and throwing out industry gossip like confetti—loud enough to make sure everyone hears her.

I tune her out, redirecting my focus toward the cluster of players I curated for today. The real guests who matter. Every line I drop is intentional—an opening designed to shine a light on Grant and Dante's strengths, a soft pitch they can knock out of the park.

And they were doing so well. Until now.

Corrine raises her voice again—on purpose, I'm sure.

"Grant's father," Corrine says to the reporter with a wistful little smile, "was the true cornerstone of this firm. Tireless. Focused. The kind of man who didn't need the spotlight—he just built empires quietly while others talked."

She touches the reporter's forearm like she's letting him in on a secret.

"And Grant's the same. First one in, last one out. Carries the firm on his back, just like his father always did. That kind of dedication is rare these days."

A perfectly timed pause. Then, with a laugh so light it stings:

"Of course, not everyone has the stomach for that kind of grind. Some people think a quick smile and a night at a club can replace actual leadership."

The jab is razor-edged and aimed with precision.

"And Vegas?" she goes on, with a dismissive wave. "I'm sure you heard about that."

She cuts her eyes to me.

"Grant handled that like it was nothing more than a little boardroom miscommunication. All cleared up now, thank God."

My stomach knots.

Dante's knuckles whiten around the grip of his club.

Grant speaks up—finally—but not where it counts.

"My father is a wonderful man, and I'm proud of the foundation he built," he says, tone smooth, polished. "I wouldn't be where I am without him. He laid the groundwork for everything I'm trying to preserve."

It's a beautiful deflection.

And a brutal omission.

No mention of Dante's father. No recognition of the equal partnership that shaped the firm. Just Grant, standing tall in his father's shadow, using it like a shield.

Dante doesn't say a word.

He just turns, stalks to the cart, and slams his club into the bag hard enough that heads turn.

I move to follow, but Grant steps in. "Dante," he says under his breath, "keep it together."

Jesus, Grant. *Wrong move.*

Dante spins, fury simmering just below the surface.

"I could—if you ever acted like a partner. If you defended me for once instead of always kissing your princess's ass and pretending that bleach job of hers makes her qualified to open her mouth."

We're far enough away the others can't hear—but that won't last long at this rate.

"Okay," I snap, stepping between them. "We're done for the day."

"Gladly," Dante mutters, already storming down the path toward the clubhouse, tension trailing behind him like smoke from a fuse that never fully extinguished.

I hesitate, torn—until Corrine beats me to it.

"Grant? I've got the charity organizer waiting at the next hole for a photo op," she purrs, turning her calculated stare at me, knowing she's won. "Old family friend. I'm sure you understand."

Grant shoots me a look—apologetic, guilty.

"I'll be right there."

I step in close enough for only him to hear.

"I'm going after Dante. But don't think for a second that you've dodged the fallout."

He frowns. "Eve—"

"No. You listen now," I cut in, voice low, steady. "Today mattered. This was your first public appearance together since Vegas, and we were building something real. Something clean. Don't blow it because you can't find your spine when she's around."

His eyes flick to Corrine, then back to me. "It's not like tha—"

I lean in one inch closer.

"You're sitting on the fence between two people right now. But that fence won't hold forever. Eventually, you'll have to pick a side."

My eyes harden.

"And you'd better be ready to live with the consequences —whichever way you land."

I leave him standing there, Corrine still waiting for him to join her.

And I go after the man who deserved defending.

Chapter 11
Dante

The sun's too bright. The air's too still. And every second Grant spends entertaining Corrine while I stand here like an idiot makes me want to put my fist through something polished and expensive.

We had one job today. One.

Play nice. Look solid.

Rebuild a little trust in the firm we nearly torched in Vegas.

And it was working—until she opened her mouth.

Now I'm at the valet stand, jaw tight, heartbeat louder than the overpriced jazz spilling from the club's speakers.

I dig into my jacket pocket and pull out a cigarette.

Flick the lighter. Shield the flame with one hand.

The tip catches fire, and I take a long drag.

The first inhale cuts through the pressure sitting on my chest like a weight plate. The second makes it easier to keep my hands at my sides.

Footsteps echo behind me—measured, calm, sharp against concrete.

I don't need to turn around to know it's Eve.

The engine growls as my car rounds the circle—

a silver-blue McLaren GT, sleek as sin and just as temperamental.

It glides to a stop like it knows better than to test me today.

I flick the cigarette to the pavement and blow one last stream of smoke into the breeze before stepping forward.

Opening the passenger door, I don't say a word.

Eve doesn't ask me to.

She slides in like she's done it a hundred times before—like we discussed this ahead of time.

I round the front, drop into the driver's seat, and slam the door shut with more force than necessary.

The second the door clicks, my foot is heavy on the pedal. The tires protest. The engine snarls. And we leave everything else behind.

Eve doesn't fill the silence.

Doesn't try to soothe it with soft-spoken sympathy or dig for details about what set me off.

She just sits there—serene, composed, legs crossed, eyes half-lidded—as the hills blur past her window. Like we're not cutting through winding roads at a pace that should fray nerves.

The woman has control. I'll give her that.

It's the second time in two days I've watched her wield it like a weapon.

And fuck, she looks like a siren doing it.

"You look good on my seat," I say, eyes on the road, one hand gripping the wheel tight as I lean into the next curve. Because, like I said, it's easier to fuck than feel.

From the corner of my eye, I catch the slow spread of her grin.

"I'd look even better on your cock."

That's my girl.

Heat flashes low and hard in my gut. The tension Grant lit in my chest funnels south, pooling sharp and fast behind my zipper.

Goddamn this woman.

This is what always happens.

Grant pisses me off until I can't fucking see straight—then I end up balls-deep in someone until I can.

That's why the Black Ledger prints money off me.

Because I don't talk it out.

I fuck it out.

Hard. Rough. Repetitive.

Today won't be any different.

Except this time, the distraction already happens to be in my car.

Smart. Controlled. And just dirty enough to make me wonder how far she'll take it before she reminds me this is all part of the job.

And I respect that.

The brains behind the charm.

The plan she's clearly putting into motion, piece by piece, trying to glue me and Grant back together. For the world's sake. Not ours.

But it doesn't change a thing.

I'm still pissed.

And I'm still hard.

And neither one of those problems is going to fix itself.

In my penthouse's building, the second the elevator doors slide shut, she's on me.

Fingers in my hair, nails dragging at the nape of my neck as she yanks me down to her mouth—open, hungry, wet.

I take her tongue with mine, taste the groan that builds in her throat as she arches into me like her whole body's been begging for this since we left the course.

She pulls back just enough to speak, eyes bright, lips kiss-bruised.

"I've been needing a good, hard fuck," she breathes. "And you're just pissed-off enough to do the job properly."

That's all it takes.

I spin her around and shove her toward the elevator wall, her palms slapping against the polished mirror surface as she braces herself.

Our reflection stares back at us—her skirt hiked high, my hand wrapped in her hair, jaw clenched tight with restraint I don't plan to keep.

Her stance is wide. She knows exactly what she's offering.

Her ass grinds back into my cock, and I growl low in my throat, tightening my grip in her hair until her head tilts just right.

My other hand slides beneath the hem of her tennis skirt.

Satin shorts. Useless.

I push past them, fingers slipping straight through her slick pussy.

"Fuck, Eve," I mutter against her ear. "You've been wet for me since the car."

She exhales—sharp and shaky—as I drag the wetness up, circle it slow around her clit.

"You thought about me fucking you the whole ride up, didn't you?"

Another grind from her hips, a breathless yes caught between her teeth.

"You know I did."

I plunge two fingers into her without warning, her moan echoing off the glass like music designed to undo me.

"Fuck, that's it," I growl, thrusting deeper. "Piccola."

The doors are still closed. The penthouse is still floors away. Thirty seconds. Maybe fewer.

But it's enough.

I yank her skirt down and let it pool at her ankles, giving her ass a single smack—tan, round, fuckable—but I'm on a mission.

My hands move with purpose. One slips between her thighs, parting her pussy lips with practiced ease. The other flicks over her clit—fast and precise—in a way I know will make her come fast.

She gasps, rising onto the tips of her tennis shoes, fingers splayed wide against the glass.

I watch her reflection.

Her eyes flutter shut, lips forming a soft, perfect "O."

Her brows arch—flushed, desperate—as the orgasm barrels into her faster than she expected.

"Fuck—Dante—don't stop," she moans, voice breathy, ragged.

"Why the fuck would I?"

Her thighs tremble, her breath stuttering through the high. She rides it out, panting against the mirror, body humming with release.

And just as it fades—

Ding.

The elevator opens.

I turn her, lift her, her legs wrapping around my waist like muscle memory. Our mouths crash together again—messy and hungry.

Behind us, the elevator doors close—and with them, Eve's discarded skirt.

Her hair falls around us in a curtain—soft and wild—but I don't break stride. I know every inch of this place.

We move straight to the bedroom—because I'm nowhere near done.

Her feet hit the floor for only a second. Just long enough to kick off her shoes and yank her shirt over her head.

She's hungry for this. Clawing for it.

And for some reason, that keeps the fury from today simmering at the surface instead of fading. It sharpens it. Makes it useful.

Eve doesn't wait. She grabs my shirt and rips it open, buttons scattering across the hardwood like shell casings. Her mouth is on me in the next breath—hot, open, biting down around my nipple.

She's not gentle. And good. I don't fucking want gentle.

I growl low in my throat as I hook my arms under her

thighs and lift her. Her body wraps around me like silk on fire.

I latch onto her breast, biting her until she calls out, back arching, nails scoring my shoulders.

Then I drop her—unapologetically—onto the edge of my bed. The mattress dips under her weight, the dark sheets catching the sheen of her skin in the low light.

"Lean back." My voice is gravel. "Feet at the edge."

She does—no hesitation.

The position spreads her wide. Puts her on full display. I step closer and reach for my belt, sliding it slowly through the loops with a hiss of leather.

Her eyes find mine—molten heat behind long lashes, her chest rising and falling with anticipation.

"Boundaries," I murmur, wrapping the belt around my fist.

She grins like the predator she is.

"You want to know what I won't do? Not much," she says, voice like honey over a blade. "So, tell me what you're into, and I'll tell you when to stop."

Goddamn.

This woman's going to get me in trouble.

And I'm going to let her.

I take a moment just to look at her. Laid out across my bed. Legs spread, waiting. Every inch of her daring me to push.

"I've got something I think'll look beautiful on you," I murmur.

She doesn't answer—just watches me as I head for the bar built into the corner of the room. I pour myself a bourbon—two cubes. Let them clink against crystal before taking a slow sip. Let it burn on the way down.

I open the drawer beside it, metal whispering against velvet as I pull out a chain. The sound it makes—sharp, deliberate—echoes behind me as I walk back.

Eve sees it.

Her eyes flick from the collar to my face. She reads me. Doesn't even think it through. She just tilts her chin up and says softly, "Do the honors."

I take another drink, finish the glass, and set it down on the floor beside me as I kneel between her thighs.

She stays exactly how I left her—legs wide, hands braced back on the mattress, waiting.

My hands slide up her stomach, to her breasts. I palm them both—rougher than I need to be—rolling her nipples between my fingers until she gasps.

"You should get these pierced," I murmur, watching the peaks swell under my touch.

She smirks. "If I ever do... your mouth gets them first."

I growl and reach for the chain.

The first piece is a black leather collar—sleek, elegant, laced with dark silver hardware. I wrap it around her neck and pull it snug, letting her feel the slow drag of control before I fasten it.

"How's that?" I ask, voice low.

"Good," she breathes. "Tighter."

I smirk and pull just enough. I take one last sip of the bourbon, then let the glass hang in my hand for a second. The two remaining cubes glisten, half-melted in the amber. An idea forms.

I set the glass beside me and lean in, mouth claiming her breast again. I lick around the nipple, then suck it between my lips—hard and slow. She gasps, arching into me.

I reach down, pluck one of the cubes from the glass, and roll it gently around her nipple. The reaction is immediate—her back bows, her hips jerk, a moan breaking free.

I follow it with my mouth again, warming her with my tongue, before trailing to the other breast. I repeat the motion—mouth, ice, mouth again—until she's trembling beneath me, skin pebbled, breath erratic.

When I know she's on the edge of begging, I reach for the clamps.

But I pause.

Hold one between my fingers.

"You'll tell me if it's too much," I say.

She nods, lips parted.

"Words, piccola."

"Yes," she breathes. "I'll tell you."

I let that sit for a moment, watching her eyes. Then I attach the first clamp. She lets out a high whimper, a shudder racing through her. The second follows, and her hands fist into the sheets.

A delicate chain sways between them, connecting nipple to nipple, each movement making her bite her lip as sensation hums through her body.

Her chest is flushed. Her thighs are slick. And her pussy is soaking the edge of my bed.

"Lay back," I tell her, voice rough. "Keep your legs spread. I want to see you gleam while you wear my chain."

Chapter 12

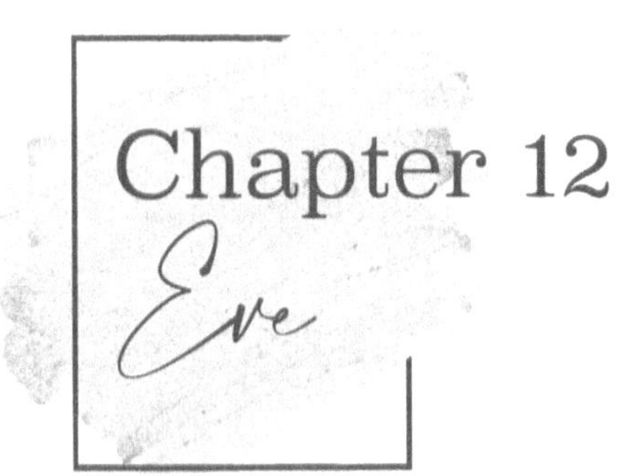

Dante lowers down my body like a man approaching worship.

Every brush of his stubble, every graze of his mouth down my stomach, makes the blood roar in my ears. His fingers stay curled around the insides of my thighs, spreading me wide like a gift he's unwrapping just for himself.

When he reaches my center, he pauses.

And breathes me in.

A long, guttural inhale—nose nearly touching my clit, lips hovering—like he needs the scent of me the way other men need oxygen.

"Christ," he murmurs, voice rough. "You smell like you're already wrecked for me."

I open my eyes in time to watch him drag his tongue slowly—so slowly—up the length of my pussy. His moan vibrates into me, so deep I feel it in my ribcage.

My head falls back on instinct. "Oh, fuck."

He doesn't say anything at first, just keeps licking. Long, reverent strokes that part me, lap at me, claim me. His tongue is firm, deliberate, and when he circles my clit the first time, my hips jolt.

He growls, low. "Keep still, *piccola*. I haven't even started."

He shifts lower, tongue teasing my entrance, licking into me slow and wet. His hands tighten on my thighs. One shifts down to grip my ass; the other pulls gently on the chain between the clamps—and the added tension sends a jolt straight through my core.

I cry out.

"That's it," Dante murmurs, mouth wet against my cunt. "You want more, don't you?"

"Yes—yes, Dante—more—"

He sucks my clit into his mouth and flattens his tongue over it, flicking fast, merciless. It's filthy and precise, and I swear I see stars behind my eyes. I'm panting, writhing, overwhelmed—but then he eases off, letting the tip of his tongue circle lazily.

"Sensitive already?" he taunts, voice smug. "I thought you said you needed this."

I glare down at him, breath catching. "I do."

His mouth is back on me in a second.

The pressure builds fast and tight—too tight—until I'm arching against the mattress, fingers in his hair, the chain tugging, and the clamps biting just enough to send everything over the edge.

I come with a sob, a curse, Dante's name gasped from my throat like a prayer and a warning.

He groans like he's the one climaxing, tongue softening but never stopping, riding out every twitch, every pulse of pleasure as I pant and shake beneath him.

When I finally collapse back into the bed, boneless and throbbing, he kisses my inner thigh.

Then, casually, darkly: "You taste even better when you come for me."

I don't have the breath to speak yet.

But I know I'll be ready to answer him when he fucks me next.

"I'm going to eat this pussy so much tonight."

My body's still pulsing when Dante comes back up between my thighs. I don't even have time to catch my breath before sharp, shocking cold glides over my clit.

"Fuck," I gasp, hips bucking instinctively as my legs twitch to close.

But his hands are already there—firm on my thighs, spreading me wider.

"Easy," he murmurs, voice like smoke. "You can take a little more."

I open my eyes and see it: the cube between his fingers, melting slightly from the heat of his skin. Then his mouth joins it—hot tongue tracing the same place he just iced, a devastating contrast that makes me whimper.

He does it again. Ice. Tongue. Ice. Tongue.

My clit throbs, hypersensitive and aching, and just when I think I'm going to come again, he eases off with a dark chuckle.

"No," he says softly. "Not yet."

The word coils inside me like a command, because the

bastard knows. Knows I'm right there—quivering on the edge—and he's holding me back like it's his favorite game.

I don't have time to beg before he's reaching for the small silver clip attached to the chain on my collar.

I freeze, breath caught.

"You still want more, *piccola?*" he asks, voice low, deliberate.

I nod once, then again, and whisper, "Yes."

His lips curl as he leans in and affixes the clit clamp carefully—precisely—fastening it just tight enough to make me gasp and moan all at once.

Pleasure bursts like sparks across my nerves.

"Oh my God—Dante—"

He watches me squirm, watches my hands fist in the sheets. His thumb brushes the chain that runs from the collar to my breasts and now my clit, a beautiful silver Y bisecting me.

The touch alone makes me come as he pulls and moves the chain until I'm moaning with each twitch of my legs.

"You look ruined already," he says, voice thick with hunger. "And I haven't even fucked you yet."

I almost say *then do it*, but I don't need to.

He rises, grabs a condom from the nightstand, and I watch as he tears it open, rolls it on.

This cock is massive. Thick. And all mine for the night.

God, I love my job.

His eyes stay locked on mine as he crawls back over me, one hand wrapped around the chains, the other guiding his cock to my entrance.

He fills me in one smooth stroke—deep, tight, perfect—and pauses when he's fully inside.

We both groan as I work to breathe around the monster he's just slid into me.

But before I can move, his fist closes around the chain and pulls—gently, but firm enough to make the clamp on my clit tug and the ones on my nipples tighten. I call out on instinct.

"Don't come," he warns, eyes blazing. "You want to come? You ask."

I bite my lip, already trembling. "And if I don't?"

He leans down, dragging his teeth along my throat. "Then I'll stop and spank this beautiful ass with my belt."

He moves then—deep strokes, slow but merciless—hips grinding with every thrust, his grip on the chains keeping me high, on edge, on fire.

"I know how badly you want my fat cock fucking you."

I moan. I writhe. I beg.

He fucks me through all of it.

And never lets me fall.

I lose count of how many times he edges me.

It's everything—his cock, his hands, the chains biting into my skin when he pulls, the throbbing ache of the clamp between my legs. Every inch of me is tuned to him, responsive, strung tight like a wire threatening to snap.

His hips grind into mine as he fucks me deeper, harder. His rhythm is relentless—made of frustration and fury—and I know without asking:

He's not just fucking me.

He's exorcising Grant from his bloodstream.

His hand slides up from my breast, past the chain at my collarbone, and curls around my throat. Not tight. Not yet. Just enough to let me feel it.

"You close?" he rasps, eyes blazing down at me.

I nod. Whisper, "Yes."

He tightens his grip.

My breath catches, my body instinctively tightening around him. The edges of my vision blur, and the pleasure spikes. My pulse pounds beneath his fingers.

And just when I think I'll come anyway—he lets go.

I gasp, air rushing in, and the orgasm fizzles out, leaving me whimpering.

"Not yet," he says. "Again."

He does it again.

And again.

I'm soaked. Shaking. My body begging while he controls every second of it.

When he finally lets me come, it's with his hand around my throat, cock driving deep, and his words growled against my ear: "Now, *piccola.*"

"Choke my dick with your tight pussy, baby."

My release slams over me—blinding and full—and just as it begins to crest, he tugs the chains and removes the nipple clamps in one fast, practiced flick.

"Ah—fuck!" I cry out, the sharp sting turning instantly into another wave of pleasure, rolling right over the last one like a thunderclap.

I don't even have time to breathe before he's fucking me through it, controlling every pulse, every contraction. My mind blanks. I don't know my own name.

I barely register the next—until he finally, finally reaches between us and slides the clit clamp off.

And then I see stars.

My body convulses, hands clawing at his back as I scream his name, my legs trembling with the aftershocks. My vision goes white. I am undone.

I've had every kind of sex imaginable. Every kind of orgasm, too. But nothing has ever shattered me like this.

Never so hard it feels like dying and being reborn at once.

I barely register the sound of his groan, the way his hips stutter, the chains still taut around my neck as he pulls them, anchoring himself to me while his own release takes him.

His body is over mine. Our breaths heavy, faces so close our noses brush each other.

"Perfect." He steps back first.

Wipes his mouth with the back of his hand like he's tasting what's left of control.

Then he reaches for his bourbon like we didn't just fuck the world sideways.

I let out a stunned laugh, dragging a hand down my face. "Jesus, Dante. That was… I mean, I've been fucked—but that?" I shake my head, lips curving. "That was criminal."

He smirks, chest still rising and falling. Doesn't even try to deny it.

I roll toward him, voice low and teasing. "How many rounds can you go?"

He reaches for his bourbon, takes a slow sip, and meets my gaze like he's already inside me again.

"You want to know my limit?"

"I'll fuck you until you tell me when to stop."

I grin, lips swollen and thoroughly satisfied. "Then get more bourbon."

My body feels like it's somewhere in the stratosphere, floating beyond the confines of this penthouse bed—even though I'm lying right beside him. Muscles: nonfunctional. Skin: humming. My breath has finally stopped stuttering out in ragged bursts, but the aftershocks still dance across my thighs like little electric ghosts.

We face each other on the bed, the sheets a tangled wreck beneath us. Both of us wrecked too—but in the best fucking way. Like we've emptied each other out and siphoned every last drop of control we had left.

At some point—hours ago—we stopped just long enough to devour Thai takeout, eating like it was fuel and we were engines in heat.

Now, we're just... here. Still naked. Still wired.

Sweaty as the sin we just enjoyed.

Not with tenderness. Not with affection.

Just with the sharp-edged awareness that we're very good at this.

I arch a brow, curiosity breaking through the quiet. "How the fuck can you keep going like that?"

Dante's mouth tilts in a half smirk—lazy and knowing. "I've perfected orgasming without finishing."

That earns him a skeptical lift of my chin.

"Ah," I answer teasing. "Now I know why your Companion survey rating was so high."

He shrugs, tenderly dragging his fingertips down my thigh, still proprietary even in the silence. "Men think orgasm and ejaculation are the same thing. They're not. You practice for it—learn how to control it. No refractory period, no crash. I can come as many times as I want... just like women can."

I blink. "You're a fucking unicorn."

He smirks. "You're welcome."

The quiet falls again.

But this time, it isn't weighted in sex or sweat. It's heavier. More rooted.

My mind edges back to yesterday. To the question he wouldn't answer. And even now—after he's fucked me over and over again—I still want the one answer he keeps avoiding.

So I ask, quieter this time. "Does he know you love him?"

A pause.

Then: "Yeah."

The weight of it sits between us.

I study his face. "Do you think he loves you back?"

Dante's jaw tightens. "I used to think so. Now I'm not sure."

I nod slowly, letting that settle. I reach up, brush a finger along his jaw, then meet his eyes again.

"Then let's see if we can pull the two of you back together."

Chapter 13

Grant

The sun is a little too bright this morning.

It slants across my office like it has something to prove, spotlighting the untouched glass of orange juice on my desk and the two aspirin beside it. I haven't taken them yet—still deciding if I want to fix the headache or lean into it.

I pinch the bridge of my nose, trying to quell the pressure building behind my eyes.

On my laptop screen, Eve's media contact has delivered a masterpiece.

And it's fucking glowing.

The piece looks like it belongs in *Forbes* or *Fortune*—clean, compelling, curated to within an inch of its life. Pictures of Dante and me standing shoulder to shoulder on the white carpet she staged in the gallery. The lighting makes us look golden. Polished. Powerful.

Exactly what we're supposed to be.

Partner CEOs. Aligned and unshakable.

Which would be easier to believe if my phone screen didn't currently show the exact opposite.

I glance down at the tabloid still open in my other hand, jaw clenching. That prick Corrine let hang around the charity golf event—some influencer with an orange spray tan and teeth too white to be real—the one hiding paparazzi in the damn trees.

The result is grainy, unflattering shots of Dante looking like he's about to murder someone. Or fuck someone. Or both. And none of it screams *stable corporate executive*.

I exhale hard and scan the headline again:

"CEO or Savage in a Suit? Dante Marchesi Rage Stroke on the Greens."

Fucking perfect.

My thumb hovers over Dante's name, brushing the edge of the screen like it might summon the courage I don't seem to have this morning. The call I should've made last night. Or the night before.

Movement outside my office draws my eye.

The glass double doors open, and he walks in escorting Eve with a hand at the small of her back. A guiding touch that should be polite. Should be professional.

But it isn't.

Not when that hand drifts lower—inch by inch—sliding down until he's nearly cupping the curve of her ass like he fucking owns it.

She lets him.

Eve struts in six-inch heels like she invented gravity, the curve of her pencil skirt a goddamn weapon. As she passes in front of him, she runs a pointed fingernail down the center of his tie, eyes flashing like a dare.

She looks like sin.

And they fucked.

They absolutely fucked.

It's written in every languid movement, every teasing glance, every subconscious brush of skin against skin. My jaw ticks as the image forms without my permission—Dante's body glistening with sweat as it moves over hers. His mouth, his hands, his control.

Eve's face, blissed out and unrepentant.

My pulse surges—and suddenly I'm there. Not watching.

Participating.

Right next to him.

My hand sliding down the smooth skin of his back. Gripping his ass as we both—

I blink. Once. Twice. Like it'll clear the static.

When my vision refocuses, I catch movement again—Corrine, standing across the bullpen, watching them too. But then she turns, catching me in the act of catching them.

Her expression says everything she doesn't.

I told you so.

When Corrine makes a beeline for my office doors, I decide it's as good a time as any to pop the aspirin. Washed down with what's left of my orange juice—now lukewarm and useless.

The door opens without a knock. Closes with a soft click.

"We need to talk," she says, about to launch into what a piece of shit Dante is. Crap I've heard before.

But I don't give her the floor. "We do," I agree.

I tap the screen of my phone, flipping it toward her across the desk. The headline stares back in tabloid-bold font—obnoxious and impossible to miss.

"What the hell is this?" I ask, tone sharp. "Because it sure as shit doesn't look like nothing."

Corrine's eyes take it in like she didn't see it before she got here. "I haven't seen that," she says, but her fingers lift to toy with the solitaire diamond on its thin gold chain around her neck.

It's the necklace she wears every day. And she always fiddles with it when she lies.

"This kind of press doesn't just hurt him," I say, voice low and hard. "It hurts me. It hurts the company. You want the board to take me seriously, but this? This doesn't help."

She seizes the opportunity like I handed it to her on a silver tray.

"Well, let's talk about Dante then, shall we?" She gestures toward the glass, to the empty space where he and Eve stood moments ago. "You saw it just like I did. What do you think that's about?"

"She's doing her job," I snap. "She's a consultant, Corrine. She was brought in to clean things up—make us look like the united front we're supposed to be."

God knows I can't tell Corrine what other specialties Eve comes with.

"You really believe that?" Her tone is soft but scathing. "Grant, you're being naive."

I grit my teeth.

She leans in slightly, eyes locking with mine. "Dante's

making his move. Probably the exact one I told *you* to make. Only now, he's a step ahead. What if he brought her in to distract you while he and that woman throw down a marriage certificate in front of the board? What if they vote to push *you* out?"

"He wouldn't do that," I argue.

But something twists in my gut.

A sliver of pain at the thought. Would Dante really do something like that to me?

He is the one that holds the contract with Eve, and I never asked to look at it. I scold myself for the oversight.

I should have asked to see the terms.

Then again, if he *were* trying to steal the company from me and use a Ledger Companion to do it, they certainly wouldn't write that in the comments section of the agreement.

Corrine watches the doubt flicker across my face like she's been waiting for it.

She reaches for my hand, the movement slow, careful, and measured. I move it to the side, pretending to reach for a pen.

Her hand ends up on my knee instead, rubbing gentle circles like she's comforting me.

"Your mother believed in you, Grant."

My stomach turns.

"She always said you were the son who would lead with vision. The one who could change everything. You need to be that man now. Be the man she saw when you didn't even know yourself yet."

I hate when she does this.

Reaches for my mother's memory like it belongs to her. Like she has the right to summon it as leverage—to wrap her voice around something sacred and wield it like a blade designed to cut through all my resistance.

But the truth is—Corrine doesn't know who my mother saw when she looked at me.

No one knows that but me. The secret I'll take to my grave because it sent my mother to hers.

That vision—whatever it was—died with her. And the man left standing in her place has never been sure if she would've loved him if she'd lived long enough to process what I had done.

It flashes then—quick, but sharp.

The intake of breath.

The way the door had slammed behind me, closing in what was about to happen.

The sound her body made when it hit the floor—softer than I expected.

The blood that spread across the marble like ink in water —slow, blooming, irreversible.

My jaw clenches, and I force the memory down, shoving it into the same dark corner I always do, where I keep the worst parts of myself out of reach. But it still hums beneath the surface, no matter how deep I bury it.

I glance toward the bookshelf like I'm looking for something to anchor me, and my eyes find the photo of her. My mother. Framed in silver, frozen in a moment that feels like another lifetime.

She's smiling in the picture. Her eyes are soft, touched with warmth that's almost maternal.

Almost.

Not like the last time I looked into them.

That final stare—wide, startled, not yet accepting the truth of what was happening—haunts me. I watched the light fade from her gaze, saw the exact moment her soul slipped away. And I've carried it with me every day since, like a bruise that never heals.

The anniversary is coming soon. It always makes the ghosts louder—more vivid—like they've been saving up their strength all year just to drag me back into the worst day of my life.

It was the day I stopped being a son.

The day I became the kind of man who knows exactly what blood feels like on his hands.

The kind of man who built his life on the memory of his mother's last breath—and the secret I bury that took it.

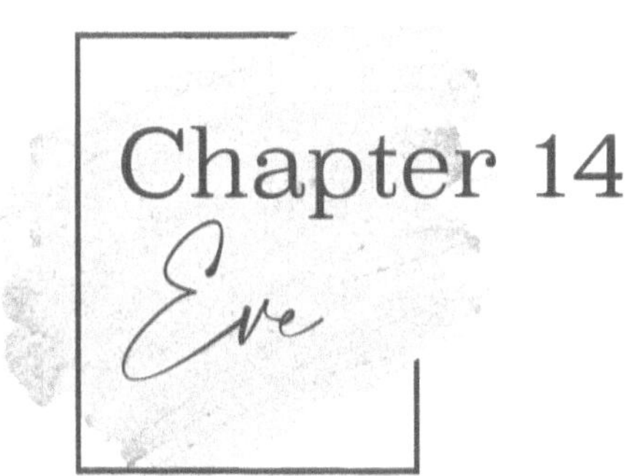

Chapter 14

Eve

I should've knocked.

I definitely shouldn't still be standing here, holding the handle like I forgot how doors work.

But Corrine's voice—low and deliberate—has me rooted in place.

Grant can't see me. She's standing just perfectly to block his view of the door, her posture just casual enough to hide how carefully she's delivering her words.

"We've always protected each other, Grant. Ever since that day."

That day.

The way she says it—weighted, like a code only the two of them understand—makes something tighten in my gut.

I don't know what she's referring to, but I know a veiled threat when I hear one. And I know leverage when I see it.

Whatever *that day* was... it matters. Enough to make her lower her voice. Enough to make him still as stone.

And now it matters to me.

Because secrets like that don't stay buried—not forever.

And I'm very good at digging.

Too much time has passed, and I need to make my presence known before I get caught eavesdropping.

I pull the door back into place just enough to feign a proper knock—one-two, polite but firm—then swing it open with an air of professionalism so smooth it might as well be choreographed.

Corrine startles like she's been caught red-handed in someone else's jewelry box. She straightens instantly, turning toward me a bit too fast for someone with nothing to hide.

Grant looks guilty. Of what, I'm not sure.

Could be the *day* Corrine just mentioned.

Could be the fact she's clearly up to something.

Or maybe it's the shitstorm on the greens yesterday that's still trickling through the tabloids.

Whatever it is, I won't uncover it right now. What I *can* do is get rid of Corrine.

"Grant," I say, offering the barest trace of a smile, "it's time for our meeting."

I wait, expectantly.

Corrine jumps in before he can speak, her voice syrupy with concern. "Maybe I should stay," she says, leaning closer to him, like they're about to share a secret. "I'd love some insight on the manner of your consultations, and Grant can sometimes be distracted around the anniversary."

My gaze snaps to her.

Anniversary.

Maybe that was the day she meant earlier. Or maybe it's

something else entirely. Either way, the word is loaded—and she knows exactly what she's doing.

What she doesn't know is that I've had enough of her games for one morning.

"Corrine, I can manage." Grant finds a piece of back-bone, at least. I wish it were a bit firmer.

"And," I say, calm but unwavering, "my contract has a firm nondisclosure clause exclusive to Grant and Dante. I'll have to ask you to step out."

Shock flickers across her face, quickly followed by irrita-tion. She blinks at me like she's trying to compute what just happened.

Then her eyes cut to Grant.

She's expecting backup.

But he doesn't give it.

He keeps his gaze on me for a beat longer than neces-sary. Then, with a quiet inhale, he stands. Rounding the desk slowly, he moves like a man making a decision in real time.

When he reaches Corrine's side, he gestures toward the door—chivalrous, polished, impossible to argue with. "Eve's right," he says simply. "Give us the room, please."

Corrine's mouth tightens.

She doesn't move at first. Just stares at him like he's betrayed her, then turns that same scathing look on me—like I'm the piece of gum she just scraped off her heel.

Then she storms out, sharp heels clicking across the marble, the office door left wide open behind her like a final insult.

Grant doesn't need a lecture.

He doesn't need a mirror held up or a therapist's tone of understanding.

What he needs is to come to terms—with Dante, and what he feels when Dante is near.

Maybe it's his sexuality. Maybe it's just him.

Maybe he's spent his whole life shoving everything soft, everything vulnerable, into a locked box. Dante being the key he's refused to acknowledge.

But I know better than to confront a man like Grant with his own truth.

If I ask him outright, he'll shut down. Retreat behind that cold veneer and drag the conversation into a war of words I'll never win—because Grant doesn't lose battles of the mind.

No.

The trick isn't to get him to admit it.

It's to make him feel it.

To provoke a response he can't explain away.

Something his mouth can lie about, but his body never could.

And when he's standing on the edge of that precipice—aroused, conflicted, furious—I'll push him just far enough to make him look down.

He won't fall yet. But he'll know the drop is there—and that he's been standing at its edge far longer than he wants to admit.

I move toward the desk, waiting until the silence stretches just long enough to become uncomfortable before I speak.

"So," I say, tone light. "Are we going to talk about

Corrine, the tabloid, or the fact that you looked like you wanted to launch her through the window?"

Grant exhales, slow and sharp. "Corrine is... complicated."

"That's one word for her."

His jaw flexes. "She's been around a long time."

"So has mold," I murmur, crossing one leg over the other as I settle into the chair across from him. "Doesn't mean you let it rot the foundation."

He shoots me a look—equal parts warning and intrigue. "Careful."

"No," I say, meeting his gaze. "I don't think I will be. Not with you."

His fingers drum once against the arm of his chair before he folds them neatly. Controlled. Restrained. "You said you had a meeting agenda."

"I do," I nod. "But let's not pretend we were going to discuss spreadsheets and synergy metrics."

He doesn't answer. That silence is just as telling.

I tilt my head, watching him. "You know, Grant... it's fascinating."

"What is?"

"The way you fight so hard to control the narrative. Your image. Your posture. Even your silence—it's curated. Like you think if you hold it all tight enough, it'll never crack."

His throat bobs with a swallow. "You're projecting."

"Am I?" I rise slowly, taking the long path around the desk, stopping just beside his chair. "Because I think you're terrified."

"Of what?"

I lean in, lowering my voice so it wraps around him like silk. "Of wanting something you were never allowed to want."

His knuckles go white around the armrests.

Bingo.

I don't bring up Dante. I don't need to.

This is about control. About the way Grant holds it like a lifeline. The way it's killing him.

But before I can say anything more, a flicker of movement catches my eye.

Corrine stalks past the outer corridor, not even pretending to be subtle. Her gaze cuts toward the office like a hawk in stilettos. The floor-to-ceiling glass makes the space feel open—vulnerable. And judging by the smug set of her lips, she likes it that way.

I lean in just enough to draw Grant's eyes to mine, softening my voice until it's almost a purr. "Is there a way to get a little more privacy in here?"

He nods slightly. "The windows fog. There's a switch near the door."

He starts to rise, ever the gentleman, ever in control—but I lay a light touch on his forearm. Just enough pressure to still him.

"I've got it," I say gently. "Let me."

His eyes drop to my hand. His throat works around a slow swallow.

I smile and pull away, crossing the room in deliberate steps. Not rushed. Not coy. Just present. Owned.

I glance over my shoulder once, then again as I reach the door. Temptation in motion. An offer wrapped in silk.

Then—with a click, the world outside the windows fades in a breath. Glass shifts to clouds, the clear view replaced by frosted walls of fog. No one can see in.

We can't see out.

Much better.

I motion toward the sitting area—two leather chairs angled toward each other across a low, round table. "Why don't we get comfortable while we talk?"

Grant hesitates for a beat, then nods. Always so polite. Always so careful.

I reach for the crystal water set arranged like a still-life centerpiece. The glass is heavy in my hand, cool. I pour a clean stream into one of the tumblers, turn, and offer it to him.

He looks at it, then at me. "No, thank you."

I set it down anyway—just beside his armrest. "In case you change your mind."

He doesn't respond. But his eyes stay on mine as I take the seat across from him, crossing one leg slowly over the other.

"I wanted to talk about something today," I begin, folding my hands loosely in my lap. "Something personal."

He arches a brow, teasing. "Well, never expected that."

I smile softly. "Sex."

The temperature in the room shifts. Not much—but I feel it.

He leans back slightly, jaw ticking. "I don't see how that's relevant."

"Frustration. Tension," I say smoothly. "They're often

the result of repression. Or a lack of release. And nothing releases pressure like a satisfying, consistent sex life."

Grant gives a humorless huff. "Not all problems are solved by sticking your cock into something."

"No," I agree, tilting my head. "But some are eased. Or at least clarified."

"I work. I run. I spend time with my father," he says flatly, like a checklist he's used before. "That's how I decompress."

I nod. "Good relationship with your dad, then?"

Something in him eases. He nods, shifting his arm on the chair. "Yes. I admire him. He built everything we have. Taught me discipline, work ethic. Loyalty."

I wait a beat, then ask quietly, "And your mother?"

The air shifts again—this time sharper. He stiffens, just enough for me to feel it.

"She died," he says simply.

"I'm sorry," I offer, and I mean it.

He brushes it off with a wave of his fingers. "It was nearly sixteen years ago."

Still, it's recent in the lines around his eyes. The silence that follows tells me everything his words won't.

The weight of her isn't gone.

Just buried.

I let the quiet linger a moment longer. Let the weight of her absence settle into the corners of the room like dust. Then I smooth my voice into something softer—silkier—as I guide us back.

"Let's go back to sex," I murmur. "What you like. What you want."

Grant gives a faint frown. "What I want?"

I smile, slow and coy, sliding to the very edge of my chair. "Preferences, Grant." I slip one heel off, then the other, lining them neatly beside my chair. "Surely you have them."

He watches warily. "What are you doing?"

I don't answer. Not directly.

Instead, I lower myself—graceful and deliberate—onto my knees. The cool bite of the floor on my skin sends a pulse through me. I crawl toward him, letting my hips sway, my shoulders roll, every movement intentional.

Calculated seduction.

His eyes darken.

"Do you like to give or take?" I ask, voice a breath. "Do you like to control... or be controlled?"

He doesn't move.

I reach his chair and settle back on my heels, knees spread just a little too wide. The stretch of my pencil skirt strains, so I slowly push the fabric up, inch by inch, until it clears the tops of my thighs. I know what he can see now.

Just the hint of bare pussy. No lace. No barrier.

His gaze drops—finally.

And stays.

His jaw is tight when he runs his tongue along his bottom lip. His hands are gripping the arms of his chair like he's clinging to his control.

And I love that. Because I'm about to take it from him.

I let my hands glide up the insides of his thighs, starting at the knees and working higher, massaging as I go. Slow, teasing circles. My thumbs drag just shy of his groin, pressing into the firm muscle there, careful not to rush.

"I wonder," I murmur, eyes still locked on his, "if you'd like to tell me what to do. Where to put my mouth. How soft. How deep."

His breathing changes—sharper now, tight in his chest. He's getting hard. I feel the shift. The heat of him, the shape forming beneath the fabric. But it's not just arousal I see in his eyes.

It's discomfort.

He doesn't want to be worshipped. Doesn't want a pretty little thing on her knees, waiting for instruction.

So, I shift.

My smile curves inward, knowing. I rise—slowly, smoothly—and trail my fingers up his arm, across the crisp line of his chest, then down again, letting my palm drift across the bulge in his pants.

"You wouldn't like that," I say, voice low, circling behind him. "You don't want to command."

I lean in, letting my breath trace the shell of his ear as I wrap my hand around his cock—firm and aching beneath his slacks. I squeeze, just enough to pull a sound from him. He exhales, a heavy appreciative breath, his body betraying what his words never could.

"You want to be broken open," I whisper, stroking him now, slow and possessive. "You want someone to take the reins. To make the decisions for you. To give you rules so you can feel what it's like to let go."

His hips twitch. His cock jerks in my hand.

"You want to be taken apart by someone who isn't afraid of what they'll find when they do."

I keep stroking, using the pad of my thumb to tease the

head through the fabric. His head falls back, lips parting slightly—fighting it and failing.

Then I stop.

Pulling away like nothing happened, I straighten.

"Give me the water."

He fumbles a second before he grabs it, like a man starved for orders. Just like I thought.

I take it with a slow smile, sipping it without breaking eye contact.

When I'm done, I give it back, and my hand trails down again. This time, I don't toy. I take.

My fingers close around him once more—hot, thick, needy.

I lean in, voice just above a whisper.

"Good boy."

He groans.

Not a quiet one. Not subtle.

A deep, involuntary sound that rips from his chest and coils straight into my core. His hands clamp tight around the carved wooden arms of his chair. Eyes closed. Jaw slack. He looks undone.

I keep stroking him—slow, precise—watching the tension ripple through him like a live wire straining against itself.

"I know what you want," I purr, voice velvet-wrapped sin. "You want strong hands on you. On your cock. You want to feel someone in control... someone who doesn't let you hide."

His hips lift slightly, syncing with my rhythm. His body answers before he can lie with his mouth.

"You want to be on your knees," I whisper against his temple. "Begging. Submitting. Taking what you're given."

His breath hitches.

I press closer, my grip tightening, my strokes faster now. "Tell me something, Grant. Ever sucked a cock before?"

His eyes flash open, but he doesn't stop me. He can't. "No."

"But you want to." It's not a question. A confirmation.

"No."

"Liar." I continue, voice like silk against steel. "You want to. You want to be on your knees, run your tongue up the shaft of a hard dick, and feel every vein pulse against it."

His chest is rising faster now, each breath ragged and raw. "Fuck."

"You want to take it deep. Feel it hit the back of your throat. Gag around it. Suck like the filthy little slut you're too scared to admit you are."

He grits his teeth. "No."

I clench my hand tighter around him. Stroke deeper.

"And I know whose cock you want to choke on."

"No."

"Who it is that you want to come down your throat while you milk every drop from him."

"You're wrong." He's so breathless, he's panting in desperation.

The fabric of his pants is wet with pre-cum, and he's moving with me now, chasing the release.

But he won't get it.

"I don't think I am wrong."

I wait until he's just there—just there—right at the

edge, panting like a man seconds from drowning in his own desire.

And then I stop.

He bucks forward with a choked, desperate sound. His eyes shoot open, confusion and betrayal flashing across them.

I lean down, my lips brushing his ear as I whisper, low and lethal:

"You're a liar, Grant. And you'll only come when you admit who you want to come for."

And I walk out, leaving him aching and alone.

Chapter 15
Dante

"Tell me how the fuck this happened," I snap, slapping the folder onto the conference table. The loud *thwack* makes a few heads turn before they quickly look away.

Frankie stands opposite me with her arms crossed, chewing a piece of gum like she's got all the time in the world. Red lips. Victory curls. Leopard-print heels that say *fuck around and find out.* Her expression doesn't flinch. Not even a little.

"I don't know how it happened," she says. "You said the twenty-first. I had the twenty-first."

"That's what I said. So why the hell are we finding out today that the meeting is tomorrow?"

She shrugs one shoulder. "Ask the client's new assistant. Or maybe a hacker with a really boring agenda. I don't know."

My fingers curl around the edge of the table. "I don't need sarcasm right now, Frankie."

"I'm not being sarcastic," she says. "I'm being calm. One of us has to be. Besides, I've already rescheduled your Thursday calls, bumped the weekly check-in, and ordered catering for tomorrow's pitch. You're welcome."

People are passing through the office like shadows, avoiding eye contact, ducking into side rooms. No one wants to be caught in the crossfire of a Dante Marchesi meltdown.

My hand goes to my pocket automatically, fingers brushing the edge of the cigarette pack I haven't opened. Not yet.

Frankie sees the movement. Her eyes narrow. "Tell me you're not smoking again."

I pause. "I'm not."

She raises a brow. "Then empty your pockets."

I glare. "Fuck off."

"I will literally reach in there myself."

I smirk. "What is it you're really after, Frankie? The cigarettes or confirmation that the rumors about my generous proportions are true?"

She gives me a long, unimpressed look. "Dante, if I wanted to hear about your dick, I'd kill myself first."

"You've been looking for an excuse to feel me up since your first day."

She snorts. "Penises are cute on gay men. On anyone else? Disgusting."

"I *am* gay."

"Exactly. Which is why I let you live."

I exhale through my nose, trying not to laugh. Frankie might be a pain in my ass, but she's the only one in this office with the balls to throw it back at me. She's also the only reason I haven't torched the entire building yet.

She softens just a hair. "Look. It's not ideal. But we can fix it. You know the material. The team's prepped. We'll run drills tonight and knock it out tomorrow. You've done more with less time."

I shake my head. "The models are nowhere near ready."

A pale shadow looms to my right.

Some intern—baby-faced and trembling—is hovering with a tablet clutched to his chest like it might shield him from incoming fire. His mouth opens once, then closes. He swallows. Opens it again.

I don't even look at him when I say, "If you ask me a question, you're fired."

Frankie doesn't miss a beat. "No, you're not."

"Yes," I counter, dragging my gaze toward the poor bastard. "You are. Figure it out."

The kid turns the color of chalk and disappears faster than he appeared. Smart.

And then Grant walks in.

Of course he fucking does.

He moves like he always does—slow, aware, a little too observant. Like he's reading the energy in the room and cataloging it for later. His eyes scan the tense stillness, the scuttling team, the obvious explosion in progress. But when he speaks, his voice is infuriatingly neutral.

"What's going on?"

I stare at him. "Nothing you need to worry about."

His posture stays relaxed, but there's a flicker in his throat. A tight swallow. Something brewing behind those eyes that isn't just confusion or concern. It's hotter than that. Sharper.

Well, looks like someone's had their session with Eve already.

Frankie scoops her things into her arms like a woman halfway through an exit plan. I narrow my eyes at her.

"Now is when you decide to walk out?"

She lifts a brow. "I would rather give a Brazilian wax to a silverback gorilla than stay here and listen to you two circle each other like gladiators in tight suits."

Before I can respond, she's already at the door.

"Call me when you're both done measuring dicks," she says sweetly, and disappears.

Silence falls like a trap.

I glance around the glass box we call a conference room. Half the team is still pretending to look busy while eavesdropping through the walls. I've had enough.

"Everyone out," I say. "Now."

Chairs scrape. Pens drop. No one dares argue.

"I'll have a revised directive in your inboxes within the hour," I add coolly.

The door clicks shut behind the last one. And now it's just me. And Grant.

The quiet thickens.

I'm still breathing hard, jaw tight, hands flexing and curling like they can't decide whether to punch something or dig deeper. And he's watching me.

Steady. Patient. That fucking psychologist face.

He steps closer.

"You're unraveling," he says, almost gently.

I look up. Meet his eyes.

"You're enjoying it," I reply.

"Did you come in here to exclusively scowl at me, Glow-bug," I bite, "or did you think this would help?"

"I've told you not to call me that." Grant folds his arms, posture stiff. "I *am* helping. You just don't like anyone pointing out when you've fucked something up."

"Of course. Always my fault."

His jaw ticks. "Maybe if you weren't so busy letting Eve play therapist with nothing under her coat, you would've caught the calendar shift before it became a crisis."

My laugh is sharp. Yeah, Eve definitely worked him up good. "Eve's trying to help. Just like I am. The real question is—what the fuck are *you* doing?"

Grant doesn't answer. Not directly.

Instead, he tilts his head, eyes raking over me like he's weighing the risk of saying what's actually on his mind. Then:

"You still pretending you're doing this for anyone but yourself?"

The words land somewhere beneath my ribs, raw and burning.

But I don't flinch. I lean in instead. Close enough that his breath catches—close enough to feel the heat coming off him.

"Tell me this, bug,"—the air shifts—no longer charged with anger, but something darker. Needier—"how do you know she wears nothing beneath her coat?"

I inhale the scent of his cologne, and it makes my jaw tighten.

We're close now. Too close. His breath fans against my

cheek when he exhales, tight and sharp. His gaze flicks—down. Just for a second. Right to my mouth.

I make a point to look down. Leaning my head to the side, making the line of my sight clear before I flick my gaze back up to his.

My voice drops, velvet and dangerous. "You gonna keep pretending it's her that's got you hard?" It's a whisper directly into his ear.

Grant's nostrils flare. A small, involuntary reaction. His mouth opens like he might deny it, but no sound comes out.

"Thought so."

I take a half step back—not enough to defuse the moment, just enough to let the tension simmer in the space between us. Grant stays rooted where he is, and for a second, he looks wrecked by it. His eyes are wide, pupils dark and dilated, his breath still catching like his body hasn't gotten the message that the fight is over—or that it never really was a fight to begin with.

There's something in his gaze now—something feral, something frustrated. And underneath all of that, something he's tried to deny for far too long.

Then the sharp rap of knuckles against glass slices through the charge between us.

Fucking Corrine.

She pushes the door open without waiting for a response, all tailored confidence and calculated timing. There's a practiced smile on her face, but the real expression is in her eyes—cool, assessing, and just a little too pleased with herself.

"Sorry to interrupt," she says lightly, her voice syrup-smooth as she glances between us. "Grant, we need to go over the budget revisions. You have a minute?"

That's when Grant steps back.

Not just a shuffle or a shift, but a full, conscious retreat. More distance than I gave him, more space than either of us needed—and I see it for exactly what it is. A line being redrawn. A mask snapping back into place. His body trying to pretend it doesn't remember what it just responded to.

"Yeah," he says, his tone as controlled as the expression on his face, but it doesn't fool me. There's something else underneath it—something flickering at the edges, like a fuse sparking under tension.

I can't help myself. The words come out before I even decide to say them.

"Run back to her," I murmur, voice low and loaded. "Your safe-space of lies."

Grant falters. A single hitch in his step, a fraction of hesitation he probably doesn't think I'll notice.

But I do.

Corrine pretends not to hear—or maybe she does and simply enjoys it. She glances back over her shoulder once as they walk out, her smile still in place but sharpened now, like a victory.

I stay where I am, watching the glass door click shut behind them.

My jaw ticks, a slow grind I don't bother concealing. I should sit. I should move on. I should let it go.

I plant my hands on the edge of the model table, shoulders tense, chest heaving with frustration I can't seem to swallow. The miniature skyline mocks me—precise, controlled, a perfect little world where everything goes exactly as planned.

Not like mine.

Not like this.

My fingers curl around the nearest model—a sleek acrylic tower I once obsessed over—and before I can stop myself, I hurl it across the room.

It explodes against the far wall, shattering into a hundred perfect pieces.

Chapter 16

Grant

I slept like shit. Not that I'm willing to admit why.

The board's looming vote is an easy scapegoat. So is the calendar mishap. The Wolfe of Manhattan breathing down our necks. Plenty of rational reasons to toss and turn all night.

None of them explain why my head wouldn't shut off. Why I kept replaying yesterday's argument on a loop—every word, every glance, every breath too close. And none of them explain why I checked my phone the second I woke up.

Why my shoulders dropped when there was nothing from Dante.

I left late last night. The kind of late where most of the building had already gone dark. But I know for a fact Dante and his team were still here. Lights on, voices tight, models being rearranged and reworked like salvation could be built out of foam core and reinforced glass.

I stepped in for a bit, helped one of the render teams in a

corner conference room that had been half-commandeered into a war zone of coffee cups, laptops, and tension. It was safe in there. Tucked away from Dante's mood and Frankie's no-bullshit perimeter defense.

But even in that room, I couldn't escape him. He was everywhere. In the clean edges of the façade. In the light-mapping innovations his mind engineered. In the way the layout pulled function and form into something living.

His brilliance is annoying. Mostly because I admire it.

And when I was leaving, shoulders heavy with fatigue and frustration, I caught a glimpse of him across the floor. Just a flicker of eye contact. His face remained neutral—icy calm, like always—but his espresso eyes were burning. The kind of quiet storm no one else would notice unless they'd spent far too long looking for it.

I turned away first. That's the part I can't stop replaying. The burn of his stare I felt every step to the elevators.

Now it's morning, and the pitch meeting with the client is set to begin in less than an hour. The entire firm is holding its breath—and so is the board. Everything is riding on this.

I send a text.

Just a short one. Professional. Cold, even. But it's also the second one I've sent.

Still no response to the first.

I try not to look at my phone like a teenager waiting to be noticed. Try not to care that it's unread. As the elevator rises, I focus on my reflection in the mirrored walls—tie straight, jaw tight. The version of me that doesn't care is the one I wear today.

Hours pass.

Still nothing.

My irritation starts to rot at the edges, curling into something sharp and defensive. Sarcasm coats it. Makes it easier to carry.

It only gets worse when Corrine calls me into her office midmorning. Something about expense reports—some bullshit line item she could easily delegate. I'm not sure if she's trying to bait me or distract me, but either way, I don't have the patience.

She asks why I'm in such a mood.

I don't answer.

Because I don't want to explain that the person I'm irritated with isn't even in this room—and that maybe I'm not irritated so much as… concerned. Not that I'd ever call it that out loud.

I excuse myself and head for Dante's floor.

I've looked at my phone a hundred times already, but I check again as I cross the executive lobby. Still no update. Not even the dots of a pending reply.

Frankie's behind her desk when I arrive, tapping away at her keyboard with a mug that says, *World's Best Assistant to the World's Okayest Boss.*

"Let me guess," I mutter as I stop in front of her desk. "He's passed out in a strip club somewhere. Champagne in one hand, misplaced ego in the other?"

Frankie doesn't bite. No sarcastic jab, no eye roll. Just stillness.

Her posture is tight. One foot bouncing slightly, fingers flexing and unflexing in her lap. Frankie gives a damn, but more importantly—she's used to Dante's chaos. If she's unnerved, something's wrong.

"What is it?" Chills rush down my spine in a wave.

"I've texted, called. Nothing. Even when he's drunk, furious, halfway to Milan—he picks up."

I pull out my phone and hit dial on a number I've not called in years.

Two rings and it connects.

"St. Vincent's Medical," a woman answers. "Are you a relative of the patient?"

My pulse skips. "Dante Marchesi?"

"Yes. He was admitted early this morning. Are you a relative? We're trying to locate his next of kin."

That's not good. That's never good.

"Yes, I'm next of kin," I say, already pushing toward the elevator. "I'm on his emergency contact. I need to know what happened."

"I'm sorry, sir. I can't disclose any patient information over the phone."

She doesn't wait for the argument she probably expects. "If you can come to the hospital, we'll walk you through what we can."

She doesn't even finish the sentence before I hang up.

"Dante's in the hospital," I bark toward Frankie. "Reschedule my meetings."

She bolts up from her chair. "Wait—what? Is he okay?"

"I don't know," I mutter without looking back.

And if he's not—if he's not okay—I have no idea how I'll tell his father.

How I'll walk into that man's estate and explain that his son...

No. I don't let the thought finish.

I just get in the elevator and slam the button for the lobby like I can outpace whatever's waiting for me on the other side.

In twenty minutes, I pull into valet like I'm about to rob the place—tires screeching, door half open before the car even stops. I toss the keys at the stunned attendant with a barked, "Just hold the ticket," and push through the hospital's sliding glass doors.

The front desk is too calm. Too quiet. The woman behind it types like she's got all day.

"Dante Marchesi," I say, voice clipped, breath tight. "Where is he?"

She doesn't even glance up. Just keeps typing. And typing. And typing.

My hands curl into fists at my sides. Is she typing up the goddamn Declaration of Independence?

Finally, she sighs and pops her gum with a loud *crack*. "Oh, this one."

My stomach drops. "He's alive?"

She leans back in her chair, chewing lazily. "And won't shut up."

Relief floods me so fast my knees nearly give. I brace a hand on the counter.

"What happened?"

"Ran a red light or something. Lost a battle with a dump truck." She lifts a shoulder like she's describing a minor fender bender. "Got pinned. They had to cut him out of the car."

My heart drops again, lower this time. "Jesus."

She goes back to typing. Another loud *crack* of gum. "They're still waiting on scans, but the only thing injured is his ego. Maybe his leg. He's in 804."

I'm moving immediately, heading straight for the elevators.

As I ride up to the eighth floor, I'm not sure which emotion is louder—rage that he got himself into this mess, or the shaky, low-grade relief that he's still here to piss me off.

The doors open. I step out, scanning for the room.

I find it by the nurse walking out with a chuckle, shaking her head like she's just been hit on and can't decide if she's amused or flattered.

Fucking flirt.

That pisses me off more.

I round the corner and step into the room.

Dante's sitting up in the hospital bed, pulling off gauze wrapped around his head and fussing with his dark hair. A bruise already blooming across his temple, scratches on his neck and collarbone—airbag, probably.

When he sees me, he quirks a brow. "You here to enjoy the show? Another viral video, perhaps?" He inspects his IV like he's going to pull it out.

I exhale, dragging a hand through my hair.

"I'm here to make sure you're breathing, asshole."

"Aw, *Lucciolina.*" He grins. "You do care."

Dante's lips are just starting to curl into another smartass comment when pain hits him.

His whole body seizes.

"*Merda*—" he chokes out, jaw clenched, one hand flying to his thigh.

The way his face twists—sharp pain and surprise—has me moving before I even register it.

"Hey. Hey," I murmur, stepping in close.

My hand slides over his, catching it through the blanket. I press it down—not hard, just enough to anchor him, to let him know I've got him. That he doesn't have to brace through it alone.

But his breathing is ragged now, uneven. One hand grips my wrist like a vise. His other hand fists the sheets.

I slip beneath the blanket. The warmth of his bare skin punches through me. Jesus. The muscle's locked, tight as a wire, and my fingers move instinctively—slow, steady circles just above the cramp. I keep my touch firm, careful.

His breath catches.

And when I glance at his face—

He's staring at me. *Really* staring.

Eyes heavy-lidded but razor focused. His lashes cast low shadows, but nothing dims that look—like he sees every thought racing through me. Every place my mind is going. Every place my hands have already been.

There's a pull in my chest, hot and coiled. A hum beneath my skin. Like I've grabbed a live wire and can't let go.

He's not watching me with that usual sharp-edged

mockery, but something quieter. Heavier. Something that makes it impossible to breathe.

There's a dark freckle high on his left cheek. A small scar at the base of his chin—one I've seen a thousand times but never like this. His mouth is parted, lips full, and his breathing matches mine—too fast, too shallow, like we're both seconds from something we can't take back.

I don't say anything. Can't.

Because this? This isn't banter or bravado. This is real.

His fingers tighten around my wrist.

Just slightly. Just enough to make sure I feel it.

And then he shifts.

His legs part, just a little. Just enough.

The message is clear. He's not asking.

He's offering.

And then his hand moves.

"Dante," I say again, voice lower now. Rougher.

He doesn't answer. Just holds my wrist as his body stays tense beneath mine. He breathes through another wave of pain—or maybe it's something else entirely—and then he guides me.

Slow.

Intentional.

He drags my hand from his thigh and moves it lower.

Lower.

Until I feel him.

The hard, unmistakable line of his cock beneath the hospital gown.

"Proprio come prima,"[*] Dante murmurs, voice low as sin. "So hard for you."

He presses my palm to it. Holds it there.

The air vanishes from my lungs.

Heat explodes in my face. In my chest. Down my spine. My hand under the blanket is still resting high on his thigh, dangerously close, unmoving now—but not pulling away.

I'm frozen. But I feel everything.

The pounding of my heart. The sweat at the base of my neck. The low buzz under my skin that tells me I should leave. But fuck if I can.

Dante's eyes haven't left mine. Not once.

He looks like he's daring me.

Daring me to say I don't want this. Daring me to pretend like we haven't been circling this for years. Like this isn't exactly what we both thought about more nights than we'll ever admit.

My mouth opens, but no words come out. Just breath.

Shallow. Hitched. Desperate.

My fingers twitch beneath the blanket. A reflex. My body betraying the denial on the tip of my tongue.

"Lo vuoi ancora. Anche se menti."[†]

The smallest smirk lifts the corner of his mouth as he presses my hand harder, his hips raising.

And that's when I snap.

I tear both hands away—fast and clumsy—like I've been

---

[*]   "Just like before."
[†]   "You still want it. Even when you lie."

burned. My heart's in my throat, my skin on fire. I step back so quickly I almost trip over the damn IV pole.

The door opens behind me.

A nurse walks in, clipboard in hand. "Alright, Mr. Marchesi, looks like you'll live." She looks up, noticing me mid-breakdown.

"F-Frankie'll send a car," I blurt. My voice sounds like someone else's. "To get you home."

Dante reclines back into the bed like a king who's just won the fucking war. That smug, lazy smirk blooming again. His eyes never leave me as he puts his hands behind his head.

"I'll follow up with the c-client," I add, backing toward the door. "Smooth it over."

I don't wait for a response.

I just get the hell out of the room.

Because if I stay a second longer, I won't be able to pretend I'm still in control.

And Dante Marchesi already knows that.

Chapter 17

Eve

"**R**ight," I say into my phone, twirling a pen between my fingers. "Private table, corner alcove. I want the first one seated by eleven forty-five. The second arrives ten minutes later."

The maître d' on the other end is hurriedly scribbling notes.

I shift in my chair and glance down at the sheet I've been sketching placement notes on.

"Grant Harrow will take the booth facing the east windows."

"And the second?"

"Dante Marchezi," I say, tucking the corner of the paper under my laptop. "He gets the fireplace table, center left."

"Noted."

"Drinks waiting when they arrive," I add, standing and stretching the stiffness from my neck. "Neat for one, sparkling water for the other. I'm not telling you which is which—you'll figure it out when they walk in."

The man laughs softly. "You always set a scene, Ms. Sterling."

"Guilty," I murmur, smiling. "And tell the servers—minimal interruption. These aren't casual lunches. They're conversations with stakes."

I hang up and slide my phone into my clutch before heading straight to Frankie's desk.

She's mid-email, fingers flying across the keyboard, blonde hair pinned into a flawless twist. She's rocking that bombshell-Betty vibe like she was born for it—hourglass dress, perfect lipstick, no time for anyone's bullshit.

I like her. She's direct, unflinching. No sugarcoating or fake niceties, just sharp efficiency with a side of sass. The kind of woman who'd survive any boardroom, battlefield, or back alley. And she doesn't ask questions unless she actually wants the answer.

She looks up, brow arching. "You look like you just pulled off a quiet coup."

I shrug. "Just lunch."

She doesn't buy it. "For both of them?"

"Mmhmm." I hand her the schedule. "Back-to-back on paper, but overlapping in real time. Same club, different clients—no one needs to know but us."

Frankie skims the paper, her lips twitching. "You're putting them in the same building at the same time?"

"Same room," I correct. "Just not close enough to touch."

Her eyes widen slightly. "That's either genius or petty."

"Depends on the outcome," I say, already turning away. "Block their calendars. I'll explain it to them myself."

I barely finish confirming Frankie's calendar holds when

Corrine materializes out of nowhere—smooth as a silk noose and twice as deliberate.

"Everything running well, I hope?" she asks, voice all polished civility, but the tension under every syllable is impossible to miss. There's something performative about the smile she flashes—like a chess player disguising her checkmate behind a toast.

"Perfectly," I say, not bothering to offer one back.

Her gaze flicks toward Frankie's screen, where the blocked time still lingers. "I noticed the calendar holds," she adds, tone light but eyes sharp. "Seems important. I assume I should be involved?"

I don't flinch. "Not necessary. These clients were sourced through a private network. Their interests require discretion."

Corrine's smile tightens. "As CFO, I'm responsible for all high-stakes engagements. If something goes sideways with either of them, the board will expect answers—from me."

Of course she plays the board card. Classic.

"Then you should trust that I've chosen the right assets to ensure nothing does," I say smoothly. No need to raise my voice when confidence is sharper than volume.

Her veneer slips—just slightly. Enough to show she's not used to hearing *no* without a concession attached. Her tone softens, but the words don't.

"You know, Grant and I built this from the ground up," she says, voice tipping toward something sentimental. "Every success, every loss. We protect each other. Always have."

I meet her eyes. Cool. Direct. Unmoved.

"That's admirable," I offer. "But protecting someone doesn't mean controlling them. However, I do note the side of the building reads *Marchesi & Harrow.* Not *Harrow and Ashwood.*"

There's a pause—brief, but weighted. A beat where she recalibrates. Swallows down the rage.

"I'll still need the details for financial projections," she says, re-centering herself. "These deals won't be invisible on paper."

I tilt my head just slightly. A smile plays on my lips—not sweet, not warm. Calculated. Measured. "And when the contracts are signed, you'll have everything you need."

My attention is no longer given to Corrine. I turn to Frankie, smoothly cutting out our newly arrived guest. As I bring up bullshit subjects, Corrine finally slinks back into her snake's den.

"Marry me, Eve Sterling," Frankie says, all glittery-eyed and smiling.

I blink. "Excuse me?"

She crosses her arms, deadpan. "I'm just saying. If you ever want to be the third Mrs. Lane, applications are open. Full benefits. Excellent dental. All we ask is a firm anti-Corrine stance and a tolerance for loud reality TV."

I snort, half-laughing as I perch on the edge of her desk. "You're ridiculous."

"I'm serious. Wait till I tell my wife. She's going to make me frame a photo of you after that line. 'Protecting someone doesn't mean controlling them'? Jesus. I want that on a tote bag."

"If we're making merch, I vote for '#AsCEO' in Comic Sans."

Frankie groans dramatically. "Ugh. Don't bring her voice into this moment. It's sacred."

We both laugh—easy, unguarded. A balm after all that performative professionalism.

She swings her chair side to side, then glances up at me. "Lunch? I'm starving. And you've clearly earned a reward for surviving Corrine's weaponized diplomacy."

"My treat," I say, standing and smoothing my skirt. "On one condition."

Her brow lifts. "Name it."

"You talk as much shit about Corrine as humanly possible."

Frankie grins, wicked. "Deal. But fair warning—I'm clearing my whole afternoon."

"Even better."

We walk out together, plotting the lunch menu and the roast session with equal enthusiasm.

Chapter 18
Grant

The maître d' leads me through the private wing of the country club restaurant, where the lighting is soft, the linens are starch-crisp, and the price of silence is built into the bill. I spot my client already seated—she's early, of course.

Blonde. Polished. Perfectly poised. The kind of woman whose heels never scuff, whose pearls are real, and whose bloodline probably owns more of Europe than it visits.

Isabelle Lévêque.

French banking heiress. Old money. The kind of client who knows exactly what she wants—and expects the world to rise to meet her.

"Mr. Harrow," she says, stepping close.

We greet in that familiar European style—a kiss to each cheek. Her perfume is soft but expensive. Her skin glows. She's beautiful. The sort of woman I might've been drawn to in another life. Before I became CEO. Before—well—just, before.

"I've admired your firm's work for years," she says in perfect English, with just enough accent to make it elegant. "I'm bringing a piece of provincial France to Manhattan. A full renovation of my grandfather's building on the Upper East Side. I want light, elegance... but with bones."

Her eyes narrow on mine. "Your portfolio suggests you understand history. And restraint."

"I like to think so," I say, offering a composed smile. "Marchesi and Harrow specializes in honoring legacy without compromising innovation."

Before I can flag a server, two crystal flutes of sparkling water arrive—lime wedge balanced just so. The waitress disappears with practiced ease.

Isabelle lifts her glass. "Then let's see if we're a match, Mr. Harrow."

The door opens again, and I don't see him at first. But I feel him.

A shift in the atmosphere—like gravity adjusting around a new axis. Every hair on my arm lifts before I even look up to see Dante.

Two days ago, he was in a hospital bed. Bruised, battered, a cocktail of machines keeping him monitored. My hand had been on his thigh. Then—then absolutely nowhere at all.

Now he's walking into this restaurant like the devil wears linen and good cologne.

He's dressed in a cream suit with a pale blue shirt unbuttoned just enough to hint at skin. His hair's styled like it wasn't—effortless and infuriating. He's laughing softly with the hostess, hand resting on her lower back as she gestures toward his table.

And that's when I see who he's meeting with.

Matheus da Costa.

Brazilian football legend. World-renowned. Fast, charismatic, and so absurdly gifted he makes gravity look optional. He's only a few years out from retirement but already positioning himself as a power player off the field— tech investments, real estate, fashion ventures. A global brand all his own.

He stands when he sees Dante. Broad smile. Hand extended.

They clasp forearms, pulling into one of those firm, one-armed hugs. Familiar but respectful. Close. Comfortable. The kind of closeness that makes my jaw clench.

They speak in low tones—Portuguese or Italian, I can't tell. Matheus says something that makes Dante laugh, all warm and relaxed in a way that sets my teeth on edge.

They don't sit yet. They linger. Dante leans in to say something, and Matheus claps him on the shoulder, laughing again like they're old friends or newly in cahoots.

I can't hear a damn thing.

And I hate how much I want to.

He's seated by the maître d' across the room—far enough that we're clearly here for different meetings, but close enough to see every line of his smirk when he turns and spots me.

He stills. Just slightly.

One hand, in the process of unbuttoning his jacket,

pauses on the second button. Our eyes lock. I watch the surprise flicker in his expression—real and unguarded—before he schools it down to something cooler. Smoother.

Then he finishes unbuttoning, slides into his seat with a fluid, deliberate ease, and smiles like he's just been dealt a winning hand.

I swallow the knot in my throat and try not to visibly react.

This has Eve written all over it.

Dante didn't know I'd be here. I'm almost certain. That flash of surprise—he's too good of an actor to fake it that well. Which means neither of us was expecting the other, and Eve orchestrated this.

Strategically.

Calculatingly.

Two luncheons. One location. Power players on either side. Matching times, mirrored placements. I'm seated with my back to the wall, full view of the restaurant. And him—directly opposite me. Every glance from either table now a game of discretion. Or provocation.

It's not subtle.

And it's not an accident.

I pick up my water, sipping slowly while Dante settles in, already charming Matheus. Dante leans in just a bit when he speaks. His smile is easy. Natural. His eyes spark when Matheus laughs—and maybe it's innocent. Maybe it's strategy.

But all I can see is his hand on my wrist. That burning look in his eyes.

His fingers pressing mine against the hard line of his cock as he exhales.

I shift in my seat, force my focus back to my client. Because whatever game this is, it's already started, and I have no idea what the rules are.

Or who's supposed to win.

Isabelle is elegance incarnate. Poised and immaculate in a crisp cream blouse that probably costs more than most people's rent. She leans back in her chair with graceful confidence, long fingers circling the stem of her wineglass.

"I want it to feel like Avignon," she says, her French accent soft but deliberate. "Not just in design, but in rhythm. A space that invites people to slow down. No sterile glass towers or overly industrial façades. Stone. Wood. Texture. Light." She smiles. "Charm."

It should be an easy pitch. This is what I do—translate vision into form. I've taken abstract aspirations and turned them into award-winning architecture. Marchesi & Harrow doesn't just build structures—we craft identity. I've walked clients like Isabelle through every phase from site selection to skyline.

But right now?

Right now, I can't even remember the name of the zoning consultant we're meant to loop in.

"Absolutely," I say, swallowing the tightness in my throat. "There's a historic block near Gramercy we've been tracking—quiet, residential-adjacent, and flexible enough for a mixed-use renovation. Our firm would oversee the full restoration. We'd source reclaimed materials locally but style it to echo Provence—stonework, terracotta, soft arches. Manhattan meets the Côte d'Azur."

She tilts her head, visibly intrigued. "And your funding partners?"

I blink.

My mouth opens—but nothing comes out. My brain stutters, locked somewhere between the sparkle of Dante's fucking laugh and the memory of his hips shifting under my palm.

My tongue feels like sandpaper. I blink once, twice, trying to shove the answer forward from wherever it's stuck in my brain, but it's drowned beneath linen suits and Mediterranean cheek kisses.

Because across the room, Dante Marchesi is fucking glowing.

His head is tilted just enough to show off the clean line of his jaw. He's laughing—like, genuinely laughing—and his hand is resting lightly on the table beside the football star, fingers barely brushing the stem of his glass. Matheus is practically swooning. And why wouldn't he? Dante's charming. Relaxed. Confident in a way that never feels like performance.

It's infuriating.

I drag my eyes back to Isabelle, clear my throat.

"Sorry," I say, adjusting my cuffs. "Long week."

She chuckles. "No worries, darling. Are you all right? You look—flushed."

Flushed is a fucking understatement.

Try two days of adrenaline, arousal, and the memory of Dante's thigh under my hands. His skin hot, his cock thick and hard and straining under the covers. The sound he made when I touched him—fuck.

"We can always move this meeting to dinner. Then—perhaps—something private."

Isabelle raises one pointed brow, and it looks like she's giving herself credit for my state.

I shift in my seat, adjusting the pressure against my slacks.

Big mistake.

Across the room, Dante lifts his glass to his lips. His eyes are on me—have been, I realize.

How long has he been watching?

His expression is unreadable. Perfectly neutral. But his gaze? Heavy. Intentionally so.

Like he knows exactly what I'm thinking about. Like he's daring me to keep going.

My jaw tightens.

Eve's words echo in my head, low and taunting: "...when you admit who you want to come for."

I swallow hard, grip my napkin tighter than necessary.

"Please, excuse me a moment," I say, already pushing back from the table.

"Of course." Isabelle sits back and takes a drink of her white wine.

I nod, mutter thanks, and make a beeline for the hallway. My hands shake as I shove the door open to the marble-lined bathroom—cool and echoing.

I lean over the sink. Breathe.

My pulse is a snare drum. My throat is dry.

And my cock is a fucking brick in my slacks like I'm some hormonal intern who can't keep it together over one look.

One look.

I splash cold water on my face, press my palms to the porcelain, and stare at myself in the mirror.

This is not just about Eve's little game.

This is about Dante. What happened. What almost happened.

And the part of me that's still furious I stopped it.

I don't need to look to know he's unraveling.

But I do anyway—because watching Grant Harrow try to hold it together might just be the highlight of my fucking week.

I make a mental note to thank Eve later. Flowers, maybe. Or I can sit her on my desk and make her come on my face a few times. Whatever it is, she's earned it. Because this seating arrangement? A work of strategic brilliance.

Across the room, Grant sits stiff-backed in his chair, soft tan now betraying him with the warm flush rising in his cheeks. He's run a hand through that dirty-blond hair at least a dozen times in the last ten minutes, each pass more agitated than the last. The perfectly sculpted strands now stand in rebellion, messier than I've seen them in years.

His fingers drum against the table—a pathetic little outlet for the storm gathering in those blue-gray eyes. The ones he keeps flicking over to me. Every few seconds, without fail. Like he can't help himself.

And fuck, do I love how beautiful jealousy looks on him.

Am I playing it up?

You're damn right I am.

Matheus da Costa throws his head back, laughing at some story I can't even remember finishing. We've spent the last twenty minutes talking about his three-year-old daughter and how she already has better footwork than half his team.

"Natural talent," he'd said proudly, placing a hand over his heart. "Just like her papa."

I'd leaned in with a grin, chuckled in that low way I know carries across the room. "I'd expect nothing less."

He's easy to like—charming, grounded, surprisingly earnest. And globally adored. You don't have to know football to know his face. The man's practically a brand of his own.

Grant knows who he is.

But Grant's not a fan like I am.

He doesn't know Matheus has been married to the same woman for twelve years. That he's devoted. Straight as a midfield line. That he's been proudly showing me photos of his daughter in matching cleats, babbling about how she already understands angles.

We haven't even touched the business yet.

But from the way Grant is glaring like Matheus just whispered something filthy in my ear, I doubt he knows that.

So, am I going to keep this up?

Am I going to keep brushing Matheus's arm when I laugh? Keep tipping my glass slowly, eyes low-lidded, every movement calibrated just enough to hold Grant's attention without being obvious?

Abso-fucking-lutely.

Because I have a damn good idea where Grant's mind keeps going.

And if I'm right—and let's be honest, I usually am—it's straight to my cock.

I shift slightly in my seat as the memory from two days ago floods back, vivid and electric. The way he whispered my name—Dante—breathless and low, like it had been dragged from somewhere he didn't want to admit still existed. Like it hurt just to say it.

His hand had been on my thigh. Then higher. The slight flex of his fingers when he brushed against me—like he wanted to wrap his whole palm around my shaft and hold on for dear life. Until he pulled away too fucking soon.

I told Eve, of course.

She asked for every detail.

And last night she played it out for me.

Let me close my eyes and walk her through it—all of it—while she wrapped her mouth around my dick and sucked me like she'd been born for it. But it wasn't her mouth I was thinking about. Not really. Not when I came down her throat saying his fucking name.

So, when I glance up and catch Grant shifting in his seat—his arm dipping just slightly under the table—I know. I know.

He's hard, just like I am.

And he's trying to adjust himself without anyone noticing.

Too late, *Lucciolina.*

His jaw clenches. His gaze snaps away. And a moment later, he's pushing back from the table like the linen's caught fire beneath his fingertips. "Excuse me," he mutters, the words stiff and uneven as he stands.

He walks too quickly.

Shoulders tense. Gait too clipped. That desperate kind of pace that's trying so damn hard to seem normal, it screams everything but.

I wait and count to five.

Maybe six.

"You order our appetizers while I use the restroom."

I rise, patting Matheus on the shoulder twice before walking away from the table.

Our families have been members of this club for decades. Grant and I were practically raised in its halls. Sunday brunches and pool days and tie-optional dinners where we'd sit across from each other. As we got older, we pretended we weren't both wondering what it would feel like to fall out of step—just once—and touch.

Never in a million years did I think I'd be following Grant Harrow into the men's room, hard as a fucking rock, with every intention of making him moan my name.

Grant doesn't hear the door open.

He's too busy bracing the counter, fingers splayed wide against the marble, head hung low like he's trying to breathe through the storm.

But he hears the click of the door shutting.

He jerks upright, catching my reflection in the mirror

just as I lean back against the door, leaving it unlocked behind me.

"Meeting a little harder than you anticipated, bug?" I ask, smirking as I take a step forward.

His eyes narrow. The heat flares.

"What do you want?" he snaps.

I huff out a laugh. "You're the one watching me like a dying man in a desert. Don't act surprised when I come offer you water."

His jaw works like he's chewing down a dozen things he doesn't want to say. But he doesn't move. Doesn't deny it. Doesn't even try to hide the fact that he's still fucking hard.

I tilt my head. "How much longer are you going to keep pretending?"

"I'm not pretending anything."

"No?" I arch a brow. "So, you weren't thinking about the hospital room?"

His mouth opens—closes.

I keep going, taking a step closer.

"You weren't thinking about the way you said my name? The way your hand moved on me?"

His shoulders stiffen.

"I'm curious." I step closer.

He backs into the cold stone wall behind him.

"Would you have sucked me off, Grant? If the nurse hadn't walked in?"

He glares at me, voice tight. "I wasn't thinking about the hospital."

"Hmm." I drag my eyes over him slowly, lingering on the

hard line pressing against the front of his tailored slacks. "So, if I grab your dick right now, it won't be hard as stone?"

He doesn't have to answer because I reach for him anyway.

And fuck me—he's hard.

Rock-fucking-hard.

"Mmm." My fingers flex over the thick ridge of him, stroking through the fine silk of his pants. He gasps—sharp and involuntary—and grabs for my wrist with one hand.

But I move before he can do anything else.

My free hand snatches his, slamming it up against the marble wall above his head. I hold it there, pressing my body into his, crowding him while my other hand keeps stroking.

"Because I confess, *Lucciolina,* I would have let you."

He curses under his breath, chest rising like he's trying to find enough air to push me back.

"Fuck."

But he doesn't move. He can't.

Because he doesn't want to.

"You can lie to yourself all you want," I murmur, lips inches from his ear. "But your body tells me the truth, Harrow."

Grant's voice breaks when he finally speaks. "Stop," he breathes—barely more than air. "Dante..."

My name. Said like that.

Like a fucking prayer.

I press in, close enough that my breath skims his cheek, and he shudders.

"I've waited so long to hear you say my name like that, bug."

My hands drop to his belt. He jerks—but not away. Not enough to stop me.

He fumbles, grabbing at my coat instead, fists twisting in the lapels as I pop the buckle.

"Knock it off," he says, trying to sound stern, but it lands somewhere between desperate and dazed. "I'm not interested."

I lift my eyes to his and smirk.

"Then stop looking at me like you want to be fucked."

His cock is hard when I take it in hand—hot, heavy, aching against my palm. I groan, letting the sound hum low in my throat.

His skin is soft. Too soft for how hard he is. Like silk over steel.

I spit into my hand and stroke him, slow at first, deliberate.

Grant curses, head hitting the marble wall with a quiet *thud.*

His eyes squeeze shut. His jaw clenches. And when he exhales, it's all breath and no control.

"Have you ever had your dick sucked by a man before?" I ask, voice husky with want.

He snaps his eyes open at that. "You know I haven't."

I smile, pleased. "Good."

My hand moves faster now, rewarded with another choked-off breath, his thighs tensing where I've pressed between them.

"Have you been waiting for me, *Lucciolina?*" I murmur, watching him fall apart.

His only answer is a low groan, hips barely lifting into my fist.

I lean up, mouth brushing his ear.

"Perché io sto ancora aspettando te, amore mio."

*God, what I wouldn't give to fuck him right now.

"Ever since that day." My hand never stops working him, but those words—the reminder—make his breath stutter.

"Dante,"

"What you lied about."

Then I drop to my knees, not wasting a fucking second.

The instant his pants are down, my tongue is on him—long, slow, deliberate. I lick up the underside of his cock, tasting the salt of his skin, the heat of him pulsing against my mouth. I don't blink. Don't breathe. I just watch.

"Oh, God." Watch what it does to him.

Grant's head tips back, throat tight, one hand braced on the wall like the air's been knocked out of him. His breath punches out on a curse. My cock aches just from seeing it—seeing him like this. Coming apart because of me.

"Dante," he grits out. "Fuck. Someone could walk in."

I don't pause. Don't even hesitate.

"I would fucking love it if they did."

Because I want them to see. Every single person in this goddamn club. I want them to know exactly who he belongs to—who he's always belonged to—even when we were

---

*   "Because I'm still waiting for you, my love."

stupid kids pretending we didn't notice the way our eyes lingered too long.

I work his cock with my mouth, slow at first. Long pulls down his shaft, then back up again, lips tight, tongue teasing the slit until he groans—a rough, broken sound that sends a thrill straight down my spine. I hum around him, letting the vibration hit him deep.

"The whole fucking club can see me on my knees for you," I growl between strokes, my voice ragged. "I wouldn't care."

Because this—us—has never been about hiding. It's been about fighting. About years of pretending it didn't burn between us like crackling electricity.

I take him deeper, choking slightly as he hits the back of my throat, and fuck, I love it. I love the way he tastes— familiar and new all at once. Love the way he trembles, trying to stay quiet, but he can't. Not when my mouth is on him like this. Not when I'm savoring every goddamn second like I've waited my whole life for it.

Because I have.

I've thought about this moment for years. Since the first time I saw him looking at me like he wanted to kiss me but didn't have the balls to do it.

Grant's hand clamps the back of my head, fingers threading into my hair. Fisting it. He could pull me off. He says he wants to. Says it under his breath like a warning, like a plea. "You need to stop, Dante."

But then his hips jerk, thrusting forward, pushing his cock deeper into my throat like instinct overrides everything else.

Like he needs this just as bad.

"F-Fuck."

He puts pressure on the back of my head, not to stop me —but to keep me there. To anchor me to this moment, like it's the only one that's ever mattered.

And maybe it is.

Because this? This has been forged into our lives for nearly twenty goddamn years. It's been simmering beneath every joke, every fight, every near miss that left us both aching.

When I was a teenager, jerking my cock to the thought of my best friend—the way he'd come out of the shower, towel low on his hips. The way he'd laugh and then look at me, all heat and confusion. Every time I caught him watching me like he wanted to close the distance between us and fuck it all up.

This has always been inevitable.

If Grant would only stop fucking fighting it.

"No."

The word leaves his mouth in a breathless stutter, punched out between clenched teeth and ragged moans. "No—Dante—no—"

But it comes with every thrust of his hips, every desperate roll forward that buries his cock deeper down my throat.

"Fuck."

"Oh, fuck. Dante," He's pulsing his hips as I suck. "Fuck. Fuck... don't."

"Ah."

"Stop."

With every suck of my mouth on him, it loses strength. Loses meaning. Until all that's left is the way he trembles—then locks up.

"Oh, my fucking god." His breath catches. His body goes taut and his fist tightens in my hair. "Ah."

"Ah, God."

And then he's coming—hard—his warm pleasure spilling down my throat as I take every drop because every part of him belongs to me.

I slow my pace, tongue dragging through each pulse of his release, savoring the way he shudders from the over-stimulation. I don't rush it. I worship it. I want him to feel everything. Every beat of his heart inside my mouth.

When he's spent and breathless, I pull back just enough to let his cock fall from my lips.

I look up at him—at my oldest friend, my longest rival—and run my tongue one last time under the base of his shaft. Long. Slow. Cleaning the last of his mess like it's sacred.

When our eyes meet, the war between us rages there.

Still burning. Still unresolved.

But today, I won the first battle.

And I'm going to win the next.

And the next.

Until Grant fucking Harrow finally admits what he's been lying to himself about for five years—that he's mine.

Whether he's ready to say it or not...

his body already has.

I rise slowly, never breaking eye contact, letting the silence stretch thick between us. My thumb drags across my lower lip, then slips into my mouth as I taste the edge of him once more before sucking my thumb clean with deliberate calm.

I don't say a word.

The moment doesn't need it.

I back away, leaving him alone in the restroom—wrecked, breathless, and reeling.

Chapter 20

The Harrow estate is a monument to appearances. The stone façade rises like it was carved from pride itself—sharp lines, manicured hedges, iron gates that whisper wealth without having to shout. Everything about it is curated. Perfect. And emotionally sterile.

Even the breeze feels rehearsed.

As I step out of the car, the staff is already in place. Gates open. Door ajar. The housekeeper, Elaine, greets me with the same warm smile she's worn for as long as I've been alive. But it never reaches her eyes—not when she looks at me.

Not anymore.

"Welcome home, Mr. Harrow," she says gently, like I'm a guest. Like I don't still carry the ghosts of this place in my skin.

I nod, offering a polite smile, and walk through the grand foyer where the scent of fresh polish tries—and fails —to mask the memory of lilies. My mother's favorite. There were so many filling the house after she died. Now, for sixteen years there's only one vase. Always with a full bouquet. Always white.

My father is in the study—where he always is at this hour. The door is open, fire lit even though it's warm outside. He's a man of habits. Routine. Control.

I suppose that's where I get it.

"Grant." His face lights up as I enter, all warmth and pride and subtle worry, perfectly wrapped in the image of the loving patriarch. "You made good time."

I nod, letting him pull me into a brief hug. It's real, but it's rehearsed, too. My father loves me—I don't doubt that. But he's also spent the last decade and a half loving me around the edges of a wound neither of us speaks about.

We settle into two leather armchairs facing the fireplace. He pours drinks from the decanter between us, just like always. His movements are steady. Practiced. It should comfort me.

It doesn't.

The study hasn't changed. Books line the shelves in neat, intentional rows. Family portraits hang on the walls, a gallery of curated legacy—wedding photos, posed holiday shots, a painting of my mother in her favorite blue silk gown. She looks serene. Regal. Down to the fine detail of the solitaire necklace around her neck.

My chest tightens.

Not just from the memory of her—but from yesterday.

From what happened at the country club. What I let happen.

What I wanted to happen.

Dante on his knees. His mouth around my cock. My groans echoing off marble and mirrors and polished wood like a fucking confession. Like I wanted the world to hear it.

Anyone could've walked in.

Anyone.

The Marchesi heir sucking off the Harrow legacy—like some sick fantasy pulled from the forbidden corners of our history. I should've stopped him. Should've shoved him away the second he dropped to his knees and looked up at me like he knew I wouldn't.

Because I didn't.

And fuck, it felt so good I almost forgot we were in public. That the door wasn't even locked. That if anyone recognized us—

It wouldn't be just a scandal.

It would be the collapse of everything our families have built.

And still...

Still, it wasn't enough.

Because I wanted more. I *want* more.

And that alone makes me pissed.

My father shifts in his chair, the firelight dancing across the lines of his face. He's aged in the way people do when grief becomes a long-term tenant—still strong, still composed, but hollowed out in places no one else can see.

He doesn't bring up what happened to her. He never does.

Like always, he'll talk business soon.

It's how he survived it—burying himself in the firm after my mother died. Throwing himself into meetings and acquisitions and early grooming speeches, as if fast-tracking my inheritance would make us forget the blood on the marble.

I was only sixteen. Too young to drink but not, apparently, too young to sit in boardrooms and learn the architecture of empire.

And I didn't complain because it kept him focused. Kept him from asking too many questions.

Even now, I can hear the sound of his scream. That guttural, broken sound when he found her.

She was lying in the foyer. Blood soaking into her yellow cardigan. Her eyes wide open and unseeing.

And I—

I was standing at the top of the landing, staring down at them.

At her.

At him.

At the aftermath of what I did.

He never asked me what I'd been doing just before. Why I was there, and breathless.

Maybe he couldn't bear to know.

Or maybe he already did and chose to pretend.

He did his best. That's the truth. He didn't fall apart. He just… diverted. Built walls. Gave speeches. Took me to networking dinners and introduced me as a man long before I was one.

He was a father in mourning, and I became a son in performance.

And now here we are—sixteen years later, still playing the same roles.

He clears his throat across from me. "I wanted to talk about the Vegas situation."

There it is. The turn. The safe ground. The clean ledger.

I nod, keeping my expression smooth even as my stomach twists.

Yesterday, I let the only person who's ever really seen me —who's ever gotten close to the rot—pull pleasure out of me in a public bathroom like it was a birthright. And I let him.

No—I wanted him to.

And still... it wasn't enough.

Because no matter how far he goes, how deep he takes me—

He hasn't seen all of it yet.

Not the worst part.

Not the part my father screamed over.

The part I watched from the stairs, heart pounding and hands still shaking from what came before.

And if Dante ever finds out—

If anyone ever does—

They'll never look at me the same again.

They'll finally see what she saw in her last breath.

And I don't know if I'll survive that.

I knew he'd bring it up eventually.

The CEO title—dangling like a blade over my head, one wrong move away from slipping out of reach forever.

My father's voice is calm when he mentions it. Not accusing. Not panicked. Just measured concern, like everything else he does.

"There's... been talk," he says, swirling the amber liquid

in his glass. "Board members get nervous when they smell blood. Especially when it comes from the top."

"I know," I say, already slipping into the answer I rehearsed on the drive over. "Dante and I are working things out. We've brought in a specialized consultant—someone with crisis-negotiation experience. It's... helping. Honestly. We're in a better place than we've been in a long time."

I can't tell if I'm lying or not. Maybe both things are true.

My father nods once, not quite convinced, but not probing either. "Good. Because this firm doesn't survive divided leadership. And you know as well as I do—the Marchesi-Harrow legacy isn't just a name. It's a promise. A future we've built brick by brick. You let that fall, and it won't just be your name that cracks."

It's not a threat, but it lands like one.

I nod and take another slow sip of my drink. The scotch burns less than it should. Or maybe I've just burned too much already to notice.

"Your mother always said you'd wear the crown one day," he adds after a long pause, eyes flicking to her portrait above the fireplace. "She knew you had it in you. The discipline. The vision."

He doesn't say the darkness.

"I miss her," I say quietly, because I should. Because I do. Because there's guilt crawling up the back of my throat, and I need to press it down with something real.

His jaw tightens. Just a fraction. But I notice.

"We all do," he says. His voice is steady—almost too clean. "She was... delicate. But strong. The kind of woman who saw the best in people, even when they didn't deserve it. The kind who trusted instinct. Sometimes too much."

My gaze lifts to his face, but he's looking away now. At the fire. At nothing.

The air thickens, lingering on that last sentence—*sometimes too much*—and I can't tell if he's aware of how loaded it sounds. If it was deliberate. If it was directed.

If he suspects, or if I'm just projecting.

I shift forward, glass balanced between my knees, elbows resting on them like the weight of what I'm holding might collapse me otherwise.

There's a moment. A crack where I could say it.

I could tell him the truth. Or part of it. Or at least enough to explain why I haven't slept a full night in sixteen years without waking in a cold sweat, my hands clenched and aching.

He's right here.

And for all his coldness, for all the distance he drowned us both in after she died—he did try. He was grieving. So was I.

And maybe he deserves to know.

Maybe I need someone else to carry it.

"Dad..." The word stutters out before I know I've said it.

His eyes come to mine. Calm. Curious. Open.

For once, I see the father I knew before the funeral. Before the boardrooms and the legacy and the weight of her name.

My chest tightens. My jaw locks.

Say it.

Tell him.

"I'm... trying," I say instead, swallowing down everything else. "To fix things. To make it right."

He nods again, the moment closing like a door that was never fully open to begin with.

"I know you are," he says gently. "Just remember who you are, Grant. And what you were born into."

I do.

Every goddamn day.

I was born into legacy.

And I might've killed it with my own two hands.

Chapter 21

Eve

When I open the door, I'm barefoot, braless, and already five seconds away from murder.

"If you don't have cheesecake, you're getting a stiletto to the eye."

Jaxon Kane grins at me like he wants the threat to be real.

"Good thing I brought two," he says, holding up a bag in one hand and a bottle of something French and expensive in the other. "Peace offering. For interrupting your sacred Saturday sloth time."

I sigh dramatically and step aside. "Fine. Enter, peasant."

He strolls in like he owns the place—tall, stupidly good-looking, and entirely too comfortable in his own skin. His dark hair's a little messy, like he just rolled out of a king-size bed with someone equally gorgeous. His jaw's freshly shaven, and the sleeves of his expensive Henley strain against arms that could throw me across the apartment if he felt like it.

Of course, he never would.

Because under all the money and muscle and menace, Jaxon Kane is one of the few men I trust implicitly.

Which says more about my judgment than it should.

I shut the door behind him and pad back toward the kitchen in my sleep shorts and oversized tee.

I eye the plain bag suspiciously. "This does not look like it's from my bestie, Elena."

"I took a pass at baking it myself!" he says, full of boyish pride.

The look of absolute and pure terror that must be on my face makes him bust out laughing. "I'm just kidding. Couldn't carry it on my bike without fucking it up, and I knew that would be punishable by death."

I let out a relieved sigh.

"You baking would've been the first sign of a psychotic break."

He smirks and sets down the wine. "I outsource emotional manipulation. Like a sane person. And order takeout."

Our friendship has always been like this—snark served with a side of genuine care, buried too deep to name. He's been a client of The Ledger for years. Never one of mine, technically, but close enough to make me his handler on more than one occasion. Somehow, we slipped into this thing we do now—late-night texts, check-ins, the occasional wine-fueled vent session on my couch.

And for reasons I've never fully understood... I feel responsible for him.

Like I'm beginning to feel for Grant and Dante.

It's not just about business anymore. Not with them.

There's something broken buried beneath those two—Grant Harrow and Dante Marchesi—and the cracks are starting to show. Not just in their company, but in them. Their partnership, their dynamic, whatever storm they've been circling for years... it's escalating.

And for some reason, I can't stop thinking they're supposed to come out of it together. Not just as CEOs. But as something more. Something real. Something that looks a hell of a lot like love—if they'd stop fighting it long enough to see it.

I can't explain it. But I feel it. In my gut. In the silence between their glances. In the ache they both try so hard to hide.

I want to fix it for them.

Just like I always want to fix things for him.

Jax leans against my granite countertop, watching me with a look that's far too observant for a man who pretends to be bored with everything.

"Wine glasses?" he asks.

"In the cabinet above the microwave. Where they always are, Kane."

"I like watching you get annoyed."

He pulls down two glasses anyway and pours, like we do this every Saturday. Which, lately... we kind of do.

If there's anything in this world that doesn't need my protection, it's Jaxon Kane.

He's tall. Built like a weapon. Trains with Lucian Vale, which means he could break ribs in his sleep. Fights in underground rings like he needs the cash—which he absolutely does not—and walks through life like the rules are a suggestion he's already declined.

He's richer than God and twice as bored.

But here he is. In my kitchen. Bringing cheesecake. Getting ready to teach me how to be a hacker.

That may be a little dramatic. Some light online stalking, if anything.

"So, whose life are we ruining? Do we get to erase any identities today? Because that is one of my favorite things to do."

"Jaxon Kane!" I scold like I'm a mother.

That thought gives me shivers down my spine.

Me. A mother. With actual living kids.

Gross.

Absolutely not in a million years.

"What?" He shrugs like he's innocent. "I give them back."

I look at him, deadpan.

"Most of the time."

"I'm not hacking anyone." I hop up on a barstool and flip open the box. The cheesecake is perfect, of course. Fluffy, creamy, a little tart. *Elena, you are a goddess among immortals.*

The first bite is perfection, and I close my eyes, letting it carry away the weight of the world for just a moment.

"I just need to know how to look up someone's history. Like birth records, doctors' visits, schools, neighbors, maybe. Who nannied them—if you're feeling generous."

He laughs softly, already helping himself to my laptop. "Jesus, Eve. You want me to teach you how to read someone's soul, too?"

I shrug. "If you've got time."

"You know I can't say no to you."

I arch a brow. "Because I'm cute?"

"Because I'm scared you'll stab me in my sleep."

Fair.

"You got a name?" he asks, eyes already flicking across his screen.

I do.

"Grant Harrow."

The moment I say it, Jaxon's fingers pause mid-keystroke, and that particular gleam sparks in his eyes—the one that means trouble is about to be fun.

"Well, well," he drawls, already opening new tabs. "Now that's a name. Harrow money goes back generations. Rumor has it the original patriarch was part of some underground secret society. You know—skull rings, blood oaths, sacrificing firstborns at midnight. Old-money weirdness."

I roll my eyes. "Save the tinfoil hat for someone who believes the moon landing was staged. I'm not here for conspiracy theories. I'm looking for the break."

Jaxon tilts his head. "Break?"

"The fracture," I clarify, leaning forward and pulling the cheesecake closer like it's fuel. "Something happened to him. Something formative. Dante's a flame. He lashes out, burns hot, doesn't know how to hold back. But Grant—he's quiet. Controlled. He compartmentalizes like a machine."

"So?"

"So, machines don't build themselves that well unless they've been broken first."

Jaxon makes a low, thoughtful sound, like he's enjoying watching my brain spin. "Where do you want to start?"

"The beginning."

The cursor blinks like it's daring me to keep going.

Grant Harrow, age sixteen.

It should've been the year everything accelerated—early college credits, prestigious internships, interviews about legacy and leadership. Crafted sound bites over champagne flutes and monogrammed cufflinks. The fast track to becoming everything the Harrow name demanded.

Instead, there's a void. A silent rupture in the record.

That's where it starts.

One obituary.

Sylvia Harrow, beloved wife of William Harrow, passed suddenly at home. Survived by her husband and son.

But Jaxon was able to find digitized police reports.

Cause of death: blunt-force trauma sustained during a fall over the second-story railing.

"That sounds sketchy AF." Jax scans the files with me, both of us invested in the history now.

Aside from this, there are no headlines. No scandal. No follow-up interviews. Just a cold fact buried beneath a list of charitable donations made in her honor and a closed-casket funeral held four days later.

But it's the location that catches me.

The Harrow family home.

Inside the home.

The kind of fall that can shatter the skull and break the neck—clean, instant, fatal.

I pull up the archived floor plan of the estate—something from a decades-old architecture feature. The house is sprawling. Cold. Symmetrical in that old-money way that prizes aesthetics over warmth. The grand staircase cuts through the center of the foyer like a spine.

"If Grant's father was here," I point to the study, "and she fell here..."

"There is no way the dad could have done it."

He reported he had been holed up in his study for hours. Phone records and surveillance logs back him up—timelines neatly arranged, like a spreadsheet prepared for grief.

"Unless someone is lying." I tap my fingernail on my tooth, thinking.

Every single detail hinges on Grant's word.

It's Grant who called emergency services.

Grant who told the responding officer his father was in the study when it happened.

Grant who testified—privately—that he came out of his room to see her at the bottom of the stairs.

Just in time to see her.

But not stop her.

Not catch her.

Not save her.

My fingers hover over the keyboard. Something feels... off. Too rehearsed. Too precise.

Jaxon reads the report beside me, brows low. "You said you were looking for the break."

"This is it."

Because even though the father's name was cleared, even though the case never made it past the inquiry stage—the timelines don't make sense.

Not unless you account for something else.

Because based on the layout of the house, the study is nearly forty feet from the top of the staircase. William Harrow would've had to sprint—full speed, without a single soul seeing him—to get out of sight before Grant found her.

He didn't.

He couldn't.

And someone wanted to make sure the report made that very clear.

But the glaring omission slams into me like a second impact.

Grant clears his father.

Not once—not in the witness report, not in the follow-up interviews, not in the press—does he ever mention where *he* was before the fall.

There's no detail. No location. No denial.

Just a single statement:

"I heard her fall. I saw her on the first floor. I called for my father. He came from the study seconds later."

I stare at the words, reading them again and again.

Grant never says what he was doing or what room he was in.

He never says he didn't touch her.

It's not an omission that screams guilt.

It's the kind of silence that only happens when someone knows the truth wouldn't make sense out loud.

Something happened in that house.

I don't say it out loud, but the words are practically tattooed on my tongue now.

Jaxon scrolls beside me, leaning his chair back just far enough to tempt gravity. "There's more here. You want me to keep digging?"

I nod slowly, eyes still locked on the cold, clean report from sixteen years ago. "Yeah. But this time, try the name *Ashwood*."

He quirks a brow. "Is that your new bestie who wears a full face of Chanel to brunch and looks like she's planning your funeral behind her mimosa?"

"That would be the one," I mutter. "Corrine Ashwood. She's been leeching onto Grant since childhood. If there was ever a moment he was vulnerable—this was it."

Jaxon types the name in, pausing only to sip his wine like this is a casual Tuesday.

"She irritates you," he says dryly.

"She slithers." I stab my fork into the last bite of cheese-cake. "There's a difference."

But as the search results populate... there's nothing.

No mention of the Ashwoods connected to the Harrow family during that year. No press. No records. Not even a passing quote about a neighbor or family friend stepping in during the funeral.

It's like they weren't there at all.

"Convenient," I murmur. "She's tied to Grant's entire

life, but nowhere to be found during the single most traumatic moment of it?"

He clicks into another archived database, this one more obscure, and hums. "Huh. Okay, this is juicy."

I glance over. "Please don't say *juicy* while we're digging into dead people's secrets."

"A year before Sylvia Harrow's death," he goes on, ignoring me, "there was a murder-suicide on the same street. Looks like one of the neighbors."

But I'm not listening anymore, because my thoughts are already turning to someone else.

Dante.

Where the hell was he?

He and Grant were inseparable back then. Practically glued at the hip by age ten. There's no way he wasn't around. Not with how close their families were.

"Pull up Dante's name," I say suddenly.

Jaxon gives me a look. "First names now? You sound like a woman ready to spiral."

"Shut up and do it."

He opens a new tab, searching *Dante Marchesi* and filtering for the same narrow window of time.

For a moment, there's nothing.

And then—tucked in the corner of a blurry, badly archived *Page Six*–style socialite blog—he finds it.

"Here," he says, highlighting the line. "Right there."

"Marchesi Heir Transfers to UK Boarding School"
That's it.

No fanfare. No scandal. Just a one-paragraph blurb

wedged between an engagement announcement and a charity gala recap.

Dante Marchesi, previously enrolled at The Dalton School in Manhattan, has transferred to St. Audric's, an elite boarding school in the UK. The young heir will prepare to begin his studies with the fall semester.

Posted: one day after Evelyn Harrow's death.

My stomach dips.

A mother dies under suspicious circumstances.

Grant gives the alibi.

Dante disappears overnight.

And Corrine is completely invisible.

Jaxon whistles low. "That's a lot of smoke for there not to be a fire."

But I already know. I feel it in my bones.

This wasn't just the trauma that shaped Grant.

This was the moment that broke something.

Whatever happened in that house didn't just kill Sylvia Harrow.

It fractured the boy she left behind.

And the silence they've buried it under is starting to rot.

I push the laptop away, grabbing my notebook off the counter. Flip it open to a clean page and click my pen once.

Two names.

Grant.

Dante.

And below them, one question in bold strokes:

What happened in that house?

Chapter 22
Dante

The end of the charity golf tournament always means one thing—excess.

The ballroom at the Four Seasons has been transformed into a high-roller's fever dream. Poker tables straight out of Vegas. Roulette wheels spinning. Craps, blackjack, Texas hold 'em—you name it, it's here. Crystal chandeliers hang like icicles made of money.

Every cocktail is handcrafted. Every smile, rehearsed. Manhattan's finest dressed in custom tuxedos and couture gowns, all here to drink, gamble, and drop seven figures in the name of philanthropy.

And later—after the games end and the masks slip—we'll all sit down to a five-course dinner where every plate costs more than a college education.

Just another night in the empire.

Usually, at events like this—where Marchesi and Harrow are both expected to smile for the cameras—we orbit each other carefully. Deliberately. Grant keeps to his side of the room. I keep to mine. I bring a Ledger companion. Sometimes two. Just enough skin, just enough laughter, just enough whispered filth into a perfectly attentive ear to make sure he sees it.

We never talked about it. Never had to.

It was just a game.

Unspoken rules. Silent power plays.

But tonight, I'm playing a different game.

And I'm looking for the long-legged brunette I enlisted to help me win it.

A white-gloved server approaches with a tray. "Your bourbon, Mr. Marchesi."

I take the glass with a nod of thanks, the cut crystal heavy in my palm. Good burn. Smooth finish. Nothing but the best for the men who rule this city and the women who wear gowns as well as they wear secrets.

I'm mid-sip when the crowd shifts—and then parts.

And there she is.

Eve Sterling.

She's impossible to miss in Ledger red.

In *that* dress. Fuck.

A fitted sequin gown hugs every curve like it was sewn onto her body. The slit running high up one thigh flashes skin with every step. And when she walks, it's like she's hunting something. Or someone.

Christ.

That leg.

That leg could ruin a man. Could break him open and leave nothing behind but worship.

I want to feel it wrapped around my head while I feast

on what she's hiding between her thighs. Slow. Filthy. Grateful.

She sees me before I reach her.

I take another sip of bourbon, let it linger on my tongue as I make my way through the crowd—never taking my eyes off her.

She doesn't look away either.

We meet near the roulette table, where some hedge-fund vampire is bleeding money like it means nothing. I wrap an arm low around her, my face turned into her neck and taking an appreciative pull of her perfume.

"Stunning." I place a light peck just below her ear.

Eve gets straight to our shared purpose for the night.

"Grant's here," she says, voice low, smooth as the liquor I haven't finished yet. "But he ran into a leech."

I smirk around the rim of my glass. "Corrine?"

She nods once—sharp and knowing.

Of course it's Corrine.

She's like a rash you can't treat.

No matter how far you push her, she always finds a way to cling to Grant like she's owed him.

I set my glass down on the velvet edge of the table and pull a deck of playing cards from inside my tux jacket.

"Do you carry cards everywhere you go, Mr. Marchesi?" Eve asks with a flirty smirk.

"Perhaps," I say, giving them a slow, deliberate shuffle. "You never know when luck might strike."

She watches the way my fingers move, the crisp snap of the deck between them.

I fan the cards and then cut, the way I was taught as a boy by men who played for more than money.

When I set the deck down between us, I look at her, eyes daring.

"Feel like playing a game tonight?"

Her eyes flick to mine, interested. "Always up for a fun time."

We each draw a card.

Mine's higher.

I can't suppress my grin as I lay it down on the felt—smug and slow.

"I was hoping to win," I admit, reaching inside my tux once more. This time, I pull out a slim, matte-black case no bigger than a pair of sunglasses.

Eve's brow arches, instantly suspicious. "You pack light."

I slide it across the table to her. "I'm a man of priorities."

She pops the latch and lifts the lid, and her smile widens.

Inside, nestled in foam padding: two sleek, rose-gold toys. One slim and curved, the other more substantial with dual-stimulation points.

She lifts the vaginal toy with gloved fingers, examining it with clinical calm. The anal plug stays untouched because she knows who that one is for.

"Nothing like a charity gala with the rich and famous," she muses, "without a little voyeurism, I suppose."

"Exactly my thoughts," I murmur, taking the toy from her hands and setting the case aside.

"This game," I say, tearing open a discreet lube packet

from the corner compartment, "is called *Can Grant Find Who Has the Remote?*"

Eve chuckles low in her throat, unbothered—aroused by the danger of it all. Her eyes are already heating with anticipation.

"So, this is why you tortured me with wearing panties tonight." Eve's gleam is just as dark as mine.

The toy is beautifully designed—curved to hit the G-spot with precision, the external suction piece shaped like the whisper of a kiss. Expensive. Remote-controlled. Fully rechargeable. Waterproof—though I doubt we'll need that feature tonight.

I apply the lube with practiced fingers, coating the smooth silicone while she watches me work.

Then I glance up, voice low. Coy.

"May I?"

Her lips curl at the corner. "Be my guest."

I step in closer.

The high poker table shields us from view, leaving just the upper half of our bodies visible to the rest of the room.

She shifts just slightly, angling her hip toward me in quiet invitation—and I take it.

With one hand, I slip the toy beneath the delicate lace band of her panties, the other holding my bourbon steady on the table. The bulb meant for her G-spot rubs against her clit first, letting me smear the lube I just applied across her slickening skin.

On the table, my phone's already open—screen aglow with the app I synced earlier.

One press, and the toy purrs to life.

Eve's inhale is sharp but controlled. Her lashes flutter, eyes falling shut for a single second as I work the toy against her with slow, deliberate precision.

I keep her just on the edge.

The moment her thighs start to tense, I kill the vibration.

She opens her eyes and glares at me.

I smirk. "We're going to have fun."

Sliding the toy fully into place, I take my time adjusting it so the curve sits flush inside her, right where it needs to be. My knuckles graze heat and silk. She clenches down on instinct, breath shaky.

Then—another press of my thumb turns it on again.

Her body shudders so slightly it's almost imperceptible.

Almost.

I lean in, close enough to breathe her in.

Then I tap the clit stimulator.

A tiny gasp leaves her lips—no louder than the creak of a leather shoe against marble.

Her grip tightens on the edge of the table. The other hand finds my elbow, nails biting into fabric as the toy works inside her.

"Find Grant," I murmur against her ear. "Help him with the plug."

She lets out the softest sound—half moan, half laugh. My lips brush the side of her neck, and I feel her start to come. Quiet. A soft squeak tucked into my collar.

"Okay?" I ask.

She nods—barely.

"Okay."

"Good girl."

I shut the toy off with a flick of my thumb and withdraw my hand as smoothly as it entered. Her body stays close to mine another beat longer, legs trembling like a thorough-bred held at the starting gate.

I press the closed case into her hand.

My phone slides back into my pocket.

"I'll see you out there on the floor."

She turns and walks away, that slit in her dress swaying with every step. But she doesn't get far before glancing back.

As if she knows me already.

She knows what I'm about to do.

I stir my bourbon with the fingers that were just inside her—slow, indulgent, like I'm savoring the flavor of the night.

Then I bring them to my mouth and lick them clean. I smile as I take a long sip from my glass.

She disappears into the crowd, looking for our third player, while I'm already imagining what comes next.

"Let the games begin."

Chapter 23
Eve

The case is light in my hand, but it may as well be ticking like a bomb.

In my other hand, I snag a champagne flute from a passing tray, letting the cool glass anchor me as I drift deeper into the room.

The place is alive — velvet and smoke and money, wrapped in tuxedos and couture.

It doesn't take long to spot Grant. Not being drained by Corrine, for once.

He's standing with a man I recognize instantly from the hours I've spent spiraling down internet rabbit holes. Same build. Same broad shoulders. Same storm-gray eyes. His father.

They're laughing—really laughing. His father tosses his head back at something Grant says, a hand on his son's shoulder, clearly proud.

The sight tugs at something in me. Something tender.

But then, like a gargoyle perched atop a Gothic cathedral, I feel Corrine lurking—watching.

She's not at Grant's side. She's hovering by a blackjack table she clearly has no interest in: not a single chip in front of her, not a glance at her cards.

She's staring at Grant with a look I can't quite name.

Not longing. Not jealousy.

It's... almost worship.

There's a dreamy daze in her eyes, like she's watching the life she was supposed to have unfolding without her—like a child staring through a shop window at a toy she was promised and never received.

It unsettles me.

Because suddenly I'm not sure this is just some toxic, clingy childhood friendship. There's something else here. Something deeper. Possessive.

Even still, I can't resist. Not with her standing there, practically salivating over him from twenty feet away like some couture-clad ghost. So I drift closer, sipping my champagne as I slow to a stop at her side.

"You look lovely."

She startles, clearly too absorbed in her surveillance to notice me approach.

Her eyes snap to mine, lips curving into a smile that doesn't reach them. "Thank you."

She doesn't return the compliment—I figured she wouldn't.

I glance toward Grant and his father—still deep in conversation, still laughing like nothing else matters.

Tilting my head, I ask, "So... what's his dad like? You must know him well."

Corrine hesitates only a second, but I catch her stammer over the words. "Barely. I've only really met him a handful of times."

Her fingers betray her nerves—lifting almost automatically to toy with the solitaire diamond at her throat.

Grant's father seems to spot someone he recognizes and, with a pat on his son's shoulder, makes his way across the room. I take advantage to steal my target.

"If you'll excuse me."

As Mr. Harrow disappears into the crowd, I slide into his place without missing a beat—my hand slipping easily into the crook of Grant's arm.

He turns to look at me, a touch surprised, until his eyes catch the deliberate curve of my body pressed to his side.

"Didn't want you to get lonely," I purr, tilting my head. "Though I'm not sure it's safe to leave you unattended in this tux. You look a little too tempting tonight, Mr. Harrow."

His gaze drops to the slit in my dress—and stays there. I shift ever so slightly, accentuating the exposed line of my thigh. A ripple of tension passes through him, low and unmistakable—apparently, Grant Harrow is a leg man. Noted.

He licks his bottom lip, gaze flicking to my mouth. "You look..."

I arch a brow. "Beautiful?"

"Addictive," he answers.

We hold our stare, neither of us looking away, both agreeing where this conversation is going.

"Walk with me?" I ask, already guiding him toward the edge of the ballroom.

We stroll in a slow, unhurried arc around the perimeter, the buzz of conversation and music fading beneath our own quieter rhythm. We aren't looking at the party. We're looking at each other.

"Can I ask you something?" I say softly.

"You can ask," he replies, eyes flicking down again—this time catching the dip of my neckline before returning to my face.

"Why haven't you taken advantage of the full terms of your contract?"

His steps pause. He got the implication.

"I never actually saw the contract," he admits. "Dante handled that part. I had no idea. Then you showed up on his arm and..."

"And?"

"At first, I was surprised. Maybe not pleasantly," he says, giving me a sidelong glance. "But now..."

His eyes dip again and linger on my cleavage. He doesn't even try to hide it.

I smile. "Now you're imagining all the things you didn't realize you paid for."

His jaw flexes. He doesn't argue.

"You know, Dante took the contract out in both your names," I say lightly. "You each have equal access to the full package."

He raises a brow. "Meaning?"

I guide us gently, deliberately, down a quiet corridor just

off the main ballroom—the kind of space no one pays attention to unless they need a moment alone.

Grant glances around, a little wary, rubbing the back of his neck. "So does that mean... uh—"

I turn smoothly and press him back against the wall, one hand firm on his chest.

"Does it mean you could bend me over right here and fuck me in this corridor?" I whisper. "Yes."

His breath hitches. His eyes drop again, darker this time —arousal eclipsing hesitation.

I press my body flush—and feel the unmistakable hardness straining beneath his slacks. Perfect.

I lift one leg against him; his hands are on me instantly —one sliding down my thigh, the other gripping my waist.

"If you wanted," I murmur, brushing my lips along the shell of his ear, "we could even see what fun you, me, and Dante could have together."

Grant groans, pulling me tighter. I roll my hips once and his hands grip harder.

"What makes you think I would share?" he growls.

"Who says you'd be sharing me?" I whisper, letting my mouth hover just shy of his. Each word is a promise. A threat. A challenge.

"Maybe..." I breathe, "we'd be sharing you."

Then I kiss him.

He groans into my mouth—hungry, desperate, searching. I taste the frustration, the desire, the need he didn't know what to do with until now.

I don't have to guess how turned on he is. I can feel him

throbbing against me, so I grip his cock *over his pants* and massage. Because right now, he's mine to play with.

I bite at his bottom lip as I pull away, slow and deliberate, tugging just enough to make him chase my mouth again. I don't let him catch it.

"I want you to do something for me, Grant," I murmur, voice low and liquid with promise.

His eyes remain fixed on my mouth. "What?"

I take his hand—large, warm, eager—and guide it between us. Beneath the slit of my dress. Under the delicate band of my panties.

With a hum, his fingers slip in, and I see the exact moment he finds it—his breath catches, his whole body goes taut.

"Feel that?" I purr, keeping my gaze fixed on the ballroom.

An elderly couple ambles past the corridor entrance, laughing softly, oblivious. They don't see us—but they could. And I fucking love that.

He presses a little deeper, testing the shape of the toy inside me, and I shiver.

"I have one for you to wear too," I whisper.

I pull his hand from my panties, lift it to my mouth— one then two fingers—sucking them clean like a dessert I've been craving all night. My other hand returns to his cock.

His jaw tightens. His erection twitches. And I smile.

Without a word, I loop my arm through his and lead him back toward the ballroom, our pace unhurried but his breathing anything but.

I lean in, letting my lips brush his ear as we rejoin the edge of the crowd.

"Have you ever enjoyed anal play before?" I ask softly, ensuring no one else can hear.

He's quiet—for a moment, I think he won't answer.

Until he finally does. "Yes."

My lips curl.

"And did you enjoy it?"

His gaze flicks to my mouth. "Yes."

I hum, pleased, and slip the discreet black velvet case from my clutch into his jacket pocket.

Then I rise on my toes like I'm going to kiss his cheek— and do.

But my words are anything but innocent.

"Then go be a good boy and put this in," I murmur, lips brushing his skin. "Then come find me."

I let my lips linger one heartbeat too long, then turn and walk away without a backward glance.

Because I don't have to look. I know he's going to do it.

I spot Grant before he sees me—lingering near the edge of the crowd, tall and lethal in a black-on-black tux. Tension in his frame, hunger in his stare. But he doesn't move—until I smile. Then he comes closer.

I'm standing at the center of the craps table crowd, one hand wrapped around a champagne flute, the other resting below the table's edge. Hidden. Secret. Just like the game we're playing.

Or at least... he thinks he is. Because I'm not the one holding the remote tonight.

Grant doesn't know that yet—but he will.

Dante's on a streak—the kind of winning run you only see in movies. Every toss of the dice is perfect. The crowd is euphoric, throwing chips and shouting praise. But the real show isn't the money.

It's us.

When the toy inside me flickers to life, I gasp. And across the table Grant's lips part at that exact moment—and I know he's wearing it. I mouth, "Good boy," and watch his pupils dilate.

He doesn't understand yet—that it's synced to Dante's phone, that every wave of pleasure is coming from the man he swore to hate.

I glance at Dante. He doesn't look at me, not yet—just grins like a king. But I know he's watching.

Grant follows my gaze—just as the plug's rhythm deepens inside me. The one in him must match, because I see the shift in his posture—chest rising faster, grip tightening, jaw ticking like he's trying not to reveal everything.

The next roll comes. Dice clatter. Pleasure spikes.

I must set down my glass. My fingers tremble, bracing on the table. I fight not to whimper. My clit stimulator kicks in — pulsing, sucking, dragging me toward the edge—and Grant... poor Grant... is right there with me.

He's blinking rapidly now. His throat bobs. He looks down, then up. And that's when he sees it: Dante's phone on the table—his finger circling—exactly in sync with both our escalating bodies.

That's when it hits him. Dante is the puppeteer. The man under his skin for years is about to make him come in his *fucking* pants.

And Dante—God, he looks like sin incarnate. A devil in full control.

And that's exactly when the orgasm hits.

I go first—knees shaking, head tipped down, lips parted as wave after wave rocks me. I barely stay standing, clinging to the table like it might save me.

I regain enough calm to watch Grant. The moment it rips through him... his eyes go wide, stunned, humiliated, wrecked. He jerks once, twice, then goes frighteningly still— save for a slight shoulder tremble. It's subtle, but we're watching. We know.

Dante picks up his phone, silencing it, sliding it into his pocket. The buzzing inside me fading into afterglow. I smooth my dress, gather myself, and circle the table.

Grant doesn't move. He can't. He's still shaking.

I press in close. My perfume surrounds him—sex and power and victory. I run my finger up the inside of my thigh, gathering the slick trace of what Dante just did to me... and to him.

I grip Grant's chin, tilt his face toward me.

"See, baby..." I purr, letting my arousal coat his bottom lip.

His eyes darken. He swallows hard.

"Such a fun toy for us to play with."

I turn him toward Dante just as the dice roll again. And now the game has irrevocably changed.

As I drift away, I know we have one more round left. And this time, our toy is going to come to us.

Chapter 24

I shouldn't still be hard.

Not after what just happened at the Craps table.

Not after coming so completely, I nearly collapsed against the poker chips, panting, like a fucking teenager.

But I am.

Because now I know it was him.

It was Dante—controlling the plug buried deep inside me, his fucking hand on the remote the entire time.

And the moment I realized it the orgasm hit me so hard I saw white behind my eyes and bit down on my own tongue to keep from groaning.

And now, thirty minutes later, washed up as best I can manage, I'm stepping back into the ballroom like nothing happened.

Like I haven't just been wrecked in the most humiliating, exhilarating way imaginable.

They've moved the gala into a new room—larger, moodier, candlelight flickering from chandeliers and along the mirrored walls. Waiters circulate with silver trays and practiced smiles, passing out oysters and champagne while the city's elite cluster in small, curated conversations.

I straighten my tux jacket and glance around, scanning automatically.

Of course, I see him first.

Dante stands near one of the tall cocktail tables, deep in conversation with Matheus da Costa—the club athlete from earlier this week. Seeing them together flips the switch in my memory.

The bathroom.

On his knees.

The heat of his mouth.

The best blowjob of my fucking life.

My cock twitches.

Fucking hell.

As if he can sense it—sense me—Dante's gaze flicks up.

Finds me instantly.

There's no smirk. No challenge.

Just that look—intense and unyielding—but different now.

The fire's still there. It always is. But it's not the wildfire I've always known. Not the blaze that made every interaction feel like a battle.

Tonight, it burns steady. Controlled. Like it wants me to come closer.

So, I do.

I cross the floor, weaving through donors and hedge fund managers and washed-up actors clinging to their last season's relevance. And when I reach them, Dante barely misses a beat.

"Grant," he says, voice smooth as ever, "Have you been introduced to Matheus da Costa?"

Matheus offers his hand. "From the club the other day. We didn't get a chance to meet."

"It's my pleasure," I say, shaking firmly. "And this lovely woman on your arm?"

"Vanessa, his wife." Dante says for him, already turning to me. "Twelve years married and somehow still madly in love."

She flushes, laughs. Matheus beams. And I—

I look at Dante.

Twelve years married, huh?

Madly in love, you say?

So, the flirtation earlier this week was nothing more than a performance.

Dante meets my eyes, and something smug flickers there. Not cruel. Not taunting. Just... amused.

I give him a look that says *You were pretending*?

He doesn't say anything. Just lets the corner of his mouth lift in that quiet, knowing grin.

Asshole.

And yet—

This is easier than I expected.

Like we've always stood like this. Side by side. Two halves of the same pitch.

I reach into my inner jacket pocket and pull out the small, sleek case. The one I now know belongs to him.

It's heavier again—both toys back inside.

Dante watches every move as I hand it over. He doesn't break eye contact for a second as he takes it, fingers brushing mine, deliberate and slow.

He slides it into his own pocket like it's nothing.

Then he takes a long pull of his bourbon and turns back to Matheus.

For the next hour, we work the room like seasoned partners. Never straying far from each other. At times, we greet people together—switching off who leads, who jokes, who seals the moment.

Eve lingers nearby.

Never front and center, but always close. She stands beside us during key introductions, just far enough back to let us stay in control. But when one of us lands a cutting remark or redirects a conversation with effortless command, her eyes shine with approval.

It's subtle. Intentional.

And suddenly I get it.

This is what she was brought here for. What she's been working towards.

To get us to stop waging war and start moving in tandem.

And somehow, against all odds, it's happening.

Corrine finds her way over eventually but this time I know what side of the fence I need to be on.

"Dante," she says warmly, brushing her fingers over the edge of his sleeve. "Heard you had a car accident. How are you?"

He nods, calm and cool, pulling away from her touch. "Barely scratched the bumper. But thanks for checking in."

Fucking liar.

I saw the aftermath of the car. Totaled is more like it.

Lucky to be alive¬–another phrase that comes to mind.

He's been masking it, but I've noticed the slight limp occasionally on his right leg. The way he's favoring it. Squeezing his thigh at times.

She hums, sips her drink, clearly expecting more. But Dante gives her nothing else. Just that polite wall of ice he wears so well when she's around.

Then—she pivots.

Eyes on me now. "Grant. I was thinking about that weekend in Charleston—remember the rooftop bar?"

She places her hand on my arm. Light. Familiar.

I glance at it, then at Dante.

"Actually," I say, spotting Isabella across the room, "Dante, there's someone I'd like you to meet."

Dante follows my line of sight as I lean closer. "Isabella Lévêque. She's working on something I think you'll be very interested in."

Corrine's hand drops.

Dante's already nodding. "Lead the way, bug." I feel his touch–featherlight–on my lower back and my stomach drops as deep as his voice when he says that nickname.

And just like that, Corrine's left behind—no offense, no confrontation. Just... unchosen.

It feels like a thousand pounds have lifted from my chest. No verbal sparring between Dante and Corrine with me putting out fires between them. I can't help but wonder if things really could be this easy.

We move toward Isabella like we've done this a thousand times.

And maybe we haven't.

But it sure as hell feels like we will.

The dinner table is massive—round, lacquered mahogany dressed in black velvet and candlelight. It seats twelve, all of us from the firm. Dante is directly across from me. Eve to my left. Corrine—two seats down on my right.

Each place setting cost two hundred and fifty grand. An entire table bought without blinking. The money goes to notable causes across the city—rehab centers, food banks, arts programs. But our contributions tonight are earmarked for the St. James Orphanage.

Dante let Eve pick the benefactor.

It's never been on our charitable service days hosted by the firm, so I make a mental note to look into it later.

The five-course meal was decadent—foie gras, tenderloin, sea bass in citrus butter. Wines paired with each dish. Everyone's belly is full. The lights are dim.

All eyes face the stage as a speaker begins to thank sponsors.

It only takes a second and I feel that heat crawling up the back of my neck. That static of being watched.

I turn slightly and my eyes land on Dante.

He's not smiling. Not smirking.

He's devouring.

And I'm helpless under the weight of it.

That flame from earlier—meant to warm, to pull me toward him—it's gone.

What stares back at me now is consumption.

The inferno that used to feel like war but it's different now and I'm lost to it.

He's so beautiful it knocks the breath out of my lungs. His lips part like he's struggling too. Like something primal's coiled tight inside him, desperate to break free.

Then his hands move, slipping beneath the table, slow, smooth, and out of view.

I feel my cheeks flush. I glance down the table, searching for a witness.

Eve is focused on the stage, face poised, spine elegant. Corrine's halfway through a glass of wine, legs crossed, attention fixed somewhere across the room.

No one sees except me.

And I know what he's doing.

I see it in the slow, near-imperceptible shift of his shirt fabric. The smallest motion—a rhythmic pump that has everything to do with his cock in his hand under the table.

The semi I walked in with swells into something painful. Torturous. Like I've never been this hard in my life.

I grip the edge of my chair. My thigh flexes under the tablecloth. Every cell in my body screams for friction, for release, for him.

For the very thing I've been fighting for five years.

Fuck, longer than that.

Then Dante shifts. Barely. His nostrils flare, his throat tightens, and his jaw goes rigid with tension. His mouth opens just enough for a whisper of breath to leave him— and I know.

He's coming.

Right now.

Right here.

At this goddamn charity gala. In a ballroom full of power and performance and polished fucking reputations.

Even our fathers are here—seated at a different table across the room with the old-money fossils they play golf with.

And yet Dante sits there, going still as the euphoria slides through him.

I watch the tension bleed out of him, one vertebra at a time. Then a shift of fabric as I imagine he's zipping himself up.

Jesus Christ. My cock is leaking in my fucking pants... Again.

And just as the lights begin to brighten again—signaling the end of the segment—he pulls a folded napkin from his lap.

And his phone.

With a smirk that sends a ripple straight through my core, Dante taps the screen a few times. Then darkens it.

Not two seconds later, my phone buzzes inside my jacket.

My heart punches the inside of my ribs.

No.

No way.

He didn't.

Did he?

"Excuse me, everyone," Dante says, voice low and polite

as he pushes back from the table. "It's been a wonderful evening."

I track his every step as he crosses the ballroom, his gait loose now. Relaxed. He nears the exit, passing a waste bin. I watch—actually watch—as he drops the used napkin into it, like he's tossing out a receipt.

And then he's gone. His tall, muscled form walks out through the double-doors.

I swallow hard.

"I'm going to hit the restroom," I say, already rising. My voice cracking on the last word.

I move quickly—grateful the direction is away from the lights, away from the crowd. Once I'm in the bathroom, I go straight for the last stall. The one farthest from the door. Quiet. Private.

I lock it behind me and press my back to the cold tile wall.

Heart pounding. Hands shaking.

I fish my earbuds from my pocket. Slip one in and pull out my phone.

There's a text. The first text he's sent me personally in years.

DANTE: I had fun tonight.

There's a video attached.

Jesus.

My throat tightens as I tap it.

The screen brightens. And my breath catches as it flickers to life.

I can see his shirt hem riding up, his hand sliding over himself, slow and practiced, the thick ridge of his cock gripped in his fist.

Holy shit.

He's big.

I mean, I knew that already. But watching it? Seeing the dark flush of his head, the way his hand glides up and twists just beneath the crown, coaxing slick from the tip like it's nothing?

I'm practically drooling.

My cock is throbbing, still aching from earlier. From him. From this… fucking game.

I don't hesitate. I unzip my pants, take myself in hand, and give in.

I stroke myself in time with him. His hand on screen. Mine in the stall.

The breath that leaves me is ragged. Every nerve lights up. Every thought zeros in on the heat in my palm, the image of Dante's fist sliding wet and steady down the length of his cock.

He's close.

I can tell by the flex in his forearm. The twitch of his fingers.

And then he comes.

Fuck.

His cum spills over his fingers, thick and white, streaking down his shaft to the waiting napkin in his lap.

And that's all it takes.

I bite my lip, eyes locked on the screen as I follow him over the edge. My hips jerk, release hitting me like a train.

Fast. Blinding. I choke out a breath and catch it in a wad of toilet paper, gripping tight to keep from collapsing entirely.

Shit.

What the hell are we doing?

On the screen, he strokes, long and slow until he's satisfied, then he wipes it all away.

I clean up in silence, flushing the evidence and heading to the sink.

Washing my hands. Fixing my tie. Running my fingers through my hair. I stare at myself in the mirror, chest still rising and falling, a thin sheen of sweat clinging to my brow.

Bathrooms.

Seems like they're becoming a fucking theme.

First one—admitting I got the best blowjob of my life... from my oldest friend and business partner.

Second—sticking a plug up my ass and made to come at a goddamn charity event.

Now this—jacking off in a goddamn stall to a video of his dick.

I can't keep pretending anymore.

Can't keep pretending this is anything but inevitable.

This isn't a power game anymore. It's a collision course.

And I know what it's going to make me face.

The pressure in my chest tightens—too fast, too sharp. My stomach turns.

My mother.

The smell of blood and lilies. The icy numbness of guilt I never seem to shake.

Not now. Not here.

I splash cold water on my face. Let it run down the back

of my neck. Try to force the memory out. Then I exhale, fix my bowtie and open the door.

And stop.

Because there he is not even ten feet away.

Dante leans against the wall like he owns it, bourbon glass in hand, blazer unbuttoned, smirk in full, unbothered amusement.

He knows.

He fucking knows what I just did.

What I just came to.

That I was in there, fucking my hand, watching him send me over the edge with a goddamn napkin in his lap and a smirk on his lips.

"Just wanted to say goodnight, Lucciolina." he says, voice low and smooth like the bourbon he sips.

Lucciolina. It's Italian for little glowbug. I looked it up. The name he always calls me that I have no fucking clue why. But tonight, it's not an insult. It's a caress.

He doesn't wait for a reply.

Just finishes his drink, pushes off the wall, and strolls down the hallway with a lazy, arrogant grace that says checkmate.

And I stand there, heart thudding in my throat, and realize—

This whole time, I thought we were circling the ring, both of us throwing punches.

But Dante?

He's been playing chess.

I didn't even know the board was set.

And now?

Now I'm losing.

Not just to him—but to the truth I've spent years burying.

The denial.

The lie.

Chapter 25

The end is days away.

Five years of jockeying for position.

Five years of high-stakes moves and veiled threats and nights where I barely slept because the next day could be the one that changes everything.

The board vote looms like a guillotine. Clean cut. No appeals. Just legacy—split clean down the center. Or burned to ash.

But that's not what's got me twisted up inside.

Not anymore.

It should be.

Hell, it used to be.

Everything about this firm—about our fathers, their blood, their names—it's been drilled into me like gospel.

But now?

Now it's him.

Grant fucking Harrow.

The man who's haunted my nightmares and filled my dreams in equal measure.

The man I've hated more thoroughly than I've loved anyone else.

The man who—God help me—I never stopped wanting.

Something snapped this weekend.

At the gala. At that table. Beneath the watchful eyes of the city's elite, while legacy dripped from the ceilings and money soaked the wine.

I watched him break.

Just a crack.

Barely visible to anyone else. But I know him too well. I feel him too well.

And I saw it—the moment the wall began to crumble.

The moment denial lost its grip and he couldn't lie to himself anymore.

That's what this has always been, isn't it?

Not business. Not rivalry. Not ambition.

It's been the lie.

The thing Grant refuses to say. Refuses to name.

The thing he's been running from for years, even when it's bled into every boardroom, every contract, every fucking look he gives me.

I've played my part.

I've pushed him.

Cornered him.

Tempted him until I could feel the moment he forgot to hate me.

But I can't finish this.

Not this part.

He has to be the one to come the rest of the way.

To face what happened.

To face me.

To stop hiding behind fury and fatherhood and grief and finally admit what he's done.

Because until then, this will stay unfinished.

And I'll keep walking around with my chest split open, pretending I don't care when I'm dying for him to look me in the eye and say it.

Not *sorry.*

Not *I love you.*

Just the truth.

And if he does—if he finally fucking does—then maybe we stop fighting.

Maybe we stop bleeding each other out just to prove we're still alive.

Maybe we begin.

But if he doesn't?

Then I was wrong.

And we were never going to survive this anyway.

The elevator rises like a slow climb toward a fall I can't stop bracing for.

I check my phone again.

For the hundredth time since Saturday night—but still nothing.

No call. No text.

Not that we've ever been a phone call kind of... whatever this is.

But a text? That would've made sense.

An olive branch. A simple, *"We need to talk."*

But all I get is silence.

Maybe I pushed him too far.

Maybe sending that video—stroking my cock under a million-dollar table while the city's elite clapped for auction bids—was a line too far.

But God, the way he looked at me.

The way he walked out of that bathroom like his spine was made of glass and I was the one who cracked it.

The way I know he got off to it.

I run a hand through my hair and exhale through my nose, fingers twitching near the pack of cigarettes inside my inner jacket pocket. I'm not going to smoke one, but fuck—I might.

The ding of my phone cuts through my thoughts like a blade.

My pulse kicks.

It's stupid that I still half-hope it's him.

But it's not.

Meeting Invite: CONF. B – 8:30 a.m. (Internal: Board Transition Review)

From: Corrine Ashwood

Sent: 8:31 a.m.

Fucking hell.

I roll my eyes and resist the urge to throw my phone across the elevator.

Last-minute invite. No subject context. Scheduled right now. Probably sent to everyone else a week ago.

Classic Corrine—make me look disorganized, unprepared, always two steps behind.

Grant pretends it's not personal, but it is.

It always has been.

I snap a screenshot of the invite and fire off a text to Grant:

> DANTE: Care to tell me what the hell this is?

Or are we still pretending Corrine doesn't do this shit on purpose?

The elevator slows.

The doors open to the executive floor, glass and steel gleaming around me like we're all trying to convince ourselves this place is modern, untouchable, invincible.

But all I feel is the weight of legacy. Of war. Of whatever Grant and I are.

I slip my phone into my jacket as I walk.

Two minutes late. No prep. No agenda.

Exactly how she wanted it.

I reach the conference room, fix my cuffs, and push open the door. Corrine's already seated at the head of the table when I walk in, handing out pristine white folders like she's hosting a fucking awards ceremony.

Seven board members. All eyes flick to me as I enter. No one speaks.

Except her.

"Nice of you to join us. Even late."

I don't take the bait. Not really.

"Nice of you to include me," I reply smoothly, taking the one empty seat opposite her. "After the meeting has started. Shall we get on with it?"

She offers a saccharine smile and gestures to the stack of folders. "By all means."

I open mine.

Pages of statements and itemized ledgers. At first, it looks like standard firm accounting—a quarterly breakdown or financial audit—but then I catch the highlighted charges.

Recurring. Bimonthly. Labeled as *Consulting Services*.

My brows furrow.

Wait. I know this.

"This is nothing," I start, waving the page like I'm bored. "You're wasting everyone's time."

Corrine folds her hands like a queen ready to sentence someone to death. "Before you lie, Dante, let me spare you the embarrassment. I already know what they are."

I freeze for a fraction of a second, confused what she is playing at.

She sees it. Smiles.

"If you're willing to admit it now," she purrs, "we can perhaps avoid a formal inquiry and come to a resolution the board will find... reasonable."

I lean back in my chair, voice low and sharp. "If you know what they are, Corrine, then do enlighten me. Go ahead. Make your case."

She doesn't hesitate.

"You've been funneling firm money to sex workers," she says, dropping the words like poison into the center of the room. "Paying them monthly under fabricated job titles. 'Consulting services.' Like no one would put it together."

The room goes dead silent.

A beat.

Then I laugh. Sharp, surprised, genuine.

"That's your play?" I shake my head. "You think I'm stupid enough to do something that reckless?"

But then I flip the page.

And my laughter dies.

Because the next page isn't a payment log.

It's a profile.

A site I recognize immediately—one of those platforms where people host explicit content, post their own videos, pictures, offer private sessions behind paywalls. And there's no mistaking the man in the previews.

Teddy.

Shirtless in one. Pantsless in another. On his knees in a third.

My jaw tightens. Somehow I know exactly where this is going to go.

Corrine's voice slithers in. "As you can see, Mr. Marchesi has been funding this young man for nearly a year. Tuition by day. Sexual favors by night."

I close the folder calmly. "So what? The kid's making money in a way you don't approve of. Doesn't mean he's not worthy of a college degree."

"Dante," she sighs like she pities me. "You've been paying him for sexual gratification—on company funds. That's embezzlement. Prostitution. Pick one."

I stand. "You don't get to stand on a soapbox and moralize, Corrine. You've spent your entire career stepping on the backs of better people."

Her eyes narrow, but just as I open my mouth to continue, the door opens.

And Grant walks in.

"What is this?" he asks, eyes scanning the table, then the folders, then me.

Corrine straightens in her seat too quickly, her expression cracking just enough. She didn't expect him. Didn't want him here.

Which makes it all the more satisfying.

"Well, since you're here," I say, voice sharp, "I'll spare you the spin. I pay for the kid's college. Directly. Through the university's finance office. He never sees a dollar of firm money in his account. Whatever he does to pay for the rest of his life—his rent, his groceries, hell, his dignity—isn't mine to control and certainly not yours to judge."

Grant picks up one of the folders, flipping through slowly, deliberately. I watch his brow furrow. Then he closes it.

"Corrine," he says quietly, "we talked about this."

And something in me fractures.

I turn to him, sharp. "You knew about this?"

The hurt escapes before I can choke it down.

He doesn't get a chance to answer.

"Grant," Corrine interrupts, tone dipped in false sympathy, "it's understandable you'd be fooled by Dante's lies too. We all have been."

"Bullshit," I snap. "You've been trying to shove me out of this chair since the day you took the CFO's seat."

She lets out a dry laugh. "So paranoid."

"You didn't even wait until his wife was told," I hiss,

"that her husband had a heart attack at his fucking desk before you started making calls about his replacement."

"Enough," Grant cuts in, voice tight. "This isn't helping anyone."

Of course.

Of fucking course.

There it is again—him stepping between us. Not to defend me. Never to defend me. Just to calm the storm. To keep Corrine clean. Polished. Untouched.

While I stand here with blood in my mouth.

Corrine can't fucking help herself.

"And while we're on the subject of questionable expenditures," she says, voice silky with malice, "I have reason to believe Dante has recently hired a prostitute—Eve Sterling—and has been parading her around this office for the last week under the guise of a consultant. I suspect sexually inappropriate behavior within these walls. Including in his own office."

The floor drops out beneath me and I see red.

Not just anger—but a pulsing, blinding fury that settles beneath my skin like fire.

"You want to put me on the chopping block," I say, my voice low and dangerous, "then do it with actual fucking proof. Show me the deposit trail. Show me the payment receipts."

I glance around the table, at the board members shifting in their seats. Faces unreadable. Predictably silent.

But I don't look at Grant. I can't.

Because if he had anything to do with dragging Eve into this, with making her collateral damage in this stupid war—

"I'm warning you," I continue, forcing every syllable through clenched teeth, "you leave innocent people out of this."

Corrine doesn't flinch. Even that fake-ass smile remains plastered on her manipulative face like she knows she's won.

I smooth my jacket. Breathe through the rage before I say something I'll regret.

"You've got four more days," I say, eyes locking on hers. "Four more days until the board vote. If you want me out, bring something better than this weak-ass slander next time."

I walk out of the room and leave the doors open behind me.

Let them sit in it.

Let them stew in the tension they created.

I head straight for the elevators, vision tunneling, chest tight. My hand smashes the call button harder than necessary—like the force could burn off some of the rage simmering just beneath my skin. I need air. I need out. I need a fucking cigarette and a wall to punch.

Then I hear Grant's voice.

Firm. Authoritative. And... something else.

Something I've never heard from him when it comes to Corrine.

Anger.

"If you ever pull something like this again," he snaps, "I'll have your resignation before you can finish your first accusation."

My head turns slightly, not enough to look back, but enough to feel the impact.

He's defending me. Protecting me.

That's new.

"You don't meet with my partner without me," Grant continues, each word clipped, deliberate. "I told you those charges were for the kid's tuition. And you go on a witch hunt?"

For a beat, my chest fucking opens. *My partner.*

For a second, I let myself believe this isn't all an elaborate setup.

That he's not on her side.

But the elevator dings.

The doors open, silver jaws inviting me in. I step inside, throat tight, tongue bitter.

My hand slams the *Lobby* button. I don't care where I'm going—just that it's away.

The doors start to close, sealing me into silence but just before they shut, a hand slices through the gap.

The doors jolt, then reopen and Grant steps inside.

The moment the doors seal shut, I snap.

I don't give him a chance to speak.

Don't give myself time to second-guess.

I grab the lapels of his suit jacket and pull him toward me—hard.

Our mouths crash. A collision of years. Of silence. Of everything we never fucking said.

It's not soft. It's not tentative. It's a storm we've both pretended didn't exist.

I feel his breath stutter, his lips tense—surprised for a second—

Then he kisses me back.

Fuck, he kisses me back.

It's the kind of kiss that rewrites timelines.

That makes a man believe in every god he's ever cursed.

His mouth is molten, desperate, his hands threading into my hair like he's drowning and I'm the only goddamn thing keeping him afloat.

I groan against him, walking him back until his shoulders hit the elevator wall.

He doesn't resist.

Our hands are everywhere—gripping, clawing, tugging.

He fists the fabric of my shirt, and I swear he wants to tear it off me.

I press my thigh between his legs and he ruts against it like he can't help himself.

It's messy. It's brutal. It's everything.

I don't want to stop.

I want the whole fucking building to know.

I want them to look at him and see he's mine.

But just as the elevator starts to slow, just as the ding sounds—

He pulls back.

Not gently.

He bites my lip—hard enough to make me taste blood— and shoves at my chest until I take the step back.

The doors open.

The lobby is empty as we stand there like we've just survived a fucking war.

Grant straightens his jacket. Won't meet my eyes. His chest heaves, his jaw tight.

I lick the sting from my bottom lip. Taste copper.

"Come find me," I say, voice low, raw, wrecked, "when you're ready to stop hiding."

And I walk without glancing back. Without another argument or plea for the truth.

Just the echo of the best fucking kiss of my life burning on my lips.

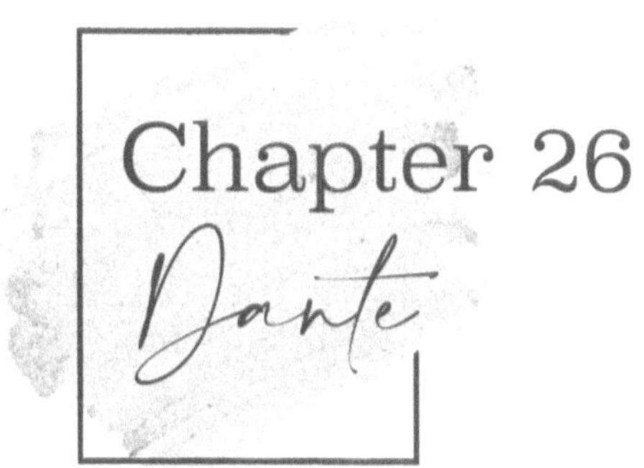

Chapter 26
Dante

The knock at my door isn't who I want it to be.

But I answer it anyway.

Eve stands there in a simple, fitted mini, strapless, holding a paper bag that smells like heaven and a bottle of red tucked under her arm.

"It's not what you think," she says before I can say anything. "I'm not here to sleep with you."

"That's a hell of a greeting." I lean against the frame, still not moving. "You're definitely here with ulterior motives, so what is it? An ambush? A bribe?"

She holds up the bag. "Fresh pasta. Real garlic. And a meatball the size of your ego."

I grunt, stepping aside to let her in. "So, definitely a bribe."

"I figured you haven't eaten. And judging by your face, probably haven't slept either."

She's not wrong.

She moves like she's done this before—uncorks the

wine, sets out two mismatched glasses from my cabinet without asking, opens the takeout, and starts plating it with the casual confidence of someone who has never cooked a day in her life.

"I'll warn you now," I say, exchanging the odd cups for proper stemware, "if this is some kind of come-to-Jesus dinner, I'm walking out of my own damn penthouse."

Eve rolls her eyes and sits across from me. "Relax. I'm not here to fix your feelings."

"So what are you here for?" I ask, standing at the counter, arms crossed, pretending like I haven't already taken three deep inhales of whatever magic came out of that takeout bag.

She doesn't answer.

Instead, she calmly plates everything with the kind of patience that makes me irrationally twitchy, and pours another glass of wine like she owns the place. She doesn't look at me, doesn't speak again until she's sitting at the table with her fork in hand and the steam curling up from real-deal pasta.

Only when I finally give in and sit down across from her does she look up.

"You had every opportunity to tell me what happened between you and Grant when you brought me in. When you laid out the contract."

I swirl the wine, watching the deep red catch the dim light. "I wanted you to figure things out on your own."

Her brows lift. "And?"

"And what?"

"Have I?" she asks, stabbing a piece of rigatoni like it insulted her.

I set the wine down and lean back in my chair. "You tell me."

Eve narrows her eyes. "There's a hole in the story. I've connected a lot of dots, but there's still something missing—and I want you to fill it."

I give a slow, amused smile. "And what do you think it is?"

She sets her fork down with a quiet clink. "Grant's mother."

That makes me pause—just for a breath—but I recover with a sip of wine, giving her nothing.

She watches me.

Waits.

"Something happened," she says, voice low but steady. "Something between Grant and his father. Something no one talks about. And whatever it was, you were sent away the very next day. Because you knew. Or you saw it."

I scoff. "That's your theory? That I witnessed a murder, and the family shipped me off before I could squeal?"

She shrugs. "I wouldn't put anything past the filthy rich."

I lean forward, elbows on the table. "Well, if I'm being suspected of homicide, I should probably call my lawyer before I incriminate myself."

"Don't deflect," she says. "I know what I'm asking. I know it's ugly. But I've already seen the rot under the floorboards, Dante. You dragged me into this for a reason. I'm not leaving until I know what the hell I'm standing in."

For a moment, all I can do is look at her and tap a finger on the edge of my plate. "That's not it."

"No?"

"Not even close."

Eve's brow furrows. "Then what—?"

I cut her off with a shake of my head. "You want the truth?"

She nods.

I look at the window, the city burning gold against the glass. "You've already figured out enough. And with the board vote a few days away... what the hell." I glance back at her. "Our graves are already dug."

"It was five years ago," I say, voice quieter now, but steady. "Right after the firm announced us as co-CEOs."

Eve doesn't speak, just sips her wine. Waiting.

"It was the night our first major architectural win went public. Wolfe Industries. The whole city was buzzing—every blog, every paper. We had reporters lined up, investors throwing money at us. It was the first time I actually believed we could do this. Together."

I look down at the glass in my hand and twist the stem slowly.

"Grant invited me back to his penthouse that night. Said we should toast the moment. Just the two of us."

Her brows lift slightly, but she stays silent.

"It started simple," I continue. "Champagne. Loosened ties. That massive sound system humming low in the background while we talked about everything—our fathers, how we got here, what it cost. All of it."

I glance up at her, let the next part land the way it should.

"And maybe the champagne made me reckless. Or maybe I'd just been holding it in for too long. But I told him."

"Told him what?" Eve asks, voice soft now. Less guarded.

"That I've always had a crush on him."

Her brows arch at that.

"It wasn't some ploy. Just... a quiet truth I'd buried," I say. "I told him I remembered seeing him again after I returned from the UK. How he looked standing there at our father's office, a man just like me. And I thought, *fuck*. He's still the most beautiful boy I've ever seen."

I close my eyes, just for a second. "He always was. But seeing him again... it was like I could finally breathe for the first time since I left."

When I open them, Eve is watching me like she's seeing something new. Not with judgment. Just... clarity.

"I tested the water," I admit. "Said it quietly. Asked if he'd ever thought about me that way."

"And?" she prompts.

"He didn't laugh. Didn't pull away. He hesitated, like he didn't want to admit it. Then he nodded. Just once. But it was enough."

The memory is sharp. Bright as fire, and I rub my bottom lip like I can still feel him there.

"I kissed him. Careful, at first. Like I was expecting him to bolt. But he didn't. He kissed me back. Hard. And then it was like years of wanting broke open all at once."

My voice drops as I speak, the memory curling around me like smoke.

"Our clothes were half off in a second. Hands were everywhere. I pushed him back onto the table, held him steady as I ground against him. My mouth on his chest, his head tipped back like he was coming apart."

I take a breath and run my hands down my face, resting my elbows on my knees—because the next part still makes my blood run cold.

"And that's when the suite door opened."

Eve tenses slightly.

"Corrine walked in," I say. "Sobbing. Hysterical. Said something was wrong."

Everything snapped.

Grant shoved me back like I'd burned him. Like kissing me was some bomb he hadn't expected to touch. The way he flinched—how fast he moved—it was like I'd just destroyed something sacred.

Corrine was already gone, her cries echoing down the hallway.

Grant chased her and I followed him. Just far enough to see the scene unfold at the end of the hall.

He caught up to her near the elevator. She was trembling, wiping at her eyes with one hand while the other jabbed at the call button like the building was on fire.

"It wasn't what it looked like," Grant kept saying. Over and over, like he was trying to hypnotize her with denial. "Corrine, please—don't leave. Just talk to me."

There was something about the way he said it—this raw desperation, this crack in his voice I'd never heard before—

that made something click. I don't know if they were ever official, but there was something there. Something unspoken. Or maybe just something Grant was terrified of losing.

Then she turned on me.

"You drugged him, didn't you?" she snapped, eyes glassy and wild. "What did you put in his drink?"

I stood there, stunned. "What the fuck are you talking about?"

"You coerced him." Her voice shook. "You've always had this... obsession. I saw the way you looked at him."

I waited for Grant to step in. To say *No, that's not true. I kissed him back. I wanted it too.*

But he said nothing.

Didn't look at me. Didn't look at her. Just stood there, frozen, like the weight of it all had crushed his ability to speak.

That silence was the break. That was the moment everything cracked open between us.

So, I left.

I didn't give him the satisfaction of a goodbye. Didn't wait to see if he'd come after me again. I just walked out of his penthouse with his taste still on my lips and a crater splitting my chest wide open.

The CFO had collapsed in his office from a heart attack. Corrine was the one who found him—said she'd come to drop off quarterly projections and walked in just as he hit the floor. It rattled her.

That's why she came to Grant's that night in a panic.

After, she stepped in to help "hold the fort," and Grant let her. Gave her the title like it was a favor, like it meant nothing. And I was too drunk and too pissed off to contest it. Drowning in a cocktail of anger, bourbon, and whoever I could get my hands on.

I made sure Grant saw it all.

Every Companion I took to the holiday parties. Every lover, every late-night scandal whispered through the halls. Male, female—didn't matter. It was punishment. For both of us.

Corrine watched, too. Always smiling. Always calculating.

She's been the wedge between us since the beginning. The only thing that's changed is her strategy. When guilt didn't work, she switched to shame. When that failed, she brought up Grant's mother. Now? She's all knives and boardroom politics.

But the goal's the same: drive me out.

And the worst part?

Some days, I don't know if Grant will ever really stop her.

Eve doesn't interject. She doesn't argue. She just watches me, calm and steady, like she's seen enough of people unraveling to know when not to push too hard.

Then, quietly: "So this had nothing to do with Grant's mother?"

"No." My eyes meet hers, and I let the sincerity bleed into my voice. "If you want the truth about that, ask Grant. Or Corrine."

She blinks. "Corrine?"

"Yeah," I say. "She was there."

Eve stills. That carefully composed mask of hers cracks for just a second.

"She was there?" It's a whisper from her lips.

"She lived with them," I add. "For a year."

The silence that falls between us is sharp. Cutting.

Eve doesn't look at me. She stares into her untouched wine like she's trying to read the bottom of the glass. Like maybe the answers are floating there, waiting to be scooped out and pieced together.

Her face gives nothing away—but I know that look.

She's reassembling the puzzle now.

Eve stands. "I'm going to hit the little girl's room," she says, voice unreadable.

I hear her voice in the hallway—low, clipped, controlled.

"Jax? Remember my new toxic bestie?"

Chapter 27

Grant

The office is quiet—too quiet. Just the hum of the AC and the dull echo of the city below.

I sit at my desk, jacket off, sleeves rolled, tie loosened like a noose I can't quite get rid of. My fingers drift to my mouth without thinking—just a brush, a memory.

Of Dante, the elevator and that goddamn kiss.

I can still feel it—still taste the blood he left behind.

I lean back in the chair and exhale, but it doesn't ease the pressure. Everything is pressing in on me. The board. The vote. The dark shadow that follows me. The truth I've spent five years burying deeper than any grave.

And now it's all clawing its way back to the surface.

The door opens.

I don't need to look up. Her heels are too familiar. Too precise.

"Still here?" Corrine's voice is soft. Honeyed. Dangerous.

She glides in without invitation, setting a bottle of my

favorite whiskey on the desk. Two crystal tumblers beside it like it's a peace offering.

"Thought you might need a drink," she says, already uncorking it.

I don't respond. Just watch her, wary.

She pours slowly. Controlled. Like always.

"I just came from visiting Mom," she adds after a beat, almost like an afterthought. "She didn't move. Obviously. Same as always."

She looks up at me with a brittle smile. "I didn't want to be alone tonight."

My fingers brush the rim of the glass she poured me, but I don't drink. I keep my eyes on her instead while she toys with her necklace.

"I should've told you what I was going to say today," she says, sliding one glass toward me. "I'm sorry for that."

I arch a brow. "That's what you're apologizing for?"

She tilts her head, that perfect mask of remorse never slipping. "I did what I had to do, Grant. For the firm. For you."

"Framing Dante? Dragging some woman into it who has nothing to do with anything?"

"I didn't frame anyone," she says smoothly. "I raised concerns. If they're unfounded, he has nothing to worry about."

I stare at her. Hard.

She shifts, smile faltering just enough to show the steel beneath. "He's always had a hold over you. Even now, you can't see it, can you?"

I clench my jaw.

She leans forward, her voice dipping. "He used you then. He's using you now."

"Stop."

But she doesn't stop.

"That day," she says, almost a whisper. "When I walked in before it went too far. I protected you, Grant."

"You didn't protect me," I say, cold. "You humiliated him. You made assumptions, accusations—and I let you."

"You let me," she repeats, eyes narrowing. "You let me because you needed someone strong enough to do it for you."

I stand. "You have no idea what you're talking about."

Her gaze holds mine. "Don't I?"

There's a long silence. The kind that echoes with everything that's been left unsaid for too long.

I glance down at the whiskey she poured, running my finger around the rim of the glass. I don't drink. Just keep it there between us like a line I haven't decided whether to cross.

Corrine doesn't sit. She paces slowly behind the chair opposite mine, hands clasped lightly in front of her. Like she's giving a presentation. Like this is all still just business.

"I'm not asking you to make any irrational decisions," she says. "The board's vote is coming. We both know that. All I'm asking is that you give it a good, clear thought. What's best for you. For the company."

I don't respond. I already know what she's circling.

Her voice softens, persuasive. "You and I... we have history, Grant. Stability. A shared understanding of what's necessary. And we've kept each other's secrets for a long time."

She finally sits. Smooths the hem of her skirt.

"I've protected you," she continues. "Your reputation. Your legacy. Even your shame."

That lands heavier than it should. I shift, fingers still at the glass.

"I never told anyone about the *other* day," she says quietly. "The day your mother died."

My spine stiffens.

She's watching me now. Carefully. Measuring every flicker of reaction.

"That it was you," she says. "At the top of the stairs. Just... standing there. Looking down at her body. It was you."

The room tilts.

She leans forward, voice low. "Everyone blamed your father. No one ever asked where *you* were. But I knew. And I never said a word."

My throat dries, but I don't let it show. I won't give her the satisfaction.

"I've carried that, Grant. For years. And not because I had to—but because I chose to. Because I've always had your back. Even when it cost me."

I say nothing. Just stare past her, past the glass, past the memory she's trying to resurrect.

She sits back, calm and patient. Like the bomb she just dropped is a kindness.

Like she thinks she's won.

But the only thing I feel right now is the slow rise of nausea curling behind my ribs.

Corrine watches me over the rim of her glass like she hasn't just shifted the ground under my feet. Like she's done me a favor.

Then, so casually it almost doesn't register, she adds, "Of course... secrets like that aren't easy to keep. One day, I might slip. Say the wrong thing to the wrong person."

My blood stops moving.

She's not smiling. She's not playing coy. She's just... floating the possibility like it's an accident waiting to happen. Like a weather forecast.

Something in me snaps.

I move without thinking. Cross the room in a single breath and grab her face in my hand—my fingers pressing into the sharp line of her jaw until her lips go tight, her eyes wide.

"You're going to threaten me now?" I say, my voice so quiet it scrapes.

She flinches just a little. "Grant—no," she mumbles, the words thick and warped through my grip. "That's not what I'm saying."

"The fuck it isn't."

Her pupils flicker, but she doesn't fight me. Doesn't even try to pull away. She just stares up at me, stunned and silent, like she finally miscalculated.

"Please." She whispers. Actual fear in her eyes. "You're hurting me."

I lean in closer, my voice razor-edged now. "You don't ever speak of that day again. Not to me. Not to anyone."

Her breath hitches.

Then I let go. Hard. Like her skin burns.

She exhales sharply, but still doesn't move.

I turn my back on her. Walk straight to the office doors, the silence pressing in from all sides. I don't look at the whiskey. I don't look at her.

I just leave it all behind—

The bottle.

The lies.

And the goddamn ghost of my mother at the bottom of the stairs.

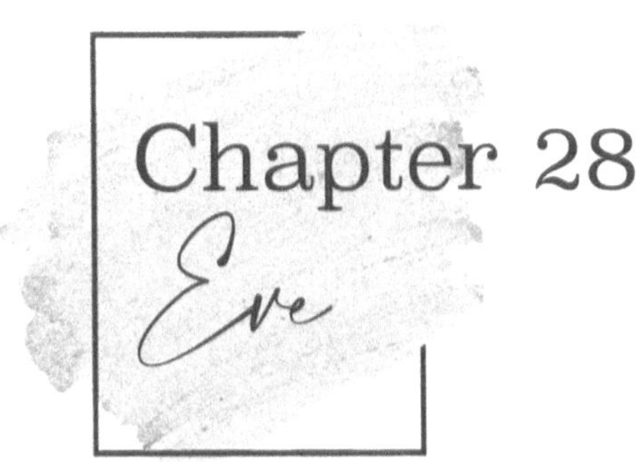

Chapter 28

Eve

The bell rings.

Dante sits low in the armchair across from me, one long leg draped over the other, the stem of a wineglass hanging loose from his fingers. His shirt is half unbuttoned, chest peeking out just enough to be distracting. His eyes, though—those obsidian pools—flick to the door, then to me.

We don't speak. We don't need to. Because we know who is here.

I rise slowly, smoothing the fitted lines of my black mini dress. Strapless. Tight. Strategic. My heels click over the hardwood as I walk to the front door and open it.

And there he is.

Grant Harrow—untethered.

His shirt is wrinkled, half untucked from his slacks. His tie hangs loose around his neck, collar spread open like he doesn't remember unbuttoning it. His hair is a mess, like he's been dragging his hands through it.

He looks at me like he wasn't expecting me to be here. Like it hurts that I am.

The bravado that carried him here is slipping. But then—his gaze drifts past my shoulder.

Dante's dark eyes, locked on him. Unmoving. Unforgiving. Unrelenting.

Grant's jaw ticks. I see the fight flash in his expression—but it doesn't last long. He's unraveling. That wall he's been holding up with spite and control is splintering.

I step forward, slow and soft, like I'm approaching something wounded. I reach up and sweep a lock of hair from his brow, my fingers trailing down the side of his face. I kiss his cheek gently. Then his neck—lingering there. He shivers.

"I know what you need," I whisper.

He looks down at me, something broken flickering in those sharp eyes. I cradle his face in both hands and ask, quietly, "Do you trust me?"

He doesn't answer right away. Just stares, like he's trying to see if I mean it.

Then, finally—he nods.

I take his hand and pull him inside.

Dante doesn't move. Still lounging in that same chair, wineglass resting on one thigh, the soft gleam of the city skyline behind him. His shirt parts just wide enough to show that golden skin and the faint shadow of a tattoo at the edge of his collarbone. He's silent, still, but that stare commands the room. Commands Grant.

And Grant feels it.

He tenses slightly as I pull him into the center of the penthouse, into the space where Dante can see everything.

I turn to face him, kick off my heels, my body brushing against his.

"What do you want, Grant?"

His throat bobs. His jaw flexes. He doesn't answer.

So I kiss him.

Soft at first. A coaxing touch of lips meant to unravel him, not claim him. He groans into my mouth, hands finding my hips, gripping like he needs something to anchor him.

"Do you want to play?" I whisper, brushing my lips across his again. "Let me help you relax."

Another nod. More desperate this time.

I smile.

Then I grip the top of my dress and slowly peel it down, baring my breasts—no bra, no pretense. Just skin and heat and want.

His breath catches. His eyes drop, hungry.

And when he looks up again, his gaze doesn't stop at me. It drifts to Dante, still seated, still watching.

I can feel how that stare affects him. His kiss grows rougher, hands bolder—gripping my waist, sliding down, cupping my bare ass as he hikes my dress up. He grinds against me, and I can feel him—hard, thick, straining through his slacks. A low growl rumbles from his chest as he presses his mouth to my neck.

But his eyes keep flicking to Dante.

Dante doesn't speak. Doesn't move. He just watches like he owns the room.

And maybe he does.

Grant's hands roam over me with a need that borders on frantic, but there's a question buried beneath all that desperation.

A silent: *Does he want me—or just want to watch me fall apart under you?*

And we all know the answer.

We just haven't admitted it yet.

Grant works my dress down past my hips, and I step out of it—completely bare now. Bare for him. Bare for both of them.

His breath hitches.

Then his mouth finds my breast, tongue swirling around one nipple as his hand palms the other, before he switches—pulling the second into his mouth with a low, hungry groan. I thread my fingers into his hair, tugging just enough to make him groan again.

When he looks up, I capture his mouth, kissing him deep and open-mouthed, then begin peeling away his layers—slipping his loosened tie from around his neck, undoing the buttons of his shirt one by one. He shrugs out of it, baring golden skin and sharp muscle, and my hands run down the ridges of his stomach until I'm palming him through his slacks. Hard. Hot. Throbbing under my grip.

His breath shudders out.

"God, you're—" he starts.

I silence him with a teasing kiss and walk him backward until the back of my knees hit the couch. He follows, letting himself be guided, lips still moving with mine.

I sink to the cushions.

My lips press against the skin of his abdomen, kissing a slow trail down. He moans softly, running his fingers through my hair as I unbuckle his belt and pop the button on his pants. He kicks off his shoes without hesitation as I tug down both his slacks and his boxers, freeing his cock.

He's already leaking.

I glance up at him through my lashes as I take him in hand, stroking once—slow and firm. His jaw clenches.

Then I grin.

My tongue runs a slick path along the underside of his shaft, from base to tip, before I take the head into my mouth. Swirl. Suck. Just enough pressure to make his head fall back with a groan.

"Fuck, Eve—"

But I'm not looking at him.

I'm looking at Dante.

Still in his chair. Still clothed. Except now one hand is lazily stroking over the thick bulge behind his slacks, his palm pressing firm over the outline of his cock. His jaw is tight. His nostrils flared. There's a tick in his cheek he doesn't bother hiding.

Oh, he likes this.

Grant moans again, hips twitching slightly beneath my mouth.

I release him with a wet pop and guide him lower on the couch. I kiss him, slow and messy, tasting his own arousal on my tongue.

Then I lean back and open my legs.

Completely bare. Completely ready.

Grant's pupils dilate. But I catch his jaw, tipping his head back toward mine.

"Show him," I whisper. "Show Dante how well you eat my pussy. Show him how hard you can make me come."

His breath catches. I feel the hesitation in his body.

And then—obedience.

He shifts, moving down the couch until his head is between my thighs, shoulders hooked under them. His hands grip my hips, and he pulls me closer, closer still, until his mouth is on me—tongue flicking through my wet pussy before flattening against my clit.

My head tips back.

And when I glance up through hooded eyes—Dante is standing.

Unbuttoning his shirt. Watching. Silent. Hungry.

Watching Grant worship me while his cock strains behind his zipper.

Watching him submit.

Grant's tongue is relentless.

Soft flicks. Deep licks. Wide, messy strokes that make my thighs shake. I grind against his face, my hands in his hair, riding every gasp he coaxes from me with skill that surprises me. No hesitation. No restraint.

"Just like that," I murmur, rolling my hips in time with his mouth. "God, you're so good, baby. That mouth of yours —fuck."

He groans against me, the vibration deep and rich. I look down and find his eyes locked on mine, hungry and desperate for more praise. I give it to him with a moan, a sharp tug to his hair, letting him know I feel every stroke.

I don't even hear Dante move at first.

Then—

A slow creak of leather as he rises. Footsteps. Deliberate.

He steps up beside us and sets a dark wooden box on the coffee table. Quiet. Heavy. The kind of box that makes promises.

I glance at it—but it's Dante who steals my attention.

His pants are next. He undoes them with precision, sliding them off and letting them drop to the growing pile of clothes on the floor. His cock is thick, flushed, heavy in his hand. He strokes himself slowly, lazily, dragging his thumb through the glistening bead of precum at the tip. Then he brings it to his mouth, tongue flicking out to taste it.

Grant groans low against my pussy—tongue still moving, licking me like he can't stop. His hungry eyes are on Dante's dick, and I'm not sure if he's starving for it or scared of it.

Dante's voice is gravel and silk.

"Feels good, doesn't it?" he says, crouching beside the couch. "You like how he licks your pussy, piccola?"

I nod, breathless. "So good."

Dante's eyes darken. "He's licking you like a good boy, huh?"

"Mhm," I hum, my head tipping back. "So fucking good."

Grant moans again, and I feel the tension in his shoulders tighten. His grip on my hips turns bruising.

Dante leans in and kisses me—slow, deep, tongue parting my lips with absolute control. One hand slides into my hair, holding me in place, while the other drags down the curve of my neck to cup one breast.

His mouth leaves mine to kiss down my jaw, my throat.

"Look at you," he whispers, lips ghosting along my collarbone. "Letting him work that mouth just to please us."

He finds my breast, lips closing around my nipple as his other hand rolls the opposite one between two fingers, pinching until I gasp. My back arches, caught between the flick of Grant's tongue and the suck of Dante's mouth.

Pressure builds.

Pleasure blooms.

"Dante—" I gasp, my whole body shaking.

"Come for us," he murmurs. "Let him taste it. Let him know how good he's doing."

I cry out as the orgasm rolls through me, wave after wave crashing over my spine. Grant doesn't stop. Not for a second. He holds me down and licks me through every pulse, every tremble, until I'm shaking and soaked and clawing at the couch cushions.

Only then does Dante rise to his feet again, cock thick and twitching as he looks down at us both.

"Good," he says, eyes on Grant now. His thumb wipes across Grant's full bottom lip, glossy with my release. Sucking his finger clean, he hums and says, "I want to see you do it again."

Dante doesn't touch me at first—just watches, eyes dark, voice a calm command that makes my body obey before I can think.

"Ride his mouth again," he says, voice smooth as glass. "Come on his face, angel. I want to see it this time."

I nod, lips parted, still trembling from the last orgasm as I shift up and off the couch.

Grant's eyes follow me, lips wet with me, hands already reaching. I swing a leg over him, straddling his face, bracing myself on the arm of the couch as I lower down.

His tongue finds me instantly.

God.

I cry out, hips jerking as he laps at me—greedier now. Less careful. He's lost in it, in me. Because this is familiar for him.

Being with a woman. Opening himself to me first, before giving it all to Dante.

I'm already close to coming again when Dante moves in front of me.

He strokes his cock, slow and thick, and holds my jaw to meet his eyes.

"Open," he says.

I do.

He slides into my mouth, inch by inch, until I'm full of him—until I can taste his salt and heat and he's groaning low in his throat.

"That's it," he breathes, thumb caressing my cheek. "Suck me, Eve. Nice and slow."

I hum around him, swirling my tongue along the underside of his shaft, taking more. He's so long I can only get half of him before he's hitting the back of my throat.

Fuck, I love big-cocked clients.

Grant moans beneath me, and my hips rock harder, grinding on his mouth.

Dante doesn't pull out.

He stays deep, letting me moan around him, letting me struggle to breathe as the pleasure crashes again—sharp and wild and too much to contain.

I come with both of them holding me down—Grant licking me through it, Dante gripping my jaw, cock still buried in my mouth as I moan and tremble and come again.

When my hips finally still, Dante strokes my jaw once more, pulling back with a wet, lewd sound. He steps back and retrieves two condoms from the wooden box, tossing one to me.

I catch it with shaking fingers.

Grant watches, still breathless, eyes wide as I slide off his face. His lips are swollen, glistening. I kiss him—long and messy and grateful—before easing him back against the couch.

"Sit up," I whisper.

He does. I drop to my knees between his legs.

I open the condom wrapper with my teeth, hold his cock at the base, and lower my mouth. Rolling it down inch by inch as I suck him, licking and teasing while he curses softly and fists the cushions at his sides.

Behind me, Dante's voice is lower now. Rougher.

"Let's stuff her full of us, lucciolina."

My heart skips.

Grant groans. His hand finds my face as I release him with a pop and rise again, straddling his lap. I kiss him as I guide his cock to my entrance, teasing him with slow rolls of my hips.

Then I slide down.

He's thick. Hot. Deep.

I wrap my arms around his neck, moaning as he fills me completely, his hands gripping my hips like he never wants to let go. He kisses me again—hungry, messy, eyes flicking over my shoulder toward Dante before returning to mine.

I ride him, slow at first.

And then—

Dante's hands.

He's behind me now, kneeling on the couch. I hear the soft crinkle of his condom being unwrapped; the slick sound of lube being applied—drizzled between my cheeks, preparing me for his fat cock.

He strokes himself slowly, watching us with that calculating hunger.

His hands are warm as they slide over my hips.

"Easy now," he murmurs, slowing my rhythm. He kisses my shoulder, my neck. His fingers spread the lube over my ass, making me gasp and tense.

The other hand finds my hip, brushing Grant's fingers. Neither of them moves. They just... stay there. Touching. Not running. Not retreating.

Just... holding.

I feel Dante's cock at my entrance.

He presses in slowly.

My mouth falls open every second it takes him to slide in, inch by inch, until I'm completely, utterly full.

"Come on, bug," Dante groans against my ear. "Let's fuck her. Let's make her scream for us."

And God—they do.

Two men. One rhythm. One purpose.

Dante's grip moves to my hips, pulling me into him. His hand drags to Grant's. Then his wrist.

Grant's gaze locks over my shoulder, and I know Dante is holding his stare with equal intensity. Dante's hand continues to slide up Grant's forearm, pulling Grant to him. Wanting to feel his fingers on his bare skin.

Grant takes the invitation, his callused palm sliding from my hip to Dante's. Grant must squeeze him, because I feel Dante let his head fall back as a moan escapes him.

Their thrusts sync—Dante deep in my ass while Grant pounds into my pussy—their hands gripping each other, gripping me, owning me, as I sob and moan and fall apart in the space between them.

My body is fire.

Every sensation—it's all too much and not enough. I can't tell where one ends and the other begins, only that I never want this moment to stop.

I'm wrecked. Gloriously ruined.

And when I come again, shaking and gasping, it's with their names on my lips—both of them.

Chapter 29

Grant

She comes hard.

Writhing. Gasping. Clenching around us like her body doesn't know which of us to hold tighter. And I swear, it breaks something loose inside me.

Eve collapses between us, a soaked, satisfied mess of moans and skin. Her breath dances across my collarbone as she shifts off my lap, leaving my cock slick, twitching, still desperate for release.

Dante hasn't come either.

I can feel it in the way he watches me—his chest rising hard and fast—as he slowly pulls himself free from Eve.

We're all flushed.

Breathless.

But I'm fucking wrecked.

Not just from the act—but from what it's unraveling in me. What I've buried for nearly twenty years. What I've lied about. What I've laughed off. What I've kept hidden, even from myself.

The wanting.

The truth.

It's not even about Dante, not really. It's about me. About finally letting go. Dropping the goddamn mask. Tearing it off, piece by piece, until there's nothing left to hide behind.

And tonight... I can't lie anymore.

Not to him.

Not to her.

Not to myself.

Dante's warm hand is still on my thigh, and his fingers flex just so before he slides his touch off me and stands.

Eve steps between us, eyes on fire, and reaches for the condoms still wrapped around us both.

She peels them off gently. Intimately. Like she's stripping away armor. Stripping us bare.

Taking both our hands, she presses them together—palm to palm.

Her voice is low. Breathless.

"Look at you both," she whispers. "So fucking handsome."

I look at Dante.

At his hand against mine. Our fingers mirroring. His thumb rubbing mine. Skin flushed. Cocks still hard and leaking between us. His dark eyes never leaving me.

I've imagined this.

Dreamed it.

Denied it.

But it's nothing like the reality.

This is raw and pulsing and dangerous.

And I want it.

Fuck, I want it all.

Eve drops to her knees like a priestess at the altar of sin, murmuring something wicked before wrapping one hand around each of us. She strokes us slow—almost reverent. Her tongue teases my tip before she shifts to Dante's, and back again, keeping us both painfully hard.

His cock is so fucking long. Thick. And God, I want it.

Eve looks so small against him, her mouth struggling to swallow down as much of his shaft as she can. Her hand circling him, but his girth still overwhelming her reach.

It's when her lips leave Dante that he threads his fingers in mine and guides me to him.

"Come here."

He grips my jaw and kisses me.

Open-mouthed.

Demanding.

And I let him.

No—I take him back. Tongue tangling. Breath catching. Our cocks pressed side by side, slick in Eve's hands as the heat between us explodes.

His hand fists in my hair. I groan into his mouth.

I kiss him like I'll never get another chance.

Because for twenty years, I didn't believe I deserved one.

But tonight—

Tonight, I take it.

The kiss ends too soon, but the heat doesn't.

Dante doesn't step away. His mouth lingers near mine, breath hot. Eve's still on her knees between us, her hands stroking us slow, her eyes dark with something deeper than lust.

Dante's hand slides lower—fingers wrapping around my cock. He strokes me once. Twice. His grip firmer than hers. A little rough. Like he knows what I like even though I've never told a soul.

Eve leans in, taking the head of me into her mouth again, tongue circling, cheeks hollowing.

Dante's hand never leaves, stroking me while she sucks me.

"Do you want me?" he murmurs, voice low. Velvet and sin.

My heart stutters. My hips twitch.

He squeezes gently, forcing the air from my lungs.

"Say it," he breathes, nose brushing mine.

I don't answer right away. I can't. My mind reels, body tight and trembling, held between their mouths and hands like a crucible. Everything I've run from pressing in all at once.

"Dimmi che mi vuoi, Lucciolina."

*I don't know what he's asking but I know I can't lie anymore.

I squeeze my eyes shut. Exhale through gritted teeth. My voice barely a whisper.

"Yes," I rasp. "I want you."

Dante groans softly—more breath than sound. "Fuck, Grant. I've been waiting for you."

He presses his forehead to mine before pulling back.

––––––––––––––

*   "Tell me you want me, little glowbug"

Eve shifts with him—eyes flicking to mine, her hand stroking me once more before letting go.

"We're going to take care of you, baby," she whispers, placing kisses on my dick, my pelvis.

Her lips part around the head of my cock again. Her mouth is wet heat and wicked rhythm, drawing shudders from deep inside me.

Dante steps behind me. His body warm and strong at my back. His breath skirting over my skin and heightening every nerve. Lighting me on fire from within.

I can't think. Can't breathe—just feel.

Eve takes me to the edge like she knows exactly where it is. Hovering there. Then dragging me back again. Only to bring me right to the brink once more.

Dante's mouth finds my neck, kissing the shell of my ear. My jaw.

His hands run down my spine, slow and steady. Down to my hips. My ass.

I groan.

His palm is firm as he strokes lower—between my cheeks—and I barely have time to register the coolness before his slick finger, coated with lube, slides inside.

I gasp, and my knees nearly buckle.

"That's it, baby."

Eve doesn't falter. Just stays right there—mouth open, breath warm around me.

"One," Dante says, his voice like silk soaked in sin. "Nice and easy."

His other hand wraps around my waist, grounding me.

Trailing up my stomach, my chest, pinching my nipple. His lips are warm on my neck as he kisses me there.

"Relax for me. Let go."

He curls the finger just right, and I jerk in Eve's mouth. She moans around me—low and encouraging.

Then a second finger.

Thicker. Fuller.

Fuck.

"Dante—"

"I've got you, baby," he croons, kissing the back of my shoulder. "Just breathe."

The first push inside me punches a moan from my chest. My grip tightens in Eve's hair, the other reaching back—blind, desperate—until I find the nape of Dante's neck and clutch him like I'll drown without it.

It's not just that it's a man touching me like this for the first time. It's that it's *him*. Dante.

The man I've dreamed of longer than I care to admit.

The one I told myself I couldn't want. Couldn't have.

And yet, here he is—behind me, fucking me open with fingers that seem to know exactly what I've been starving for.

I look back over my shoulder and our eyes lock—something inside me snapping loose at the hunger I see in his gaze.

I pull him into a kiss. Open-mouthed. Demanding.

His tongue tangles with mine, and I moan into him, lost in the taste of him, the feel of him, the way Eve's mouth keeps working my cock like she's orchestrating the whole thing.

"You're doing so good," he whispers. "But don't come. Not yet. Give me your pleasure, Grant—but don't you come down her throat."

I whimper.

Fucking whimper.

"I—" I gasp, my head tipping back to his shoulder. "I don't think I can—God—I don't think I can come without—"

"You *can*," Dante whispers, kissing the corner of my mouth, my cheek, my jaw.

His fingers still working me, and I call out at the euphoria building within me.

"I'll talk you through it, baby. I've got you."

Dante's hand snakes around me, palm pressing down low, right at the base of my cock.

"Here," he murmurs, his voice low and reverent. "Squeeze here. Just like that. Now breathe."

I'm trembling. Shaking. So close I can't hold it—don't want to. But Dante keeps whispering, coaxing me back from the edge, keeping me perched right there.

"Just look at me, baby," he says, kissing my cheek again, his fingers still moving deep inside me. "I want to watch you break for me."

And that's all it takes to hurl me over the edge.

It's not release. It's detonation.

My body convulses as the climax hits—raw and brutal and completely overwhelming.

Eve's mouth stills around me, soft and perfect. Holding me without motion, like she knows what we're doing. Like she wants to watch me fall apart just as badly as he does.

I don't come. Not a drop. But it doesn't matter.

It's more than any orgasm I've ever known.

I'm groaning, moaning, my voice cracking on his name as I arch and tremble between them.

Dante holds me together with both hands—one still inside me, the other sliding up my chest like he wants to touch every part of me.

"Fuck," he breathes, kissing the corner of my mouth. "You're so fucking beautiful like this."

I'm panting. Dizzy. Completely undone.

He brushes my hair back, fingertips tender against my temple.

"You're going to let me fuck this tight ass tonight, bug," he murmurs, kissing the hollow of my throat before licking up the column of my neck and biting my ear. "And you're going to take every inch of me, aren't you, *lucciolina*?"

And I know—I won't say no.

Never again.

Dante turns me to face him, and the moment our mouths meet again, I forget what it means to breathe.

It's not a kiss—it's a surrender.

My chest pressed to his, cocks sliding slick and heavy between us, our bodies move together like we've done this a thousand times in dreams and only now made it real.

Eve drifts toward the bedroom, tugging pillows into place on the wide bed.

Dante's hands are still on me—mapping every inch of my back, my hips, the curve of my ass, the tension in my thighs. He pulls me tighter, groaning as we grind together, the friction almost too much. But not enough.

We stagger backward, mouths fused.

He walks me into the bedroom like a man possessed.

When we reach the bed, Dante steps behind me, wrapping one arm around my chest while the other strokes me—slow and firm. His palm curves around my throat as he leans in and whispers against my ear,

"Do you trust me to take care of you, *bug*?"

I nod instantly. "Yes, Dante. I trust you."

His hand tightens a fraction. His voice drops lower.

"Am I going to be the first to fuck your virgin ass?"

The way he says it—like a promise, like a vow—makes me whimper.

"Yes."

He growls, biting down on the curve of my neck as both his hands fist my cock.

"That's right, baby. This tight little hole is mine to ruin, isn't it?"

"Yes—fuck—yes."

"I'm going to be your first and your only," he murmurs, dragging his mouth over my shoulder. "Is that what you want?"

I choke on a breath. "God, yes."

His next words rumble through me.

"Then lay down for me, beautiful boy. She's going to get you ready."

Eve waits on the bed, lit softly by the city glow bleeding through the windows. Pillows prop up my hips as I sink into the mattress—everything exposed, everything open.

She rolls a condom over my cock with the same care she

might unwrap something sacred, then straddles me and sinks down in one slow, delicious motion.

I grip her hips, moaning into the space between us, feeling every tight clench of her around me.

She rides me slow, each glide a tease.

"Just relax, okay?"

I nod, and she rolls her hips.

Between my legs, Dante kneels. His hands trail up my calves, then my thighs, spreading me wider.

He kisses the inside of one knee, then the other—like a prayer.

Then comes the lube.

His fingers—slick and sure—slide over me, coaxing me open again.

I shake. Half holding my breath, half afraid of what comes next. Not just because of what it means. Because it's a line that can never be uncrossed.

But also because Dante is fucking huge.

"You're safe," he says, voice rich and steady. "I'll stop if you say so..."

Then softer, darker:

"...but I'm going to fuck you so good you'll beg me to keep going."

The first push of him inside me is unbearable in the best way.

"Breathe, Grant," Eve coaxes as she rides me gently, Dante pushing in slowly. "Easy, baby."

My body clenches. Stretches.

Then opens.

A cry rips out of my throat—half pain, half ecstasy.

Eve braces herself on my chest as she moves, her breasts brushing against me, grounding me.

"Good boy. Just breathe through it."

He seems to enter me forever until finally, he's deep inside me, and I can feel him in my very soul.

Dante holds my legs wide, his arms locked under my knees, his body solid and sure between them.

His hands anchor my hips, guiding the rhythm with terrifying precision—slow, deep, relentless thrusts that strip me raw in the most exquisite way.

I feel every inch of him, every pulse, every stretch of heat where I've never been touched by another man.

"God," I choke out, eyes fluttering shut. "It feels so fucking good…"

Dante groans above me, the sound rough, reverent.

"You're incredible, baby. So tight—so perfect around me."

Eve leans over, bracing herself on my chest, her hands splayed across my skin as she rides me—deep and steady.

"You're doing so well, Grant," she whispers, pressing a kiss between my brows. "Let it happen. Let us have you."

I moan louder, no longer caring how unhinged I sound.

My body is burning—overstimulated, overwhelmed, and still begging for more.

Every movement inside me sends a shockwave up my spine—pleasure so intense it borders on pain.

But it's Dante.

It's him.

The man I've wanted for half my damn life.

"Don't stop," I gasp, fists tightening in the sheets. "Eve. Fuck. Dante, don't stop."

His pace doesn't quicken, but it deepens. More deliberate. More consuming.

"Not a fucking chance in hell, baby," he growls, teeth grazing Eve's shoulder. "I'm gonna fuck you through it, *bug*. You're mine now. Say it."

"I'm yours," I breathe, voice breaking. "Fuck—I'm yours."

"Good boy," he whispers, hand tightening on my hips. "Tell us, baby. Who fucks you like you've never been fucked before?"

"God. You do."

I'm a panting, moaning mess and I don't give a shit.

This is surrender, and I'm done fighting it.

"Fuck me," I grit out as they move—harder, faster, deeper.

I widen my legs more because I'm a fucking whore for this. For him.

"Jesus. Fuck me so good."

I close my eyes, my head tipping back—and just feel.

That's all I can do: feel. And hold on for my fucking life.

"That's it. Take it for me."

Dante is slamming into me, Eve rolling and bouncing in time with him like they're conducting a perfect symphony together.

"You take every fucking inch I give you in this tight, pretty hole."

Christ almighty.

"Oh my god, Grant."

Eve moans it out, working her wet pussy on me, and it's fucking heaven.

She leans down, fucking me, kissing my neck, and losing herself on my dick.

"You hear how good your cock feels in her, amore mio?"

Dante's gritting through the pleasure building in him too, his grip on my hips hardening.

"That delicious cock I sucked down my throat—and I'm still fucking starving for you, *bug*."

The pressure builds—impossibly sharp, like a wire pulled tight through the center of my body.

I'm strung out between their mouths, their hands, their heat.

Eve circles her hips on me, moaning my name like a benediction.

Dante drives deeper, hitting something inside me that sends me arching off the bed.

I cry out, wrecked and trembling.

"I'm—fuck—I'm gonna come—"

Dante's eyes lock onto mine.

"Then come, baby. Let go for me. Squeeze that tight little ass around my fat cock, Grant. We've got you."

So, God—I do.

The orgasm tears through me like fire and flood.

White-hot. Endless.

I shatter—hips bucking, voice cracking, body wrung out in a full-body quake.

My hands fly back to the headboard to hold me as my cock pulses inside Eve.

Dante never slows.

Never stops fucking me through it.

His praise is hot against my skin.

His long cock hits so perfectly inside me I see static.

"Beautiful," he growls. "So fucking beautiful when you break for us."

We collapse into it.

Eve moaning. Dante cursing in Italian.

My whole body trembling. Flooded. Complete.

After, Eve presses a kiss to my temple, brushing damp hair from my forehead with fingers that tremble just slightly.

She lingers—her eyes warm, her voice soft.

"You were fucking perfect," she whispers. "I hope you finally see it now... what it's like to be wanted out loud."

My throat tightens.

I nod, too raw to speak.

She smiles, then rises with slow grace, her body slick and glowing in the low light.

Dante wraps an arm around her waist, pulling her in close.

His other hand fists her breast, thumb brushing the peaked tip.

Eve cups the back of his head, drawing him into a kiss—deep, slow, tasting of everything we just shared.

"You were fucking perfect too, *piccola*," Dante murmurs. "You opened him up like you were born to do it. Look what we made together..."

They look down at me in satisfaction as our bodies grind to a slow stop.

Dante's hands leave her body and rub up my thighs.

"We made a ruined mess of him."

She hums against his mouth, satisfied and sated, before slipping away.

The sound of running water greets her as she disappears into the bathroom—steam already curling into the room, fragrant and warm.

But Dante stays.

Still inside me.

Still holding me.

And I've never felt more undone... or more whole.

Firm hands rub up my body, then he leans down to meet me. He pulls my hips into him, making sure we don't move from each other an inch while he kisses me like I've never been kissed before.

His mouth, his tongue, seem to pass a thousand confessions to me at once.

And then, with his eyes full of something I'm afraid to name, he says—

"That wasn't just the best fuck of my life, *lucciolina*."

He leans in closer, his voice barely a breath as he rubs his nose against mine.

"That was like coming home."

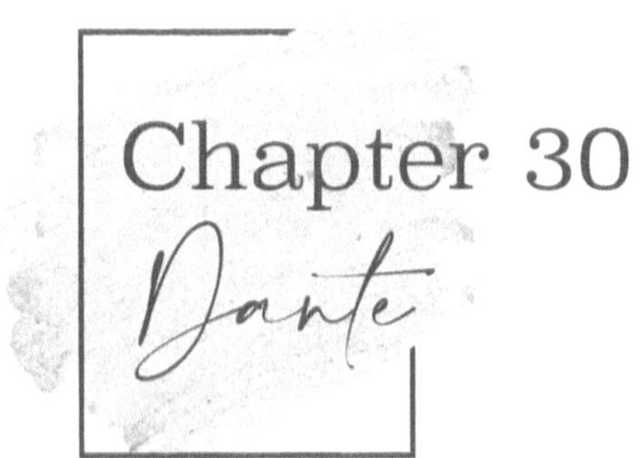

Chapter 30
Dante

Showering with Grant Harrow after fucking him within an inch of his life?

Yeah.

That's a goddamn life goal crossed off my list.

Cooking for him?

That's next.

He loves breakfast. Brunch. Anything involving eggs and carbs and too much coffee. And what else do you cook at two in the morning for a man you just broke open but eggs Benedict and mimosas?

The hollandaise is perfect. Poached eggs—soft and trembling. The ham is crisped just the way I like it. Three servings, plated hot and waiting. A chilled bowl of cubed cantaloupe rests at the center of the table. Champagne flutes sparkle in the low light, condensation beading on their delicate stems. The orange juice is pulpy. The champagne is cold. I haven't poured them yet—I want the bubbles fresh.

I'd showered fast—quicker than I usually do—leaving Eve and Grant behind. It's not that there wasn't room for all three of us. There was plenty. But she'd offered to wash his hair, pressed up against him, whispering something about how tight his shoulders were. How brave he'd been.

I knew he'd be starving when she was done with him. Starving in more ways than one.

My lounge pants hang low on my hips, towel slung over my shoulder, as I finish wiping down the counter. I'm just setting the last plate down when I hear the door open.

Eve appears first—glowing and flushed. Her long, wet hair hangs down her back, and she's wearing one of my T-shirts—oversized and swallowing her completely. She's radiant. Soft. A vision of satisfaction and mischief.

But it's Grant I really look for.

He lingers in the doorway, damp curls mussed, the waistband of his borrowed pants slung loose. He sees me and freezes—just for a second. His eyes lock on mine, and something flickers across them. Not regret. Not fear.

Bashfulness.

A pink flush rises to his cheeks.

I raise an eyebrow. A silent warning: Don't you dare backtrack. Not after tonight.

I don't know if he gets the message. But I know Eve sees it—because she breaks the tension effortlessly, slipping beside him with a teasing smile and a shoulder bump that makes him exhale a laugh.

"Sit, sweetheart," she says, squeezing his shoulders as she guides him toward the table. "I'll get the drinks."

I bring over the plates, setting hers and mine down

before returning with his. I lean in, fingers under his chin, and tilt his face up to mine.

"Eat," I murmur, brushing a kiss to his lips. Just a taste. A reminder.

He looks down at the plate like it's a miracle—then back up at me with something equal parts admiration and disbelief.

"I didn't know you could cook," he says, voice playful. His eyes drop lower, roaming my bare chest, the trail of hair leading beneath the low waistband of my pants.

I smirk. "I do have a few hobbies... other than fucking like a god."

His mouth pops open in surprised amusement, and I waste no time. I lean down and kiss him again, swallowing the sound he makes.

Then I press my lips to his ear, voice dark and low.

"Careful opening your mouth like that, bug. I'll take it as an invitation for my cock."

He chokes on a laugh. His entire face turns the prettiest shade of red.

I leave him like that—wrecked and grinning—as I cross to Eve. She's just finished pouring the mimosas, her back arched slightly as she reaches for the chilled champagne. I slide up behind her, arm curling low around her hips. My lips press to her bare shoulder, warm and damp from the shower.

"Go sit," I murmur against her skin. "I'll finish up."

She hums and lets me take the last glass from her hand. I drop a single raspberry into each flute, the crimson fruit sinking with a tiny fizz.

Then I join them at the table, lifting my glass.

"To firsts," I say. "And seconds."

Grant meets my eyes across the rim of his flute.

His smile is small.

But it's real.

We eat.

We talk.

We laugh.

It's easy. Too easy, maybe. The kind of easy that only comes after good sex and better company. The air between us feels softened—like the fight is gone, like we've wrung it out of ourselves one orgasm at a time.

Eve makes a joke about a client who once tried to pay her in rare books, and Grant laughs so hard he nearly chokes on his mimosa. He wipes his mouth, shoots a bashful glance my way—and I catch it. Just like I've caught all the others.

Sneaky little fucker.

He keeps glancing. I keep letting him.

Because we both know we need more out of tonight than our cocks. We've both danced around it long enough— whatever this is. Whatever it's becoming.

And it's coming. The moment. The reckoning.

The meal winds down. The plates empty. The bottle of champagne? Bone dry. Eve drains the last of her glass and tilts her head, locking eyes with me.

I see the message written clear across her face.

I'm overstaying.

It's time.

I nod once. Nothing more. No need for words between us.

I rise and take the plates, scraping them quietly into the sink. The water runs hot. I rinse, wash, focus on the sound of it—the scrape of ceramic, the rinse of silverware. The hum of something shifting between the three of us.

I hear the gentle scrape of her chair. Don't have to look. But I do.

Just in time to see her hand on Grant's cheek. Her lips on his.

"You don't need me anymore tonight," she whispers.

Then she's beside me, brushing her lips against my cheek. Warm. Affectionate.

"I'll be out on a personal assignment, so..." She pushes a stray lock of hair away from my eyes. "See you Friday at the board decision?"

"Fuck," I mutter under my breath. "That's coming up."

She just smiles, strutting off toward the bedroom like she owns the world, scooping up her little black dress from where it's been discarded for hours on my floor.

Grant brings the half-empty bowl of fruit to the counter and sets it down. He leans into it, exhaling like the weight of the world just let go of his spine.

But I don't let him get any further.

I shut off the water.

Then I'm turning, grabbing his hips and tugging him between me and the counter. His body fits there like it was always meant to.

One of his hands lands on the counter beside me; the other hesitates before cupping my jaw. My hands slide up his sides, fingers grazing bare skin.

"Don't you dare," I say, low and firm.

He blinks. "Dare what?"

"Start running away from me."

His eyes widen just a touch, but he doesn't look away.

"You can't run from this anymore, Grant." I keep my voice soft, steady. My brown eyes ping between the stormy gray-blue of his. "Not from me. Not from us."

He looks down, shoulders slumping ever so slightly, but his hands move—gently curling around my waist. His thumbs rub my skin like he needs the contact to stay tethered.

"I don't want to run away," he murmurs.

And when he lifts his gaze again, I see the truth there. He means it. But something still haunts him. Hangs there behind his eyes like a ghost he's not ready to name.

I cradle his jaw in both hands and kiss him.

My tongue sweeps into his mouth, and he gives me a sound—soft and desperate, a moan like surrender. I press him tighter against me, drinking in the warmth, the give, the sweetness of his lips and the promise they hold.

I fucking love kissing Grant Harrow more than I remembered.

More than I let myself remember.

I lived off that one kiss for five years like it was oxygen—and now that I have him again, I'm starving.

Behind us, the door clicks shut. Quiet. Eve is gone.

Leaving us alone.

Just the two of us and the history that shadows everything we are.

I rest my forehead against his.

"We don't have to figure everything out tonight, baby," I whisper. "I just want you to stay with me."

He nods once and swallows deep.

I take his hand, twining our fingers together, savoring how natural it feels. His palm against mine. The warmth. The rightness.

He follows me without a word as I guide us toward the bedroom.

I close the door behind us. The lights are still low. The orange glow from the electric fireplace dances across the walls, painting us in flickers of gold and shadow.

We kiss again.

And again.

Slower now. Like we're trying to make up for the years we lost.

I kiss his lips.

His cheek.

His throat.

"Are you tired?" I murmur against his mouth.

He smirks and shakes his head—but something in the smile falters.

I watch him for a beat, tension laced in the quiet between us.

"What do you need, *Lucciolina*?" I ask.

I'm patient. I'll wait.

His throat works around the words. It takes time. He's trembling, even if just inside. I see it in his eyes. In the way he blinks hard and then finally says—

"I need to tell you how my mother died."

Chapter 31

The car ride home is quiet.

Not awkward quiet—just... peaceful.

Mom hums softly, some tune I don't recognize. The radio's off. She's never really needed music when she had her own melodies to carry her through the day.

She already asked the usual how-was-school questions. I gave the usual one-word answers. If Corrine were here, the conversation would've gone longer. They would've started singing by now—something loud and theatrical. Show tunes or Fleetwood Mac. One of those duets they somehow know every word.

But Corrine stayed home today. Sick, supposedly. She texted me around noon that she was "vomiting sunshine," which is code for too tired to pretend today.

I didn't ask questions.

She's been living with us for almost a year now. Ever since...

Well. Since the day her mom snapped.

People still call it an accident. They whisper it like maybe it wasn't what it clearly was.

Her mother killed her father.

Tried to kill Corrine.

Tried to kill herself.

But she failed at the last two.

Corrine lived.

And her mother... well, she's not really alive. Not anymore. Whatever she drank—or took—burned out half her brain. Now she's just this vacant body. Breathing, blinking, tapping her fingers like some eerie metronome.

Mom says she's harmless now.

Corrine never talks about it. Acts like none of it happened. Laughs, jokes, plays along with everything.

Mom always says how well-adjusted she is. How strong.

I think she's just pretending.

Saving her tears for the dark. Mourning when no one's watching.

Mom's been talking to Dad about adopting her.

He said no but Mom will do it anyway.

She always gets what she wants. She decides, and Dad... he just smiles and lets her. He loves her too much to stop her. Probably always has.

I glance down at my phone as we turn onto the long drive that leads to the estate. A new email pings with a delivery confirmation, and my stomach flips.

Shit.

The package has been delivered.

I shift in my seat, fingers tightening on my phone.

Mom doesn't notice. She's still humming. Still driving us up the winding path like everything is normal.

I lean toward the window, trying to catch a glimpse of the front step. The way the driveway curves makes it hard to see anything past the hedges and columns out front, but I already know it's not going to be there.

We don't leave things outside.

Not in this house.

Housekeepers bring everything inside. They open packages, discard the boxes, and leave the contents arranged neatly on the round table in the center of the foyer like we're living in a damn museum.

And I never get packages.

Which means if my father sees it, he'll open it.

And if he opens it...

There's no fucking way I'll be able to explain what's in there.

My chest tightens as Mom pulls into the garage.

Before she's even shifted into park, I'm out.

My feet slam into the tile, and I move fast, cutting through the back hall into the kitchen, then through the open archway to the main atrium.

I skid to a stop at the edge of the table.

Empty.

No box.

No packaging.

No telltale stack of mail to hide it beneath.

My stomach coils.

Please no. Please. Please.

"Grant?" Mom's voice calls from the garage. "Everything okay?"

I rush past the table and tug open the massive front door.

My breath punches out of me in a wave of relief.

There it is.

Little brown box.

Untouched.

Still sealed.

I bend down, snatch it up, and call back, "Yeah! Everything's fine!"

The box is light but somehow heavy in my hands.

Like it knows it almost exposed me.

I'm already taking the stairs two at a time when I hear her behind me.

"Hold up, mister."

Shit.

I turn halfway. She's standing there, hand on the banister, still in her pale yellow cardigan and slacks, watching me with that look only moms have—the one that sees way more than you want her to.

"What's in the box?"

"Just a new jockstrap," I say quickly. "For rugby."

That does the trick.

She makes a face, waving it off like she doesn't want to go anywhere near that conversation. "Okay, well, Elaine's off today, so we're on our own for dinner."

Ah.

That explains it.

No housekeeper today. That's why the package was still outside.

Thank God.

"We'll order takeout in about an hour, so get your homework done."

"Okay," I call back, already halfway up again.

I try to walk casually once I reach the top landing, even though my heart's still beating out a frantic rhythm.

Box clutched tight.

Every step echoing like I'm walking a tightrope.

I don't stop until I'm behind my door, and toss the box on the bed.

And then I finally exhale.

I turn on the music like I always do when I study. Lo-fi beats, mellow and steady—something I can pretend to focus to. Nothing out of the ordinary.

My heart's racing, fingers twitching with the urge to move faster than I should. I drop my bookbag to the floor and reach for the box.

Stabbing a pen into the seam, I drag it down like I'm tearing open a secret I'm not supposed to have. The tape gives with a rip. The flaps pull back.

I lick my lips without thought as I stare at the dildo.

Almost too real. I reach in and lift it out like it might be delicate, but there's nothing delicate about this thing. It's heavy in my hand, thick, solid. I hold it up to my forearm for comparison, eyes widening.

"Holy shit," I mutter, a little breathless.

I wrap my fingers around it—slow, curious. Stroke once. Then again, my thumb brushing over the smooth head like I already know how it should feel. It's not warm like skin, but it looks close enough to mess with my head. The way the veins curve beneath the surface. The way it gives slightly under pressure.

I glance up.

The mirror across the room catches me in full. Shirt wrinkled, cheeks flushed, eyes bright.

"One hour," I say out loud. "Plenty of time."

My clothes come off fast, one piece at a time. T-shirt. Sweats. Boxers. Gone. I'm bare before I even think to hesitate, the air against my skin sharp with anticipation.

I reach into the side drawer and pull out the bottle of lube I keep tucked behind junk so my mom won't find it.

I think back to all the things I searched for on eBay that night—half drunk on nerves, logged in under the account I made with my dad's name. Stupid? Probably. But I couldn't stop myself. I knew what I wanted.

Eight inches.

Tan—not quite my tone. Darker. Like his.

And the suction cup. Definitely needed that.

I kneel in front of the mirror, the toy upright between my knees, my hand circling the base like it belongs to someone standing in front of me. Someone real. Someone I know.

Someone like Dante.

My throat tightens just thinking about him. His dark brows. The way he lifts one—just one—every time he catches me looking for too long. Like he knows. Like he sees me.

My grip tightens. I stroke the shaft slowly, imagining

what it'd be like to have his body close. His eyes on mine. His voice low and amused.

"You thinking about me, Grant?" I think, and swear I hear his voice in my head. *"Yeah. You are."*

I bring the toy to my mouth, testing. Licking. Exploring. The mirror watches me as I close my lips around the tip and move—just a little. Just enough. My heart hammers. My body aches.

I've never had a blowjob before.

Jessica Stammers almost gave me one at a party last month. We were outside, making out in the dark near her pool when she asked if I wanted one.

She got far enough to jack me off a little and one lick before her parents came back early and busted the party up.

It wasn't until I was zipping my pants that I saw Dante watching from under a tree. The orange ember of a cigarette lit his face in the dark just enough for me to see he was looking at me.

That got me harder than Jessica did.

I think about that lick—but not on my cock. On his.

I moan, softly, dragging my tongue along the side, then back up to the head. I wrap my lips around it and push it into my mouth until I gag on it, then I pull it out, blinking away the tears in my eyes.

After a deep breath, I press the suction to the hardwood, checking the grip. Firm. Steady.

With a line of lube into my palm, I slick it over the toy with slow, deliberate strokes, coating it from base to head. It glistens as afternoon sun brightens my room, practically begging.

I hesitate—just for a breath.

Then I lean over and turn the music up. A few notches louder. Enough to cover the sounds I might make.

I position myself over the toy, bracing a hand against the floor, the other at the base of the dildo.

And slowly, carefully, I begin to lower myself until I feel it.

This isn't the first time I've touched myself like this. Not by a long shot.

Since the first time I ever jerked off—messy, awkward, and completely overwhelming—I've wondered what it would be like to feel more. Not just in my hand, but deeper. Inside. Where my fingers only barely reach.

I started small. One finger, then two. Experimenting late at night, under the covers, heart racing with the thrill of doing something no one knew about. Then I started trying things. Stuff from my room. Things I could hide. A toothbrush handle. Then the back end of my hairbrush.

But nothing ever quite did what I wanted. Nothing gave me that feeling I knew was just out of reach.

Until now.

I exhale slowly, easing myself down. My muscles tighten instinctively, but I don't stop. I can't—not when I'm this close. I breathe through it, one hand gripping the floor as I lower further, stretching. Adjusting. Letting it in.

And then—God.

The head finally slips past the tightest point, and I moan, loud and unguarded. My thighs tremble, but I stay. Let it sit there, just for a second, buried inside me like it belongs there.

My breath comes in short gasps now. Not from panic—but from need. From this slow burn that's turning into something sharper. Deeper.

I lift my hips—just a bit—and ease back down, repeating the motion again and again, each pass sinking me further. Until I'm there. All the way.

The stretch is intense. Full. Borderline too much.

But it feels good. So good.

I wrap my hand around my cock, already painfully hard, and stroke with the same rhythm I've built below. I tip my head back, jaw slack, hips rolling in time with my fist.

This. This is what I've been chasing. That elusive something I've tried to recreate a hundred times with a hundred things that never came close.

My eyes flutter shut as I start to move faster, breathless, each downward grind coaxing another sound from my throat. I can't stay quiet. Not anymore.

The beat of the music fades into the background as I give in to the rhythm I've found—stroking, grinding, imagining—

Dante. Always Dante.

His voice in my ear. His breath on my neck. The weight of him behind me.

It's only because I envy him so much that I think about him like this. Right? How hot he is. Confident. How all the girls at school want him and all the guys want to be him.

My pace stutters.

I whisper his name.

And I don't stop.

I don't even hear the door open.

All I hear is the gasp.

Sharp. Wet. Like it punched the air out of her lungs.

I freeze—completely still—until my eyes lift to the mirror.

And I see her.

My mom.

Her face is pale, but her eyes—her red-rimmed eyes—are wide with shock. Tears stream down her cheeks like she's already been crying, like she walked in on something she never imagined and still didn't see coming.

"Oh my God," she chokes, voice jagged with disbelief.

The door slams shut behind her like a gunshot.

And she's gone.

"Fuck," I breathe, the word scraping out of me like it's got claws.

How the hell am I supposed to explain that?

That it's not what it looked like? That I wasn't—

I slide off the toy too fast and wince, my whole body clenching. Still shaking. Still hard. The cold rush of panic slaps everything else away.

"Mom!" I call, voice cracking.

I grab the towel I laid out earlier—now sticky and pathetic—and throw it over the dildo, yanking the whole thing off the floor and tossing it behind me. My shirt and shorts come next, arms fumbling through the sleeves as I hop into my clothes, not bothering with boxers. There's no time. I need to catch her before—

"Mom, wait!" I shout again, but I can't hear her over the music. I stab at my laptop to silence it, the sudden stillness ringing in my ears like an alarm that already went off too late.

I wrench the door open, tugging my shirt down as I bolt into the hallway.

"Stop, Mom!"

But the sound that stops me isn't hers.

It's a yelp.

Choked and terrified—then a heavy thud.

A sound I'll never unhear. The kind of sound that empties the air from the world.

I run.

Faster than I've ever moved, feet pounding down the hall, using the railing to catch myself as I reach the landing.

I look over.

Expecting to see her on the stairs. Still running. Still angry.

But my eyes catch yellow.

Her sweater.

And I already know.

Before I even turn my head fully, I know.

She's on the ground.

Crushed against the marble floor. The white stone cracked beneath her head, red bleeding out in all directions like a blooming nightmare.

Her legs are twisted wrong. Her arm—I can't even see it. It must be pinned underneath her. But her face... her face is turned up.

Right at me.

Her eyes—brighter than mine ever were—are open. Still wide. Still shocked. Still... accusing.

"Mom."

It barely makes it out. A whisper. Cracked in two.

Her chest jerks. Once.

Her eyelids flutter like she's trying to stay awake.

But I see it.

The moment she stops.

The moment the light in her eyes fades just slightly. Enough to know she's not trying anymore.

She's gone.

"What is it, Grant?"

Corrine's voice comes from the side hall.

I turn my head so fast I almost lose balance. She sees me —just the look on my face—and her smile drops instantly.

"What—" she starts.

But she doesn't finish.

Her eyes follow mine. Over the railing. Down.

And the scream that comes from her splits the air in half.

It's raw. Gut-deep. Horrified.

My dad barrels out of his study seconds later, doors slamming open so hard they bounce back on their hinges.

"What's happened?" he shouts, voice like a blade.

His eyes scan everything—Corrine. Me. The landing.

And then he sees her.

The noise that leaves him... I'll never forget it.

It's not just pain—it's undoing. A sound like someone being torn apart from the inside.

He stumbles across the foyer, dropping to his knees in the blood forming around her like a halo.

"Sylvia," he breathes, trembling as he presses a hand to her forehead, lowering himself to her body, breaking.

"Sylvia," he says again, and then he just sobs. Wracked, broken sobs.

I don't move.

I should.

I should go back to my room.

I should do something—anything. I'm standing right over where she fell. Right over the edge she must've hit.

Then I look at Corrine again.

And the look on her face tells me everything.

She thinks I pushed her.

She doesn't have to say it. It's in her eyes. Wide and glassy and full of something worse than horror—belief.

Belief that I killed her.

"Corrine, I—"

I didn't.

I can't even speak. I can barely breathe as tears burn hot in my eyes, and I blink to try and clear them.

I didn't push her. But I might as well have.

If she hadn't walked in—if she hadn't seen what she did, the shame of it, the panic—if I'd just locked the door, or waited another hour, or—

She wouldn't have run.

She wouldn't have fallen.

She wouldn't be down there with her skull cracked open, and my dad sobbing in a puddle of her blood.

I didn't lay a finger on her, but I still killed her.

And I don't know how I'm going to live with that.

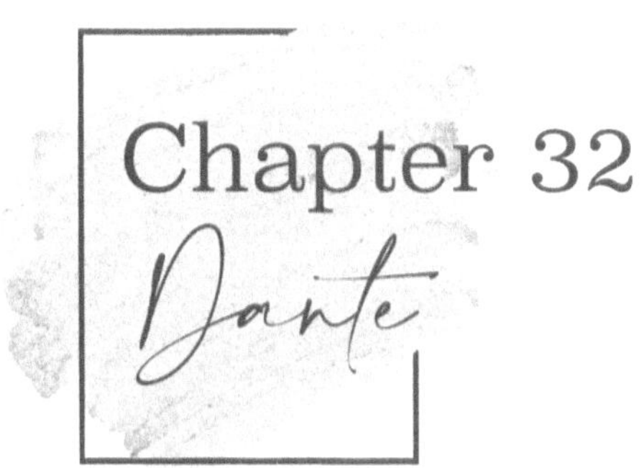

Chapter 32
Dante

Fuck.

He finally told me.

And it's not even close to the story I imagined. Not even in the same stratosphere. I thought I knew what happened that day—thought I had all the pieces, just not the right order. But this? The way his voice cracks when he says, "I killed her"—it guts me.

He's sitting on the edge of my bed, his shoulders curved forward, lounge pants low on his hips. His skin catches the amber light from my fireplace—the kind of light that makes everything look softer than it really is. Like it can't possibly hold the weight of what he's about to say.

"When my mom died," he says slowly, "I didn't just lose her. I lost the version of me I thought she saw."

My chest tightens. But I stay quiet.

"I blamed myself. Still do." He swallows hard. "Not because I pushed her. I didn't. But... if she hadn't seen me like that. If I'd just locked the fucking door. Or waited."

He trails off. I watch his hands flex where they rest on his thighs.

"I'll never forget her eyes. The way she looked at me." His voice cracks. "Not angry. Just... confused. Like she didn't recognize me at all."

I want to pull him into me. I want to tell him she was wrong. That he didn't do anything but exist in a way he wasn't ready to show the world. But I don't interrupt. Because there's more. I can feel it.

He takes a long, shaky breath.

"And then," he says, almost whispering now, "when Corrine walked in on us... it was like it was happening all over again."

I frown. That moment being one of the darkest nights of my life.

"I didn't see her, Dante. Not really. I saw my mom. Standing in that doorway again. Watching me." His jaw clenches. "And I panicked."

The pieces start falling together—slow, then all at once.

He looks at me now. Really looks. Eyes red-rimmed and glassy. "I need you to know... I didn't even realize what she thought. What she accused you of. Not until the next day. She said it again, and I was already so messed up from what I saw—what I relived—I just... shut down."

The breath he lets out trembles.

"I should've corrected her. I should've explained. But then you..." His voice softens. "You had girls with you. The men. All the time. And I thought you didn't care."

My chest tightens. "I did it to get to you."

He blinks.

"I wanted you to hurt." I say it simply, honestly. "I wanted you to feel what I felt when you looked through me like I didn't matter. Like I hadn't mattered that night. So I flaunted them—every damn one of them. And the more you acted like it didn't bother you..." I swallow hard. "I've been going fucking insane."

"It did bother me. Every time." His voice is quieter now, wrecked in that way only truth can be. "I couldn't stand seeing you with anyone else. I just thought I deserved the punishment."

I look at him—really look at him—and I realize I can't wait anymore.

I can't go another second letting him think he deserves anything less than the world.

Because he's here, in my room, in my life again—and if I don't say this now, I'll never forgive myself.

He just told me the worst day of his life. And all I want to do is pull him out of it.

Not with logic or reassurance.

But with something real—something that's been buried beneath the wreckage of us for so many goddamn years.

I shift closer on the bed, resting one hand lightly against his thigh. He's trembling—still somewhere in that memory.

"Hey," I say softly, "do you want to know why I call you glowbug?"

His eyes flick up to mine. And for a second, he doesn't speak.

But I see the curiosity he never admitted. The frustration in the name he never understood. The way he always flinched like it carried more weight than it should've.

He doesn't answer, and he doesn't have to.

"I know you hate it," I say, "and part of the reason is because you don't remember where it came from."

He swallows, throat bobbing. Still quiet.

"The day your mom died," I continue, "my dad brought you to our house. Your father was being questioned by the police, and my parents didn't want you left alone in your home."

Something shifts in his face. A flicker. A shadow of recognition like light catching on glass.

He remembers.

"The glowbugs," he says under his breath.

I nod.

We sat under the willow tree in my backyard—two boys side by side, your grief a living thing between us. And then, all at once, the field lit up around us like the universe was trying to say, *You're not alone.*

"They were everywhere," I whisper. "Thousands of them. Like they were drawn to you."

His lips part slightly. He's somewhere between memory and disbelief.

"I wanted to tell you that night," I say. "I looked at you— and I swear to God, Grant, you were the most beautiful thing I'd ever seen. Sitting there with your eyes red from crying, wrapped in the gold of the setting sun, surrounded by light." My voice dips, reverent. "You looked like magic."

He blinks hard. A tear slips free.

"I was going to kiss you. I was going to say it—I even started. I said your name."

He nods slowly. "You did."

"But then my dad came out and called you inside." I smile, bitter and aching. "And you turned around, still glowing, and said, 'You'll tell me when I get back?'"

His breath shudders. "You said—"

"'I will wait for you.'" I say it again now. Steady. Sure.

I rub the inside of my forearm where the ink lives—my one permanent truth. The moment I tattooed on my skin to never let myself forget.

"I found out that night my parents were sending me to the UK," I say. "They didn't tell me because they knew I wouldn't go. They knew I wouldn't leave you. My mother was worried I would put you before my future. The firm. So they sent me away."

The ache breaks through in my voice. I let it.

It took me a long time to forgive them. But as soon as I got back and saw Grant that first time, I knew nothing had changed.

"I tattooed the day I left and my promise, right here." I thumb the dark ink on my forearm.

I shift off the bed, drop down to one knee in front of him, and take his hands in mine.

He looks down at me like I've turned to light myself.

So I say what I should've said five years ago.

"Grant Harrow," I breathe. "I love you."

And then I give him everything.

"I've tried to burn it out of me. With other people. With time. With anger." I laugh, quiet and broken. "God, I tried so fucking hard. But it never worked. Nothing erased you."

He looks like he's holding his breath. Like if he exhales, he might fall apart.

"You live in my ribs, Grant. You haunt my skin. You're the voice in my head and the ache in my chest and the only thing that ever made me believe in something like fate." I shake my head. "And it's not just love. It's ruin. I would burn down the world if it ever touched you wrong. I'd go to war with God himself if He asked me to live without you again."

My voice drops, fierce and reverent.

"I would die for you. Gladly. But more than that—I'd live for you. Every day. I'd fight like hell to be the man you deserve, because loving you isn't hard, Grant. Losing you was."

He still hasn't moved. So I lean in, press my forehead to his, and close my eyes.

"I love you," I whisper. "I love you so much it makes me stupid. Makes me cruel. And if all you ever let me do is love you from here—if this is all we get—then it's enough."

Tears stream down his cheeks now. But he's smiling through them.

"I don't care what's behind us. I just want whatever's next. As long as it's you."

He doesn't speak at first.

Just looks at me. Like he's trying to memorize my face— or maybe find the pieces of himself I shattered five years ago. His lips part, but no sound comes. His throat works like the words are there—just stuck in grief or fear or disbelief.

And then, softly—barely more than breath—he says, "I tried to stop too."

That's it. Five little words, but I feel them like they're carved into my spine.

He's not looking at me anymore. He's looking down,

fingers twisting together in his lap, like he's afraid I'll vanish if he says too much too fast.

"I tried to stop loving you too," he continues. "Tried to hate you. Tried to replace you."

My heart doesn't just beat—it rages.

"But you were still everywhere," he says, voice unraveling. "In everything. In everyone."

He looks up at me again, and fuck, I've never seen him like this. Open. Raw. Eyes glassy, red-rimmed, like he's been holding this back for so long it got tangled in his bones.

"I've loved you since before I even knew what love really was," he says, both hands reaching out to cup my jaw. "And I never stopped. Not for a second."

I can't breathe.

"I thought I broke us," he goes on, quieter now. "And then you went and broke me right back."

A broken laugh. A half-sob.

"But you're still it for me. You've always been it."

He leans in, forehead pressed to mine again, like he's trying to tether himself to something real.

And then he whispers the only words I've needed since the day I lost him:

"I love you, Dante. I love you so goddamn much it ruined me."

My eyes slam shut. I feel it everywhere—in my blood, in my teeth, in the ache behind my ribs.

And just like that, the war is over.

No more pain. No more lies. No more pretending we didn't belong to each other this whole fucking time.

I smile, just a little, as I whisper back, "Good."

Then I kiss him.

Not like the first time.

Not like the last.

This kiss is like none we've had before.

I'm still on my knees.

He's still perched on the edge of my bed, chest rising like he can't catch his breath. Like I knocked the air from his lungs with my mouth alone.

I pull back just far enough to look at him.

We're both breathing hard. Both of us wrecked—and starving for more.

I smirk, still tasting him. "I have a question, though, Lucciolina."

For the first time, he grins at the name. A real one. Not embarrassed. Not scowling. Just... Grant. And fuck, it makes me grin too.

"Why eight inches?" I ask.

His face goes red in a heartbeat. A full-body blush that starts in his cheeks and spills down his throat.

I tilt my head, gaze fixed on him. "No, no. You have to tell me. You said it more than once. So why was the dildo eight inches?"

He groans and throws himself back onto the mattress like I've just mortally wounded him. Arms over his face. "Dante..."

I crawl up over him slowly, deliberately, until I'm straddling his hips and leaning in. "Answer me, Lucciolina. Why?"

He lets out a long breath. "Because..." He hesitates, then

mutters, "Because I overheard you in the locker room after rugby practice one day."

I raise a brow, waiting.

"You said you measured yourself hard," he says, face flaming, "and it was eight inches."

My smile is slow. Sinful. The kind that would tempt angels to fall.

I kiss him again, biting his lip just hard enough to make him gasp before I pull away.

"Oh, baby…"

I stand, tug him upright by the hands, and watch as he sits back up on the edge of the bed, blinking up at me with flushed cheeks and parted lips.

Then I shove my lounge pants down and step out of them.

My cock—hard and heavy—springs free, hanging thick and proud right in front of his face.

"That," I murmur, brushing my thumb along his bottom lip, "was when we were sixteen, Lucciolina."

He stares.

"You'll find," I say, voice dropping, "I'm quite a bit longer now."

His breath catches. His eyes drop, taking me in with slow, reverent hunger. His hands slide up my thighs, warm and steady.

He wets his lips—and my cock twitches at the sight.

He looks up, grinning now. Seductive. Confident in a way that makes my chest tighten.

Then, without a word, he closes his eyes and finally takes his first taste of me.

Grant sucks me like he's dying.

Like he's been starving for this—for me—and finally, finally has permission to devour.

All breath is sucked out of my body with each pull of his sinful mouth.

My head falls back, a groan tearing out of me as pleasure hits like a goddamn freight train.

"Fuck—Grant, Cristo, così bravo*," I choke out, fingers threading into his hair. I try to be gentle, but the second he tries to take me deeper—all the way down—I lose the ability to pretend I have any self-control left.

"Sì, amore mio†... just like that."

I fist his hair and start to thrust—slow but deep—and he lets me. No flinching. No hesitation. Just wide, wet heat and soft moans that vibrate down my cock like he wants me to lose it.

And fuck me—I might.

He feels like heaven.

But I want to see his face. I want to see the hunger in his eyes—the same hunger clawing through me.

I pull him off with a gasp, and he lets go with a wet, obscene pop.

His lips are swollen. His eyes wild. His cheeks flushed like he's drunk on me.

"Look at you," I murmur, brushing his messy hair back, voice wrecked with need. "You're fucking starving for me, aren't you?"

---

*   Christ, *so good.*

†   *"Yes, my love."*

He nods, breathless.

"Good," I say, pushing him back onto the mattress. "Because I'm starving too."

I crawl on top of him, chasing his mouth every inch of the way. Kissing him like I need to taste myself on his tongue. Like it's the only thing that will keep me tethered to this earth.

I shove his pants down and off, tossing them somewhere I don't care to remember.

We're both naked now. Both of us hard and aching.

I don't even know who reaches for who first, but suddenly we're shifting, twisting—his head at my hips and mine at his. A perfect, messy tangle of mouths and want.

I take him into my mouth and he gasps.

I groan around him as he sucks me down again, our bodies moving in rhythm, in sync. Two halves of a desperate, frenzied whole.

It's overwhelming—too much and not enough.

He moans when I swirl my tongue. I groan when he swallows me deep. Our hands clench. Our thighs tense. We're close—so fucking close.

I pull off just long enough to pant, "Don't come, just orgasm. Not all the way. I want to fuck you until the sun comes up, Lucciolina."

He lets out a strangled sound around my cock, and I feel him twitch on my tongue.

We work each other like men possessed—neither of us holding back. We want to please each other. Wreck each other.

And when the moment hits, it's like lightning.

My climax rips through me, raw and relentless, just as his hips stutter in my hands.

He only comes a little—just a taste.

And I don't waste a single drop.

Grant is breathless beneath me as I kiss my way up his body—slow, reverent. Tasting every inch of his skin, every shiver. His chest heaves. His fingers tremble where they tangle in the sheets. In my hair.

He's trying so hard to keep it together, but I can feel him unraveling for me.

When I reach his mouth, I pause, hovering just above him.

"I want to watch you this time," I murmur, voice wrecked. "When I slide into you, I want to look into your eyes."

His hips jerk. A soft, helpless sound escapes him—somewhere between a moan and a whimper. He's grinding up against me now, needy and desperate, chasing any kind of friction.

"Fuck," I hiss, "I can't get enough of you."

I sit back on my knees between his spread thighs, taking in the sight of him—flushed and panting, pupils blown wide, stroking himself with shaky fingers as he watches me.

I don't look away as I lube my cock—slow, deliberate— letting him see how slick and ready I'm getting for him.

His breath catches with every movement, his eyes glued to my dick. He's obsessed. And I love it.

"You watching, Lucciolina?" I murmur, voice low and rough. "I'm going to fuck you raw."

He gasps, hips twitching.

"Forever," I add. "Because this tight little hole? It's mine. It belongs to me. No one else gets to touch. No one else gets this. No condom. No barrier. No one between us. Ever. You understand?"

He moans—loud—his whole body trembling. He nods, frantic.

"Say it."

"It's yours," he whispers. "Fuck, Dante, please. I'm yours."

That's right.

I slide my fingers between his cheeks—rubbing, teasing, circling his entrance—until he's squirming. Begging. His voice breaking as he pleads for more—for me.

"God, please, I need you inside. Need your cock—fuck, Dante, please." He begs as I tease his mouth with my tongue.

I press in—slow and careful—watching every flicker of emotion cross his face. I ease past that tight ring of muscle, groaning as I finally sink into him.

Fucking hell.

He's so tight I see stars.

I give him time, sliding in and out with deliberate care. My hands grip his hips, my forehead pressed to his as he adjusts. We breathe together. Move together.

This isn't just fucking.

This is us.

When I finally bottom out—chest pressed to his, legs tangled, mouths inches apart—we freeze. Eyes locked.

And then I start to move.

Slow. Deep. Intentional.

"You feel that?" I growl against his mouth. "Feel how fucking deep I am?"

Grant arches, mouth falling open in a perfect cry.

"This cock was made to ruin you. To stretch this sweet hole open and keep it open. Every inch of me inside you until you can't fucking breathe."

He moans—high, broken, perfect.

"I'm gonna fuck you senseless, Lucciolina. Gonna make you forget your name. Gonna fill you so full of my cum, it'll be leaking out of you for days."

He claws at my back, eyes rolling as I drive into him over and over.

"You love it, don't you? Love being my little fuck toy. Love knowing I own this body now. No one else gets to touch. No one else gets this."

"Dante—oh fuck—yes," he cries, legs tightening around me.

"That's it, baby. Take it. Take all of me. Be a good boy and take what I'm giving you."

I grab the headboard, knuckles white, using it to pound into his tight, perfect fucking ass—knowing he's ruining me as much as I'm ruining him.

And when we come—it's chaos.

There's nothing soft about it. No muffled sounds or quiet sighs.

We shout.

We curse.

We break.

He clenches around me as he spills between us, and I

drive deep—grinding in—filling him with everything I have.

My name on his lips.

His name on mine.

And nothing between us at all.

Except the love we finally get to live.

Chapter 33
Eve

The houses here all match. White fences. Clean windows. Lawns so symmetrical they look AI-generated. But Corrine's is a step above creepy-perfect. Her mailbox is so polished it probably has a skincare routine.

Jaxon leans over to whisper as we sneak through the lawns to her house. "Who even lives like this? Her lawn has stripes. Is she okay?"

"Focus, Jax."

He grunts, pulling his black-hoodie tighter. "This is breaking and entering. You know that, right? I'm rich. I can't go to prison. They'd put me in minimum security with no tech. I'd have to play board games with dentists who didn't pay their taxes."

"And yet you still got in my car when I told you to wear something dark," I mutter, grabbing the small-black device he'd been fidgeting with since we left my apartment. "Tell me how this thing works."

"Excuse you." He snatches it back with an offended gasp. "One of us is the world's youngest tech genius and the other can run a mile in six-inch stilettos. Watch and weep."

He crouches by the keypad near Corrine's front door, squinting at it with the concentration of a bomb-defusal scene in an action movie. The device clicks softly, then emits a quiet series of beeps—three short chimes.

Jaxon grins like he just hacked the Pentagon. "Boom. I'm amazing. The alarm's down. Door's unlocked. And by the way..." He steps back with a dramatic bow. "Security feed has been recording on a loop for the last hour."

I don't waste time and push the door open like I own the place.

The air inside smells faintly of pine cleaner and smugness. It's cold—crisp in a way that screams no one lives here full-time. Too curated. Too untouched. Every pillow fluffed. Every picture frame perfectly aligned. It's the kind of place that looks staged, like a model home frozen in time.

Jaxon steps in behind me. "How long do we have?" he whispers, eyes darting from room to room like he expects the walls to sprout hidden security cameras.

"You know you don't have to whisper, right?" I roll my eyes and head straight for the kitchen. "I told Frankie to keep her at the office as long as she could. No promises."

"Great," he mutters. "Love a vague ticking clock. That always ends well."

Corrine is hiding something. I absolutely know it. She's been in everything too much, but at the same time in nothing. Too invisible for it to be a coincidence.

And we're going to find out what it is—tonight.

"This woman alphabetized her vitamins." Jax is staring into a cabinet, hands on his hips before he reaches in.

There is nothing here, so I head upstairs.

Jaxon follows reluctantly, like a man being led to his own murder. "You know, when I said I was bored and wanted something to get into tonight, I meant like... Vegas. Or something fun like hacking the White House again and changing the President's email. Not felony trespassing in a Stepford-wife's murder castle."

The number of times I've rolled my eyes while we've been in this house should be a new world record.

"You were the one who begged me to let you in on the action," I remind him, walking into her bedroom. "This is the action."

"This is how white women die in true-crime podcasts."

"Then don't get caught."

Corrine's bedroom is just as unsettling as the rest of the house. Not a single wrinkle in the sheets. Closet doors shut. Everything staged like it's waiting for a real person to move in.

I open the closet and immediately regret not bringing gloves. Not because I'm worried about fingerprints—Corrine's too busy manipulating lives to dust for those—but because everything in here is pristine. Like museum-exhibit pristine. Her shoes are lined up like soldiers. Color-coded. Heel height descending from left to right.

This woman orgasms off control. "She is a fucking psychopath."

I dig through the drawers inside the closet island, scanning for anything out of place. Hidden compartments. Documents. Keys.

Behind me, Jaxon leans in the doorway, arms crossed over his broad chest. "This is the most aggressively beige room I've ever seen."

I don't stop searching. "Check the nightstand drawers."

"I'm not touching her nightstand. That's how you find dildos or diaries, and neither is on my to-do list tonight."

"Oh yeah, a diary would be good. Hop to it."

"Fine." He sighs and pads across the carpet. "But if something bites me, I'm running away."

He pulls open the drawer and whistles. "No dildos. Thank God. Just a Bible and a gun."

That gets my attention. "Really?"

"No."

"Ugh, Jax!"

"You think she's hiding a body in here?" he asks, reaching into the drawer and shifting a few things before closing it.

Next is an armchair by the window. He slides it about an inch to the left.

Rounding the bed, Jax tilts the table lamp's shade ever so slightly, then joins me in the closet.

"What are you doing?" I ask, watching him open a drawer that is lined with the most perfectly folded and organized socks I've ever seen in my life.

He picks one up, turns it the opposite direction, and closes the drawer again.

"This'll drive her nuts." He takes two pairs of shoes next to each other and switches their places. "You know Charles

Manson had his freaks do this. Break into people's houses and do nothing but move their shit juuuuuust a little."

Jaxon spends a good bit of time rearranging her jewelry drawers while I pause and take in the space, looking around for the one thing that doesn't belong here.

It's like everything is so perfect on purpose—to distract from something. I just need to figure out what.

"Who knew one woman needed so many beige trench coats." Jax shakes his head as he removes a shirt from a hanger and flips it inside out before returning it.

When he reaches up to place the hanger back in its place, that's when I see it.

One thing that doesn't belong in this curated beige nightmare.

A brown—not pristine—box.

Slightly darker than everything else here, yellowed from time. A little worn on the edges. A smudge on the lid. Imperfect.

Bingo.

"Jax! Get that down for me."

He squints. "Oh, so this is why you really wanted me to come along. Taking advantage of my height?"

"Yes, now gimme."

He rolls his eyes but plucks it down effortlessly and hands it to me like he's presenting a cursed artifact. "Behold. The Box of Doom."

It's an old shoebox. The cardboard is soft in places, like it's been opened and closed a hundred times. Something about it immediately prickles under my skin.

I lift the lid and my heart drops.

Inside—dozens, maybe hundreds—of newspaper clippings. Stacks and stacks of carefully folded articles.

All about Grant Harrow.

Social pages. *Forbes* writeups. Society wedding coverage. Gala photo recaps. If there was a piece of media with the Harrow name on it, Corrine has it in this box.

He's younger in most of the ones toward the front. Late teens to early twenties. Always in a suit. Always with that practiced Harrow smile.

My stomach tightens.

They begin after his mother died. The age. The fact most of them have photos of only Grant and his father.

I pull one out and snap a picture with my phone. Another. And another. I tuck each one back where I found it, keeping them in order just in case there's a method to her madness.

The newer ones seem to be toward the back. I want to know what happened all those years ago, so I stay toward the front.

"Eve..." Jaxon's voice is tight. "This is giving serial-killer scrapbook. I'm officially creeped out."

But I don't answer. I'm already flipping through more of the stack, scanning each article like it's a clue. A map. A confession. I'm not even sure what I'm looking for yet—but I'll know it when I see it.

Why keep all of this?

What does it mean?

I dig deeper, pulling out a dense stack of folded pages, and something clinks at the bottom of the box.

Two busted USB drives.

They both look like they've been crushed. On accident or on purpose, I can't tell.

I cradle them in my palm, staring down like they might whisper something.

"Hey," I call softly, holding them up. "World's youngest tech genius. Can you do anything with these?"

Jaxon walks over, squints at them in my hand, and snorts. "I can't resurrect the dead."

"Weakling."

"I can try to recover data. But not here. I need tools. And time. And ideally, no psycho socialite showing up to murder me with her disinfectant wipes."

His phone pings and we both look at it.

"Shit," Jaxon mutters, eyes glued to his phone. "She's pulling in."

He's in full-on panic mode now—darting looks around the room like he's expecting to find a telepad to beam him out of suburbia and into a nice, safe server farm somewhere.

I stay crouched, flipping through the last stack of clippings because I've only got seconds left on the clock. We can't leave here without getting the answer.

"Eve—Eve!" Jaxon whispers, voice shrill. "This is *not* a drill. She's coming in. Like, inside the house. We need to go!"

"Two seconds," I hiss back, snatching the last few clippings and jamming them into my pocket. I'll sort them later. Or never. Who knows if we're surviving the next five minutes?

From downstairs, the unmistakable click of the front door unlocking.

Followed by the sharp *clack-clack* of stilettos on marble floors.

And then her voice, floating up like a ghost from hell:

"I swear I set my alarm this morning."

Jaxon is pacing now, crouched like a squirrel about to explode. "We're dead. This is it. I'm too pretty to die behind bars. They'll eat me first, Eve." He whispers.

"Shut up and help me," I snap, motioning wildly.

He sets the shoebox back into its spot—exactly how it was before. For once, I'm grateful for his obsession with symmetry.

Her heels are getting louder. Then I hear her on the stairs, coming up.

I meet Jaxon's eyes, then glance to the balcony doors.

He follows my gaze as I point and push his shoulder.

He mouths: *No freaking way.*

I nod. Stern frustration twists my features into a deranged look of anger as we try to make no noise at all.

We move fast—quiet as ghosts, even though my pulse is anything but silent. Jaxon sneaks open the balcony door just as we hear Corrine reach the landing at the top of the stairs.

She's not in a hurry, so at least she doesn't suspect anything is amiss yet.

The balcony doors swing shut behind us with a soft *snick* —a sound so small, so careful... and yet, to me, it may as well be a gunshot.

I flinch, instinctively ducking, then wave my arms like a frantic air-traffic controller.

Go. Go. GO.

Jaxon wastes no time. He swings one leg over the

wrought-iron railing and starts climbing down, moving fast but careful, his limbs gangly but precise. He's clearly seen too many spy movies and is living his best 007 fantasy.

I throw a leg over the edge, then the other. My palms—slick with sweat—grip the railing.

Thank God we wore black.

My heart's jackhammering against my ribs, but adrenaline sharpens everything—makes the shadows clearer, the air colder, the consequences louder.

I drop down below the line of the railing, my shoe in the first foothold of the trellis, when the dark around us becomes slightly brighter.

Corrine moves the curtain.

The golden light from her bedroom spills across the balcony, stretching out like a spotlight hunting its next victim.

Jaxon is climbing down the trellis and freezes when he hears my panicked *shhh*.

I drop my head below the railing just as she opens the balcony door and steps out.

Shit. Shit. Shit.

My body is trembling. Muscles burning. I don't breathe. I don't blink.

Corrine pauses.

Looking and listening into the night surrounding her.

I can feel her presence—so close beside me I swear I can smell her perfume in the air. I press closer to the house, praying the darkness cloaks us, that the trellis doesn't creak, that my damn heartbeat doesn't echo loud enough to betray us both.

She takes one slow step forward, then stops.

A long moment passes before she finally turns and steps back inside.

The door clicks shut behind her.

Still, I don't move. I don't trust her not to still be watching.

After an eternity, the curtains drop back into place. Darkness deepens around us once more, and I hear the distant sound of running water.

A shower.

I look down. Jaxon's eyes are wide as saucers, still clinging to the trellis like it's his emotional support structure.

Go.

I mouth—with all the authority of a SWAT commander.

We scramble down as quickly as we can. I land next to Jax with a hard thud in the grass. He doesn't wait—grabs my wrist, pulling me along, and we bolt across the lawn, slipping through the gate and around the side of the house like we were never there at all.

By the time we dive into the car and slam the doors shut, we're both panting, half laughing, half horrified.

Jaxon buckles up without a word, then finally exhales a long, dramatic sigh.

"Next time," he says, "we break into an Amazon data-center or something normal."

I grin, still catching my breath. "This was the most fun I've ever had."

He turns to stare at me like I've lost my damn mind. "You need therapy."

"Probably," I say, shifting into drive. "But after we figure out what's on those USBs."

His face falls as he pats his pockets. I feel the color drain from mine.

"I think I left them in the bedroom."

"Jaxon Kane, I will kill you if you are being serious."

"Dang! Calm down, *Murder, She Wrote.*" He pulls them from his pocket. "They're right here."

I press the gas and pull away from Corrine Ashwood's nightmare house, the shadows swallowing us whole.

"Sometimes I hate you."

Chapter 34

Grant

The lobby is quiet at this hour—*too* quiet, if you ask me. The marble floors gleam under the down-lights, polished to perfection like everything else in this building. But perfection doesn't steady my nerves.

Dante stands beside me, calm as ever, hands in his pockets like we're waiting on a cab instead of the elevator that will carry us into the most important meeting of our lives.

I reach out and fix his tie, fingers smoothing the silk against his chest.

He doesn't move. Just watches me with that annoyingly calm expression that says nothing can touch us.

When I glance up, he's grinning. Smirking, really. That crooked, infuriating, completely self-assured grin he's had since we were kids.

I narrow my eyes. "What?"

He shrugs—lazy and infuriatingly unbothered. "Just thinking about the last forty-eight hours. Best of my life."

Despite everything—the nerves, the pressure, the weight of what's about to happen—I feel my mouth twitch.

We called out of work and spent two wonderful days together. Much of it in Dante's bed but also, working. Together. Something we've not done in five years.

"You realize we're about to walk into a boardroom full of men who've spent the last five years waiting for us to fail, right?"

"Yep."

I exhale through my nose, rolling my shoulders once. The knot in my stomach pulls tighter.

"Five years," I say, quieter this time. "Everything our fathers built. Everything we've done to try and honor it. All comes down to one hour."

Dante doesn't shift. Just pulls the pack of cigarettes from his jacket—his usual tell—and turns it over in his hand. For a second, I think he's going to light one. But then, without ceremony, he crushes the pack and tosses it into the nearby trash can.

"They'll either side with us," he says, brushing his palms together, "or we'll kick them out. Either way, they'll have to pry this firm from our cold, dead hands."

The elevator dings.

I glance toward it, throat dry.

Dante steps closer.

Without a word, he takes my hand—right there in the open—and rubs his thumb across my knuckles. Slow. Steady. Grounding.

I look at him.

He's not nervous. And maybe that's what makes this

moment work. Because I've spent my whole life trying to prepare for every worst-case scenario... and he's always been the one who walks in like we've already won.

Today, we're doing both.

The elevator doors slide open.

We step inside—side by side.

Not just partners in the company now.

Partners in everything.

Dante reaches across me and pushes the button for the fiftieth floor, and before the elevator doors close, he's moving in on me, his hungry eyes fixed on my mouth.

"We have a tradition to uphold in elevators now, so give me those lips and kiss me, bug."

The elevator doors slide open with a soft chime, and I instinctively wipe my bottom lip with my thumb.

Frankie's already waiting in the atrium, leaning against the reception desk in a black pencil skirt, navy blouse, and her signature pin-up glam that makes her look like she just walked off a vintage *Vogue* cover. She's popping a piece of gum, bored and beautiful.

"Disgusto," she says, not even blinking. "You better sanitize that elevator if you plan to defile it every time you're in there."

Dante grins.

I don't bother replying.

Eve rounds the corner a second later, a vision in her

Ledger-red pencil dress, an armful of black folders and a smile sharp enough to slice through steel.

"Morning, boys," she says brightly. "Glad to see you both look freshly fucked today."

Frankie gags dramatically. "I just vomited in my mouth a little."

She pivots on her heel and starts toward the large conference room like she owns the place—which, to be fair, she kind of does in her own way. Eve falls into step beside her, and Dante and I follow.

The hallway's already buzzing with early arrivals. A few board members mill about, murmuring and sipping coffee, their gazes sharpening as we pass.

"Morning," I offer with a nod, polite but not warm.

One of them lifts a brow. "Any hints on the room switch, Marchesi?"

Dante doesn't miss a beat. "We had some last-minute changes to today's agenda."

The man frowns faintly but nods and steps aside.

It's fine. They'll understand soon enough.

We're almost at the door when Corrine comes around the corner like a storm in Louboutin heels—face flushed, breath uneven, phone still clutched in one hand.

"Excuse me," she says, voice clipped. "What exactly is going on here? Why didn't I receive a memo about the room change?"

Dante's already there, holding the door open for Eve, who breezes in like she belongs—offering warm greetings to a few board members she's gotten to know over the last two weeks. The way they respond tells me it was time well spent.

I turn to Corrine, keeping my tone neutral. "This is a meeting with the board. You do recall that meeting was today?"

Her face falters. Irritation flashes across her expression before she masks it with a tight, professional smile. She doesn't move. Doesn't speak. Just walks into the room with her spine straight and her chin higher than necessary.

She takes a seat near the end of the table—far enough to make a point, close enough to remind me she's not going anywhere.

I glance toward Frankie. "Please bring our other guests in as soon as they arrive."

Frankie nods once and disappears down the hall.

Corrine's voice cuts through the room, sharper now as she gestures to Eve. "Grant, this is completely inappropriate—"

"It's done," I say, calm but final.

She stiffens, mouth parting in protest, but the boardroom is already shifting around us.

I step forward, and Dante follows behind me, still holding the door with one hand. Just before it closes, he touches the small of my back—subtle, grounding.

Inside, Corrine sits like a statue, her eyes fixed on me with a quiet fury that simmers just beneath the surface. Anger, hurt, disbelief—layered in her gaze like sediment no one's disturbed in years.

Dante steps forward, smooth and controlled, and calls out, "Let's take our seats, please."

The chatter begins to fade.

One by one, the board members settle around the oblong mahogany table, their tailored suits and polite expressions concealing a thousand predictions and private bets about how this morning will play out. They've spent five years watching us circle each other like predators in a glass cage.

Now, they're about to see what happens when we fight on the same side.

I step up beside Dante, nodding once to the room. "Thank you all for adjusting your schedules on such short notice."

Eve moves silently through the space, a red flash of elegance and confidence, handing out the sleek black folders she and I finalized late last night.

"There will be no vote today," I continue, leveling my voice. "No discussion on a CEO transition. Because Marchesi and Harrow isn't changing hands—"

"—it's changing direction," Dante finishes, his voice easy but firm.

I glance at him briefly. We didn't rehearse that line together. But we didn't need to.

"The last five years have seen their share of turbulence," I say, turning back to the board. "Mistakes were made—on both sides of this partnership. But Dante and I spent the last forty-eight hours working through everything we let suffer. Every breakdown. Every blind spot. Every inch of ego. And what came out of that wasn't just clarity—it was vision."

Eve places the final folder and steps back beside Corrine, who did not get a one.

"Looks like I didn't prepare enough."

I absolutely *do* catch the smile in Dante's voice as he takes over.

"Modern meeting classic. Innovation rooted in legacy. Design that doesn't just follow trends, but tests boundaries —environmentally, structurally, conceptually. This is the future of Marchesi and Harrow. And we're done waiting for permission to pursue it."

As if on cue, the double doors swing open behind me, and Damien Wolfe enters like a storm in a black suit.

His presence shifts the temperature of the entire room. People sit straighter. Conversations cut off mid-sentence. Power recognizes power.

Behind him, his business partner Marcus steps in, followed by several members of their own board—all sharp-eyed and silent, radiating billionaire-level scrutiny.

After them, a new acquaintance.

Jaxon Kane.

Eve's referral. Tech genius. And apparently someone with a stupid amount of free time on his hands.

As Eve and I worked the deck, he and Dante finalized the digital renderings. He's brilliant. Slightly unhinged. And exactly what this presentation needed.

He slides me a remote with a nod. "All tee'd up and ready to razzle-dazzle." With a smirk and a wink, he steps to the back of the room, leaning against the wall with his face in his phone.

Across the table, Corrine's eyes narrow—just slightly— but enough. She wasn't briefed on any of this, and the realization is beginning to crack her composure.

We move forward to greet Damien and his team—all firm handshakes and polite nods. They take the remaining open seats along the left side of the table, directly across from several of our more skeptical board members.

I return to my spot next to Dante, posture steady, heart pounding slow but strong.

Beside me, Dante leans in slightly, his voice pitched low enough only I can hear.

"You okay, bug?"

Corrine adjusts her blazer that doesn't need fixing, her fingers stiff. She forces a smile at me—two seconds too late, two shades too tight.

Then I look at the table full of board members—ours and Wolfe's. And at the future about to unfold in the room we are finally taking back.

And I realize...

"Yes," I say quietly. "I am."

The lights dim with a quiet hum, and I press the remote in my palm.

Across the polished surface of the mahogany boardroom table, the room lights up with a low electric glow—and then the projection begins.

A full 3D model of the Wolfe Complex blooms into view, cast holographically between the board members. The city skyline surrounds it—elevations, shadow play, green space integrations. With one flick, Dante brings up the sustainability overlays. Another flick and the usage flow animates in real time, people moving through the structure in translucent motion.

It's architectural porn.

Gasps break the silence.

Chairs lean forward.

Whispers start immediately—awed and reverent.

Even Corrine leans in—jaw clenching as she eases back in her chair. She knows we're nailing this, and she hates it.

Dante's voice cuts through, cool and assured. "Sustainable energy isn't a feature. It's the foundation."

I take over seamlessly. "This design incorporates solar membrane skin, geothermal cores, and fully adaptive shading. Energy-positive. Carbon-negative. And built for resilience."

We keep going—like we've practiced for years. Revolutionary tech integration. AI-responsive infrastructure. Spaces designed not just for function but for culture, collaboration, and legacy.

The questions, the discussions, the pull-ins to show the detail and bring them into the building in a way they've never before seen on a pitch—couldn't have gone more perfectly.

By the time we finish, the room is quiet again—but this time, stunned into silence.

Then Damien Wolfe rises.

He crosses the room with purpose and extends his hand —first to Dante, then to me.

"Congratulations, gentlemen," Wolfe says, his voice low but definitive. "The city's top project deserves the city's top firm. We'll be in touch."

A man like Damien Wolfe doesn't wait for pleasantries or salutations. Those take time and—as the old saying goes —time is money.

Wolfe, Marcus, and their team exit, leaving behind a boardroom humming with murmurs and thinly veiled excitement.

Corrine doesn't move.

She's seated halfway down the table, her posture rigid, lips slightly parted like she still might try to reclaim the floor. But it's gone. The moment has passed, and she knows it.

Dante steps forward first, his tone calm but resolute. "For those still uncertain, allow me to clarify what just happened."

He gestures briefly toward the door Wolfe just exited through, then levels his gaze on the room.

"That was the most influential client in the city—and he just entrusted his legacy to ours."

I pick up from there, standing taller as the final echo of the presentation settles in the room. "Marchesi and Harrow will continue to lead as New York's premier architectural firm. That is not up for debate."

I pause—let it land.

"If the board sees fit to remove us as co-CEOs, we'll start a new firm. And our clients—Wolfe Industries included— will come with us. Because it's our names on these build- ings. Our vision they're investing in."

Dante nods once. "And we're not giving that up."

"So you either side with us or find a new table to sit around." I finish and we look each member in the eye.

Silence stretches, taut and charged.

Then applause breaks like a wave—spontaneous and growing.

Several board members rise to their feet. A few cross the room to shake our hands. Someone claps Dante on the back. Bottled waters are lifted like toasts. It's not just approval—it's victory.

Corrine doesn't clap.

She sits perfectly still, a half-laugh caught in her throat like a misfire. Her fingers twitch once before balling into a fist in her lap.

No one looks to her for input. No one waits for her commentary.

The board has made its decision.

Eve rises last—slow and graceful—the only one to glance Corrine's way. She leans in, voice a velvet dagger.

"My boys knocked it out of the park," she murmurs. "Just like I always knew they would."

Corrine's jaw ticks, but she says nothing.

Because there's nothing left to say.

I don't even need to turn to see Corrine's face. I can feel the heat of her fury from across the room. She's seething. Practically steaming through her designer silk.

Beside me, Dante leans in and murmurs, "The second this room clears, I'm pinning you to that table and making you scream my name."

My mouth drops open in pure disbelief.

He glances down at my slack jaw, then grins. "Invitation accepted, *Lucciolina*."

Before I can gather a reply, his hand slides low across my back—casual, practiced. It could almost be mistaken for professionalism... until it dips just low enough to cup my ass. A firm squeeze. Entirely unrepentant.

No one notices.

No one except Corrine and she narrows her eyes like I stabbed her in the back.

Dante steps away, all smooth swagger and lazy power, but he tosses the final dagger over his shoulder as he crosses the threshold:

"My office. Ten minutes?"

I nod, a small grin tugging at the corner of my mouth. It feels good—earned.

"Need to make a call first," he adds, and then he's gone.

The doors shut behind him, and the room begins to clear.

Corrine just stands there—on the outside. Looking in.

And for the first time... I think she understands.

This isn't just the end of her control. It's the beginning of something new.

Something she's not going to be a part of.

Not anymore.

Chapter 35
Corrine

No one notices when I slip out of the conference room.

They're too busy clapping Grant on the back, beaming with praise, drinking the Kool-Aid. The prodigal sons, returned and redeemed. All grins and glittering futures.

And meanwhile—I do what I've been trying to do for five years.

Save the damn firm.

My heels are soundless on the marble as I carefully approach Grant's office. It's still dark inside, frosted glass casting soft light around its edges. He always leaves it like that in the mornings—like he's waiting for sunlight and worship before turning the fishbowl on. Always so eager to make himself visible, transparent, open.

That's what makes him easy to manipulate.

But not Dante.

No, Dante's never been easy.

I'm not surprised to find him inside.

He's bent low behind Grant's desk, rummaging through drawers like a common thief. His sleeves are rolled, his back casually arched, like he belongs there. Like this office has always been his.

I pause in the doorway. Cross my arms. Let my weight shift against the frame, one brow arching just so.

"I always knew you were bad for him," I say, smooth as silk. Triumphant.

He doesn't startle.

Just straightens, slow and lazy, like a snake uncurling. Smirks at me—the kind of smirk that says *I already won, and I didn't even have to try.* One hand slides into his pocket. The other reaches for the bottle of whiskey sitting on the desk— the one I brought Grant Friday night.

Dante uncaps it, sniffs it once, then lifts it slightly in my direction.

"From you, I take it?" he says.

I nod, stepping into the office. Carefully. Keeping the desk between us.

He glances at the label. "Always did have good taste," he muses. "A drink?"

He already has one of the crystal tumblers from the silver tray in hand.

I decline. "A little early for me."

His smile shifts. Not polite. Not charming. He makes a face like something sour just crossed his tongue—like *me.*

He pours himself a generous glass and throws it back

like water, his eyes never leaving mine. Cold. Calculating. No pretense of civility between us anymore.

He sets the glass down with a soft *clink.* The sound of tension. Of lines being drawn.

I glance at my watch.

"I've always known you had something up your sleeve," Dante says, voice low, casual. "I have to give you credit, though. I still don't know what it is."

His gaze is unreadable. But I see the twitch in his jaw. The awareness.

This is the match I've been preparing for.

It was always going to come down to me and Dante.

He's lingered around Grant like a parasite from the beginning. A leech feeding off the Harrow legacy, riding on charm and smirks and backroom deals. But I've seen through him since day one.

"Looks like we've both been playing the same game," I say coolly. "Though I have a pretty good idea of what you intend to get out of all this."

His brow lifts, ever so slightly. "And what's that?"

I motion around the room. Around the firm.

"All this, of course. *Marchesi and Harrow* stripped down to just the *Marchesi* name on the building. You, standing beside Grant like some conquering hero. And him? Too blind to see the knife you're waiting to drive into his back."

Dante's smile turns slow. Dangerous. "Lacks creativity," he says. "But not too far off."

I step closer. One heel clicks. Then another. I hold his gaze like a challenge.

"Well," I say, tilting my head. "We both know neither of us is going to be the first to back down. So how about a wager?"

His interest flickers, but he masks it well. "And here I thought you were a walking stick-up-the-ass."

I laugh. It's sharp. Humorless.

I reach for the bottle, pouring two fingers of whiskey into a second glass.

He watches me, intrigued now, his hand already moving to refill his own.

I raise my glass slightly. "To the best player."

He lifts his own in response. "May the best man win."

"Or woman," I correct, voice soft but steel beneath it.

He drinks.

I don't.

I lift the glass to my lips, hover, and then... set it down untouched.

His eyes track the motion.

A flicker. A subtle shift in his expression. The swallow a little slower this time.

I smile sweetly and let him wonder.

Because I am playing the long game. And he has no idea when the game actually started.

I watch him for a moment longer—Dante, still leaning against Grant's desk like he owns the place—and the silence stretches between us, thick with challenge.

I tilt my head. "So? What were you doing rooting through Grant's drawers?"

"Mm, not that easy." He shrugs, casual. "Tell me yours and I'll tell you mine."

I glance at my watch again.

Almost time.

It can't hurt anything now to be a little honest. It's not like it will matter in a moment or two.

I pretend to think it over, tap a finger to my chin like I'm weighing the cost. "Sure. Why not."

"I'm also going for the firm," I say lightly. "I know. A little anticlimactic, right?"

He narrows his eyes but stays quiet. Watching.

"But you know," I continue, picking up the bottle and walking toward the bar, "it's the journey, not the destination. That's where all the fascinating things happen."

Dante blinks, clearly confused now.

I sigh, smiling. "I suppose I don't have to talk in riddles. You won't tell anyone anyway."

He coughs once, as if he didn't anticipate it. "Putting a lot of faith in my ability to keep a secret."

I flash him a smile—wide, wicked, absolutely sincere.

"Dead men tend to keep the best secrets."

His face falters and turns white as the grave.

I dump the contents casually down the sink, letting the glug of the liquor—and the poison it holds—disappear down the drain.

"You know," I say cheerfully, "it took me a trial or two to really perfect the dosing. But I was always excellent in chemistry."

I walk the room slowly, hands trailing along the bookshelves, the edge of the credenza, the back of Grant's chair. And all the while, Dante just stands there—watching me like he's starting to piece together a puzzle far too late.

"I poisoned them at the same time, you know," I say, like we're sharing secrets over coffee. "My parents. Slipped it into their wine. One right after the other."

"My father fell like a brick."

I sigh.

"Too quickly. Not dead yet, but gone. It was disappointing to think he didn't suffer."

Dante starts to cough.

Subtle, at first.

Then sharper. Harder.

"I wanted it to draw out a little. As you are experiencing right now," I continue, circling the room like I'm giving a TED Talk. "So I lowered the dose for Mom—but that backfired. It was a little too low and she vomited most of it. Even got out a call to 911 before she started seizing."

I wipe my finger along the bookshelf, as if there would be dust to collect, and pause on the picture of Grant's mother.

"I had to improvise and got the satisfaction I was looking for when I bashed my father's head in. My mother was right there. She got soaked in his blood while she went mindless. It was cathartic to watch. Then there was my acting—slamming my head against the wall and the *my-mother-tried-to-kill-me* sob story. I had to get out of there before the police arrived."

I chuckle, thinking back on the reactions when I first started reciting what had happened. No one ever questioned it.

"You know the rest of that story. She lived. If you can call it that."

"Now she sits in an asylum—slumped, drooling, blinking once every thirty seconds. They say she's still in there. Knows what's happening around her."

I tilt my head.

"That gives me some satisfaction. I visit her every week. I remind her who I am. What I did. I want her to see me. Her daughter. The one who almost killed her."

Dante stumbles back.

His glass drops from his hand and shatters against the floor.

He gasps—mouth open, sucking at the air like it's been stolen.

I keep going.

"But plans change over time. So I had to adapt."

He drops to a knee.

One hand clutching his chest as foam touches the corner of his mouth.

"I needed to be seen here at the firm. Elevated. And the old CFO was past his prime anyhow. He should have retired ages ago, but he was also a horny bastard. Just perching on his desk, showing a little leg, and he'd drink anything you gave him. Then die, nice and quietly."

Dante is quickly becoming a mess. It really is gross to watch, so I look away—out at the city skyline.

"When I came running to Grant's—fake tears and all—I didn't plan on walking in on the two of you seconds from fucking, though. It was too good. I didn't even have to lie. Just gasped, loud and wounded, and watched Grant unravel. He's always so predictable."

"All I had to do was be patient after that. Keep driving the wedge. Keep feeding the doubt. And wait."

I take a seat in Grant's chair, fingers steepled, watching the show and trying not to listen to the sounds of suffocation. "Oh, lord. You're foaming."

Pinching the bridge of my nose, I keep going with my little confessional. It really is a cathartic moment to let it all out to someone.

"As I was saying—you made things difficult. Always hovering around Grant, whispering poison in his ear. I worked hard to drive that wedge between you two. The Vegas hot mic. The staged photo leaks. All necessary escalations. But cutting your brakes?" I grin. "That one was just for fun. Too bad you didn't die in that wreck like you were supposed to."

He collapses fully now—spasming. Seizing. Eyes bulging in panic. Muscles twitching as he suffocates on nothing.

"Now you're going to die in agony. And that's your punishment. A fitting one, if I may."

His limbs jerk once—twice—then still.

Silence falls.

I take a breath and walk toward him, my heels careful on the tile. I kneel beside him and brush a lock of hair back from his damp forehead.

"Fucking finally," I whisper, looking over the corpse.

With Dante out of the way, Grant will come back to me —just like he always does. He'll lean on me in his grief, seek comfort in the one person who's never truly left his side. He'll marry me, trust me, give me everything without even realizing it's already mine.

And then, in time, he'll meet his own unfortunate end.

I'll be the devastated widow, of course. The sole bene-factor of his estate.

The firm. The wealth. The mansion.

The Harrow name will be mine.

Exactly as it always should have been.

The door slams open with the force of a tidal wave.

Eve. Grant. Frankie.

They barrel in like the walls themselves are crumbling, and for a second—I actually think they might be.

I snap to my feet, heart hammering in my chest.

"He—I think he's dead—I just found him—" I gasp, voice shaking. Just enough. Wide eyes, trembling lip. Years of performance, rehearsed panic, all summoned in a single breath.

But Eve doesn't even flinch. Her voice cuts like a scalpel as she heads to Grant's desk and removes something from its underside.

"Stop being dramatic. He's not dead."

What?

Behind me, Dante chuckles first, then opens his eyes. Sits up, wiping his mouth on his shirt.

No.

"You could've let me ride it out a little longer," he mutters with a lazy smirk. "It was sensational acting."

No. No, no, no—this isn't right. He should be dead.

"Did you take a seltzer to foam at the mouth?" Frankie shakes her head in disbelief. "Method acting. I respect it."

"Why, thank you." He actually bows his head as mine

implodes. "I thought it was an authentic touch. Thanks to Eve for discovering the poison."

My body feels locked. The air around me warps. I don't move. I can't. My thoughts scream at me to run, but my limbs won't obey. Every second stretches wide and horrible, the floor tilting underneath me like a broken carousel.

Eve holds out a slim black recorder, held aloft in her palm like a gavel.

"We recorded you," she says, voice laced with quiet triumph. "Confessing to murder. Several of them, actually. Attempted murder. Poisoning. Fraud."

No.

Dante stands fully now, brushing imaginary dust from his pants.

"That's twice now you've tried to kill me," he says, then clucks his tongue. "And during Pride Month? That's just mean. Honestly? Feels a little homophobic."

No. That fucking asshole. No!

I lunge. Everything inside me snapping into motion. I need to leave.

If I can just reach the door—if I can just make it to the elevator—I can disappear. I can still fix this. I always fix it.

But I don't make it.

Eve's foot shoots out, tripping me. My head smacks the marble floor, blood blooming on my tongue. I scream, half fury, half disbelief.

This is not how it's supposed to happen.

Grant grabs me—ruthless, unflinching. My arm is bent behind me, my face pushed down onto the floor. Cool marble against hot skin. The taste of copper floods my mouth.

The room explodes in noise. Shouts. Footsteps. Cuffs. But it's Grant's voice that cuts through everything. Quiet. Deadly.

"Game's over, Corrine. And you lost."

No.

Officers take over, their hands replacing Grant's as metal snaps tight around my wrists.

No.

This wasn't how it ends.

I feel the fury coiling in my gut, sticky and black. Police officers pull me up, and I'm upright on two feet. Warm, thick blood drips down my chin, and I watch it splat on the white marble at my feet.

"Why us?" Grant asks.

His voice is rough. Breaking. Like it costs him to ask.

"Why, Corrine?"

I look at him, swallowing the blood in my mouth.

And I smile.

Because he wants to know.

There is a reason.

There's always a reason.

Something old. Sharp. Sacred. Something I wrapped in silk and buried deep.

And if I gave it to him—if I handed it over like some desperate confession—he'd get to make sense of it all. Find closure. Heal.

No.

He doesn't get that.

I can still win this.

This one, final thing.

So, I smile wider.

Let the blood coat my teeth like war paint. Let the moment stretch, linger, choke.

And I say nothing.

Because torment makes a lovely inheritance.

And he can live with it.

Rot without ever knowing.

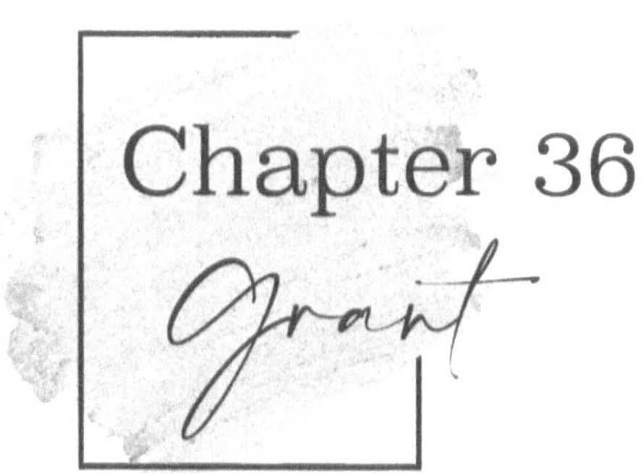

Chapter 36

Grant

The Harrow estate hasn't changed. The lawn is still perfect, the hedges trimmed with surgical precision, and the porch lights cast the same golden glow they always have. But as I pull up the drive and step out of the car, a heaviness settles over me—a weight that doesn't come from the air or the sky but from memory.

Everything looks normal.

But it feels different.

Not loud or obvious. Just... off. As if the house is holding its breath. As if it knows what today is, too.

He opens the door before I knock.

"Grant," he says, voice warm, familiar. "Glad you made it."

I offer a nod in return, stepping inside. The door clicks shut behind me, and suddenly I'm sixteen again—lost in the echo of the day that split my life in two.

"You all right, son?"

His question is casual, but his eyes are already scanning me for the answer.

"I need to talk to you," I say. "About Mom."

The words hit like a small detonation. His expression stills. The practiced warmth fades into something fractured. Like it always does when someone mentions Mom.

"Of course," he replies after a pause. "Come into the study."

He turns, leading the way down the familiar corridor. We move in silence. Not awkward—but deliberate. Like neither of us wants to interrupt the ghosts still whispering through the halls.

The study is as it's always been. Dimly lit. Lined with old books, framed accolades, and the soft crackle of a fire already burning in the hearth—even in the heat of June.

He moves to the liquor cart, lifting the decanter. The soft chime of crystal echoes, but I don't follow him in yet.

I stop just past the doorway, my attention snagged by the stretch of wall to the right of the entrance—plain, unre-markable. I've passed it thousands of times. Never once looked at it. Never knew how significant it was. But tonight, it pulls at me.

Beyond it, I can make out the foyer. The curve of the staircase. The marble floor that glints beneath the chande-lier. I know exactly where she turned and ran up the stairs for the last time.

I know the spot where she fell.

Where she looked at me before she took a final breath.

"Grant?"

My father's voice pulls me back. He's holding two glasses of whiskey, one extended toward me.

I turn to him, take it with a nod.

"Yeah."

We sit in the wingback chairs that have faced each other for decades. As a boy, they made me feel small. Tonight, they feel like prisons.

I lift the glass to my lips and let the whiskey burn a trail down my throat. It's not courage exactly, but it's close enough.

My father settles into the chair across from me, the fire casting shadows that flicker along the edges of his face. He lifts his glass but doesn't drink, watching me like he's waiting for a storm to hit.

"What's on your mind, son?"

What a fucking understatement.

I set my glass down, the sound sharp against the lacquered wood. My hand moves to the inside of my suit jacket, pulling free the short stack of photographs. They're enlarged. Matte finish. Every detail crisp. Unforgiving.

I toss them onto the table between us. Watch as they fan out—sliding just far enough for him to see a flash of skin, a desk, a face he once knew far too intimately.

He frowns, reaching for them slowly, carefully setting his own drink aside as he pulls his reading glasses from his breast pocket. He slips them on with deliberate grace, like this is just another contract, just another negotiation.

"What are these?" he murmurs.

I don't answer. Not directly.

"I'm sure you'll recognize them."

He picks up the first photo.

At first, he blinks like he doesn't understand what he's seeing. Then the color starts to drain from his face. A flicker of disbelief, followed by something that looks too much like fear—and worse—recognition.

I don't let up.

"They tell quite the story, don't they, Father?"

He exhales sharply through his nose. Grim now. His expression collapses inward as he sets the photo down with a trembling hand.

"Grant—"

"She was sixteen."

The words cut out of me like a blade, low and venom-laced. My breath comes harder now, like the effort of keeping it all in has become too much.

"That first one?" I nod at the photo nearest to him. "That's you. Laying Corrine out on your desk. Your head between the legs of a sixteen-year-old schoolgirl."

His mouth opens. Closes. Then—

"You don't understand, Grant—"

"Oh, don't I?" I lean forward, voice trembling, fury riding the edges of every syllable. "But you didn't have enough? Mom was picking me up from school, and the next photo—"

I stand suddenly, pointing behind me toward the study's doorway. Toward the blank expanse of wall that will never be blank again.

"—that's you. Right there. Your mouth on her breast. Your hand up her skirt."

He flinches, and I fucking hate him for it.

The tears come before I can stop them, burning down

my face in silence. I can't even wipe them away. My voice is shaking, gutted, nearly unrecognizable.

"She saw you."

He rises now, slow but insistent.

"Son, there's more to this—there's a lot more you don't know."

But I'm already standing. Already unraveling.

"Oh, I know it all." My voice cracks, louder now. "I know it all and I wish I could cut it out of my mind forever."

The words rip through the room, spit flying from my lips as my chest heaves with the weight of it. Of years spent trying to make sense of something that never had any.

"I thought she was upset with me." My voice breaks. A sound I don't even recognize. "But she wasn't. She saw you."

"She walked in. Saw everything."

"That's why she ran upstairs. That's why she opened my door already crying. She didn't say anything, but I knew something was wrong. I thought it was me."

"This whole time, I thought I killed her." I let that truth hang between us—shame and sorrow curdling into rage.

"But she saw you," I whisper. "She fucking saw you."

I reach for the glass, and throw it.

The glass explodes against the back wall of the fireplace, shards catching the light as they scatter into flame. The whiskey hisses, sizzling as it hits the embers.

A fitting sound, I think, for the truth I'm about to lay at his feet.

"Corrine stayed home from school that day," I say, my voice low. Controlled.

"You two had a lot of fun, didn't you? So much fun that

you didn't hear Mom or me come home. Didn't hear her heels on the floor. You didn't hear her open your study door."

He says nothing.

His fingers twitch around the rim of his glass.

"But you heard her gasp," I continue, pacing slowly now. "You heard the shock in your wife's voice as she walked in on you. Her husband. Molesting the orphan girl she brought into our home to foster."

He opens his mouth to speak, but I cut him off before he can even form a word.

"And instead of going after her—your wife—you were a selfish bastard. You yelled at Corrine to go to her room, and you ran straight to the security system. Straight to the cameras so you could erase what you did."

My fists are clenched at my sides, nails biting into my palms.

"But Corrine didn't go to her room. She waited at the top of the stairs. Hid around the corner. And when Mom came running back—shattered, sobbing—Corrine pushed her."

My throat tightens. A tear slips free.

"She pushed her."

I swallow hard, trying to hold the rest in, but the grief surges up anyway, hot and sharp.

My breath hitches.

My vision blurs.

"I thought she was upset with me," I say quietly.

"I thought I'd done something wrong."

He shifts in his chair, pain etched into the lines of his face.

"Son…"

I glance at the fire, at the dying embers flickering through smoke.

"She was so obsessed with you… so twisted from what you did to her, that she thought if Mom was gone, you'd finally be hers."

He looks stricken, pale and trembling. But I don't let up.

"She was my age," I hiss. "She was your friend's daughter. How the fuck could you?"

"She was confused," he murmurs. "Grant… Corrine was very confused at that time—"

"No," I snap. "She wasn't. She was already a killer before she ever set foot in this house."

He stares at me, bewildered.

"What are you talking about?"

"Oh, you didn't know?" I laugh, but it's hollow.

Jagged.

"She killed her parents just to come live here. With you."

He flinches. The truth cuts.

"She pursued me," he mutters, jaw clenched. "She seduced me. I told her no—again and again—"

"Don't you dare," I growl, stepping closer. "Don't you dare put this on her. She was a child, and she was broken because you broke her. You groomed her for years. You preyed on her."

"I read her diaries." I lean over him now, shaking. My voice a menacing whisper.

The fear in his eyes makes me want to kill him. Because now he realizes, I know his other secret. How sick he really is.

"When did it start, Dad? She spent so many nights in this house when we were little. How young was she when you first went into her room?"

His mouth opens, but no sound comes.

He slumps back into the chair, hands over his face, and begins to sob.

I kneel beside him—not in comfort, but to see his shame up close.

"You molested her," I say, my voice barely above a whisper. "You twisted her mind until she thought the abuse meant love. Then you discarded her—because she got too old."

"No," he says hoarsely. "No—"

"Don't lie," I snap. "I have the evidence. Pictures. Diaries. She stopped coming over when we were thirteen. But she never let go. You has already made sure of that."

"She thought she belonged to you," I go on. "She believed that if she waited long enough, you'd come for her. And when you didn't—when you tried to push her away—she spiraled."

"She killed her parents knowing Mom would take her in. That's how calculated she was. That's how obsessed. And how long did it take, huh?" I stand.

"How long until you were back in her bed?"

His voice is wrecked when he shouts back, still sobbing.

"She pursued me!" He jabs a finger into his chest. "I told her no! I told her no! She kept pushing, and I gave in. Is that what you want to hear? That I'm weak? That I—gave in?"

"It was a mistake."

I stare at him like I've never seen him before.

"A mistake is forgetting an anniversary," I say. "Burning dinner."

I look at the portrait of my mother over the fireplace, her smile soft and steady. My voice drops.

"You molested a girl for years. You warped her. Drove her to madness. And people died because of it. Mom died. *Your* wife. *My* mother."

I stare up at her, eyes burning.

"And I never noticed it before... the necklace Corrine always wears. The one she fidgets with when she lies." I laugh again, this time lower. Bitter.

"It was Mom's. She ripped it from mom's neck as she pushed her over the railing."

I look back at him slowly, my voice shaking.

"And while you were pretending to weep—"

"I did weep!" he shouts, standing. "I mourned her!"

I stare at him like the words are filth.

"You're a monster," I yell back. "You're not capable of such things."

I stare at him. At the pathetic, crumpled man hunched in the leather chair like he's the victim here. Like the weight of his sins is something he was burdened with—not something he chose.

"You mourned her?" My voice is hoarse. Raw. "You mourned the woman you let die so you could cover your filthy little secret?"

He doesn't answer. Just shakes his head, fingers clawing into his scalp like he can dig the truth out and make it disappear.

"I was scared."

"You were a coward."

He sobs again, but I've gone numb. There's nothing left inside me but ash and acid.

"You don't get to cry," I whisper. "Not after what you've done. Not after what you drove her to. You broke two girls. One is dead. The other's a murderer. And you? You get to sit here and cry?"

He collapses forward, arms resting on his knees, chest heaving.

I take one final look at him. The monster. The man I called Father and I want to vomit. I want to burn this place to the ground and the ghosts that live here.

I can't breathe.

The walls feel like they're closing in, dragging me back into memories I've spent years trying to forget. I step away, moving toward the tall windows that line the far end of the study. I need space. Air. Proof that there's still a world outside this house. That not everything is rotting behind its polished veneer.

Through the glass, the estate grounds stretch out beneath the gray afternoon sky—manicured hedges, marble statues, the gravel path I used to race down on my bike. It looks the same. But nothing is.

"I had her arrested," I say, my voice low, steady.

Behind me, I hear him inhale sharply.

"Corrine's in custody. She's talking." I pause, not turning around. "I've turned everything over to the police. They're on their way."

Another breath. This one staggered. Wet with grief or fear—or both.

"I just wanted to see your face," I add. "Look into your eyes while you tried to deny it. While you tried to pretend you were still a man."

I let the silence sit between us like a corpse.

Then I walk away.

Every step through the halls of Harrow Estate feels like shedding a skin I've worn too long. The air feels stagnant and stale, as if even the house knows something's changed. That the rot has finally been exposed.

By the time I reach the front door, my heart has slowed. My lungs fill easier. The air tastes different. Cleaner.

Outside, the wind lifts the edge of my coat, and in the distance, I hear the sirens. Wailing through the stillness, growing louder by the second.

With one foot in the car, one hand on the hood and the other holding the door, I watch. Wind blows the leaves, and a bird flies past as if nothing is happening here.

As if this isn't a house of horror.

Just as I'm about to slide into my car, a crack slices into the setting evening. An unmistakable flash shoots out of the study window and is gone just as quickly as it came. The boom of a gunshot echos into nothing.

The leather seat complains as I sit. The shutting of the car door is a far louder click than I've ever heard. Then nothing. Silence as I start the engine and drive away.

As I leave Harrow Estate in the rearview, I don't check the mirror because there's nothing left to see.

Not for me.

Not anymore.

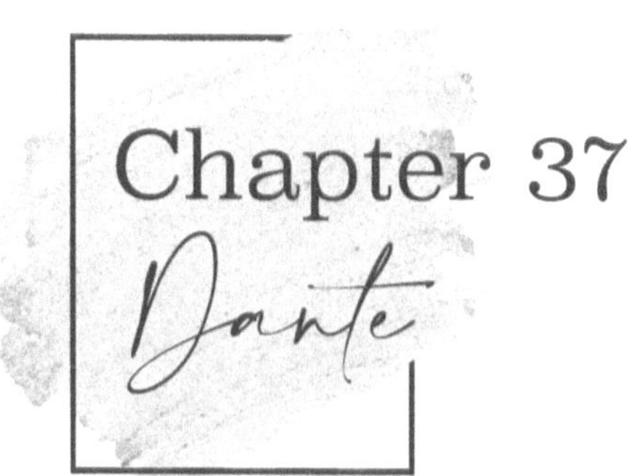

I sit low in the armchair, the highball glass sweating against my palm. Whiskey untouched. The ice has long since melted, but I haven't moved.

I'm watching the clock.

He wanted to go alone.

Told me this was something he needed to face by himself. Said it gently, with a hand on my chest and that stubborn set to his jaw. So I let him. I waited. I've been waiting—for the knock, the call, the anything that would tell me how it went.

Instead, I get silence.

For hours.

And then—finally—the door creaks open.

And the man I've been in love with for most of my life walks in.

He doesn't say a word.

Doesn't need to.

He looks like defeat made flesh—like a ruin barely held

together by bone and breath. His shoulders are slumped, his eyes glassy, the weight of everything he's carried etched into every slow, heavy step.

I'm already standing. The glass hits the table without care. I meet him halfway.

I take his face in both hands. His skin is cold.

"Grant," I whisper, but that's all I get out before I'm kissing him.

I mean for it to be soft. A welcome. A balm.

But he gasps into my mouth and clutches at me—fingers knotting in the back of my shirt, arms winding around my neck like he's afraid I'll vanish if he lets go.

He rises onto the balls of his feet, chasing the kiss, deepening it, pouring all the agony and ash and fury of today into me. And I take it. I drink it. I let him taste something other than grief, if only for a minute.

I pull him into me so there's no space left. No air. No past. Just heat and pressure and the ache of finally being needed this way.

I can feel him—every shiver, every unspoken plea pressed against me. We're both already hard. Already moving without direction, just instinct. His hips grind against mine like he's trying to forget his own name.

And maybe he is.

Maybe that's what this is.

He doesn't need comfort. Not now.

He needs to be burned down to nothing and built again from ash.

I can do that.

I will do that.

My hand tangles in his hair, the other sliding down his back to grip his waist, grounding him as he ruts against me like he can't stand not being skin-to-skin. I walk us backward, guiding him toward the bedroom, kissing him like a man who finally has permission to worship.

Because I will worship him. Every inch. Every scar.

Tonight, I'll strip him bare—not just his clothes but the haunted version of himself he brought back through that door.

And when he looks in the mirror tomorrow, he'll see something new.

Something clean.

Something loved.

Tonight, I'll give him exactly what he needs.

And every night after, if he'll let me.

The bedroom is already warm from the fire crackling in the glass-covered hearth. Shadows dance across the floor, flickering over the tall mirror that stands to the right— framed in black iron and old wood, like it's been waiting for this moment.

I guide him there, to the mirror.

To himself.

The floor cushions are arranged like I left them—thick and plush, pulled close to the fire. I'd planned for comfort. For conversation. A slow exhale after the weight of the day.

But Grant needs something else.

He needs to see.

I turn to face him. My fingers trail over the buttons of his shirt—slow, deliberate. "You're going to watch tonight," I say, voice low, calm. "Every second. Every sensation.

You're going to see exactly what I give you. What you deserve."

His breath stutters. His hands twitch at his sides.

"This," I murmur, undoing the first button, "isn't just about touch. It's about truth."

Each button undone is a peeling back of pain. A removal of shame. Guilt. Armor.

He lets me take it—his shirt, his belt, his pants. Piece by piece, I strip him until he's bare in the firelight, trembling and beautiful and so damn breakable.

I pull one of the pillows over, setting it in front of the mirror.

"Hands and knees," I tell him, my voice firmer now. "Head down, ass up. Face the mirror."

He obeys without a word, moving like his limbs are heavy with want and memory. He settles with his head on the pillow, thighs parted, his reflection raw and exposed. Vulnerable.

Perfect.

I kneel behind him, still fully dressed—dark slacks, sleeves rolled to my elbows. Deliberately untouched.

Untouchable—until now.

My hands part his cheeks and I kiss each one. My thumb toys with the ring of muscle I'm going to devour tonight and he clinches. It makes my cock twitch.

My lips keep moving across his ass, kissing, sucking and licking as I move to his center. I lean in, dragging my tongue between them with a slow, deep stroke.

Grant shudders violently.

"Fuck," he gasps, knuckles going white as he grips the edge of the cushion.

But I don't stop. Don't relent.

I devour him.

Filthy, wet, merciless—each pass of my tongue staking a claim. Marking him from the inside out. His thighs tremble. His groans crack apart in the air, desperate and sharp.

I reach under him with one hand, wrap around his cock, and stroke—slow. Steady. Measured.

He chokes on a moan, forehead pressed to the cushion, his reflection a portrait of unraveling: flushed cheeks, bitten lips, eyes fluttering half-lidded with shame and need.

And still, I don't stop.

Because he needs to see this.

Needs to witness the way he breaks for me. How his body pleads without a single word.

I feel it—the way he's spiraling, muscles tightening, hips twitching like he's fighting the edge. Trying to hold on.

"Dante—" he whimpers.

But I pull back.

Lick my lips. Sit back on my heels.

His body jolts, instinctively pushing back toward me, but I grip his hips and hold him still.

"Not yet," I murmur, voice thick. "You'll come when I say. When I decide you're ready to let go."

His breath hiccups—a sound caught between surrender and torment—and it sounds beautiful.

Because tonight, I'm not just giving him pleasure.

I'm remaking him.

I don't give him time to overthink.

One breath later, I shift—gripping Grant beneath his hips and flipping him with ease, holding him nearly upside down, his shoulders and head brushing the floor while I stay kneeling, seated back on my heels.

His ass is right in my face. A gift. A fucking altar.

"Open those whore legs for me," I rasp, voice wrecked with want. "Let me keep eating what's mine."

Grant moans, low and broken, as his thighs fall apart helplessly, spread wide with nowhere to go. He's suspended —his body arched and hanging in my grip, every muscle taut with anticipation, every inch of him mine.

Obscene. Perfect.

I don't wait. I dive in.

My tongue slides over him again, deeper this time, hungrier. I lap and lick and groan into his flesh as I rim him open, working him loose with slow, deliberate strokes. He's shaking now, sobbing breathless moans into the floor as I suck his balls into my mouth, one at a time, lavishing them with wet heat until he's delirious.

"Dante—fuck, don't stop—please don't stop," he pants, voice cracked and begging.

"I'm not stopping," I growl against him. "Not until I taste every inch of you. Until you forget anything but my mouth and what it's doing to you."

I devour him like he's the only thing I've ever wanted.

His cock is leaking, twitching untouched, and I know he's close—too close—so I ease him down, just enough to shift, not enough to give him relief.

He whines when I let go, and I smile.

I push him gently back, keeping his legs spread, his body trembling with need as I reach for the button of my slacks. One flick, then another, and I free myself—my cock springing forward, hard and aching.

"Hold on," I tell him, wrapping one of his thighs in my hand. "Keep your legs open. I want you to watch."

He obeys, breath hitching as I slide between his thighs, my cock dragging over his balls, over the spit-slick stretch of his skin. I align our cocks—his flushed and dripping beneath mine, both of them thick and swollen, pointing toward his face in the mirror.

He holds himself inverted with a grip on my legs. With both hands, I take our cocks, side by side and hard as fuck. I stroke us slow, long pulls. Then harder.

"Look at that," I murmur, eyes locked on the mirror. "Look at what you do to me. How hard I get just touching you. Just hearing those filthy little moans."

Grant groans, loud and desperate. His hands dig into the pillows as he bucks into my fist.

"You like this?" I ask, stroking them both in long, possessive strokes. "You like when I rub our cocks together like this? Make you feel every inch of what you do to me?"

"Y-yes," he chokes. "Feels so fucking good, Dante—don't stop."

"Yeah?" I lean down, voice dark and low in his ear. "You wanna come like this? Both our cocks on your face? Want to taste the mess we make together?"

His body jerks. He's so fucking close I can feel it in how he shakes.

"I want it," he gasps. "Please. Please, Dante, make me come."

I tighten my grip, stroking faster now. Filthy sounds of slick skin and gasping breaths echo in the firelit room. Grant is falling apart beneath me—open, ruined, so fucking beautiful.

Just before he breaks, I cup his jaw, force his chin up with my palm so he has to look.

"Come for me," I command. "Come on your own mouth. Don't flinch. Don't fucking hide."

His eyes flutter open. Wide. Vulnerable. And he obeys.

He comes, a strangled cry ripping from his throat, cock spurting over his flushed skin, some of it catching on his tongue, dripping over his lips. His thighs tremble as he shakes through it, hands limp, spent and shaking.

I follow a heartbeat later—groaning deep in my chest as I watch him take it, let it hit him, claim him. I pump through it, milking every drop until we're both coated in it.

Grant's tongue darts out. He licks his lips. Swallows.

And I damn near lose my mind.

"Good fucking boy," I growl, hand still wrapped around our cocks. "Look at you. Messy and mine. Fucking perfect."

Grant's still trembling when I ease him down fully onto the cushions. His head finds a pillow, and his chest rises in shallow, staggered breaths, skin flushed and streaked in our mess.

I'm on him again in a second—crawling over his body.

He barely has time to catch a breath before my mouth is crashing onto his, tongue sliding in deep, invading his space, claiming it like I've claimed every other part of him tonight. His lips are sticky, still salty-sweet from the orgasm I forced onto his face, and I groan into the kiss as we taste it together.

He moans, low and wrecked, as I lick into him, both of us swallowing the lingering traces of his release—his body twitching beneath mine, already hard again.

"God, you taste so fucking good," I growl against his lips, biting his bottom one before pulling back.

Grant chokes on a gasp as I reach between us, drag two fingers through the slick mess on his chest. I smear it lazily, then lean down and lick it from his skin—long, slow swirls of my tongue across his ribs, over his pecs, chasing every drop.

"Dante," he breathes, his voice thready, helpless.

"Shh," I murmur, closing my mouth over one of his nipples, sucking hard until he gasps and arches up into me. "You're not done. Not even close."

My free hand slides between his legs, spreading him again, and I press one slick finger to his hole, pushing in slow. He's already loose from my tongue, from my mouth, from the wreck I made of him.

His body yields like it's waiting for me.

"Fuck," he hisses, eyes fluttering shut. "More."

"You want more?" I murmur, licking over to his other nipple, biting it just enough to make him cry out.

"Yes. Please—Dante—"

I slide in the second finger, twisting, curling. His thighs shake again.

"That's it," I croon. "Open up for me. So eager. So desperate. You love this, don't you?"

He nods, broken and breathless. "Yes. Fuck—yes."

"You like when I stuff you full? Stretch you open with my fingers like the perfect little slut you are?"

His moan is almost a sob. "God, yes—don't stop."

I start fucking him with my fingers, slow and deliberate, scissoring him open with the ease of someone who knows this body like a prayer. My mouth finds his again, swallowing every gasp as I work him.

"You're such a good boy," I rasp against his lips. "So needy. So fucking filthy. Letting me use your body like this."

"Yours," he moans. "I'm yours."

"Damn right, you are."

I angle my fingers deeper, grinding into that perfect spot inside him until he jerks—hips stuttering, cock leaking again.

"That's it," I whisper. "You feel that? That's where I'm gonna fuck you next. Gonna drive into that spot over and over until you forget your own fucking name."

He's trembling—every muscle tight, every breath ragged.

"You're gonna come for me again," I tell him. "Gonna let me finger-fuck your tight little hole while you make a mess all over yourself again, just like a good little whore."

"Please," he gasps. "Please, Dante—don't stop—fuck—"

I don't.

I keep my fingers deep, thrusting hard now, relentless. I kiss him as he shatters—his body going stiff, then trembling as he comes again, untouched, crying out into my mouth like he's never come so hard in his life.

And maybe he hasn't.

Because I don't just fuck his body.

I break it.

I worship it.

And I make sure he knows it's mine.

I don't know how it's possible, but after coming twice —once on my own fucking face—I'm still greedy for more.

And judging by the look in Dante's eyes, he's just getting started with me.

The second orgasm still pulses through my body in warm, flickering waves. My limbs are slack, my brain hazy. It should be enough. It would be enough—if it were anyone else.

But this is Dante.

And Dante doesn't just give me pleasure. He rebuilds me with it.

He gives me a few seconds—just long enough to tear his shirt over his head and slide his pants down his thighs, his body carved from muscles and worship. His cock is hard, slick at the tip, thick and perfect.

God, I'm the luckiest bastard alive.

Still kneeling, still back on his heels, Dante waits for me

—his presence steady and open. I lift myself, legs spread to either side of him, and lean in to lick a path up his chest. His skin is salty and warm beneath my tongue. I take one of his nipples into my mouth, sucking gently, then harder, teasing him with my teeth.

He groans, low and deep, letting his head tip back as his hands thread through my hair.

"Fuck," he mutters. "That feels amazing."

I grin against his skin, greedy for more—but he only lets me have my way for a heartbeat before I feel the press of his slick hand on my hip, the shift of his other hand out of sight.

He was buying time. Lubing his cock while I distracted myself with worship.

And fuck, that's hot.

He wipes his hand on his discarded shirt, then grabs my wrist and pulls me to him. His palm curls around my thigh, guiding me forward.

"Come here, baby," he murmurs, voice like warm velvet. "Come ride my fat cock."

The words punch the breath right out of me.

I plant my feet on the floor, straddling him again, arms wrapped around his shoulders, forehead pressed to his.

He fists the base of his dick, steady and patient. "You ready for me?"

I nod, dazed. "Always."

The crown of him presses to my hole, and I let gravity guide me down. We groan in unison as his thick head pops inside, my whole body stretching around him.

"Holy fuck," I breathe. "So big."

"Taking me so well," he praises, voice tight. "Just like you're made for me."

Once I'm fully seated, balls to skin, I rock my hips—grinding in his lap, feeling him everywhere. He holds me steady, hands gripping my hips, thrusting up in sync with every roll of my body.

It's a rhythm. A prayer. Our eyes locked, our mouths parted, our souls—entwined.

"Feels so good, baby," Dante murmurs, cupping my face as he drives up into me. "I love you. God, I love you so fucking much."

"I love you too," I pant, riding him harder now. "But I need more. Need it rough. Need to feel you lose control."

His lips curve into something dark and reverent.

And then he gives it to me.

He shifts me again, lifting me like I weigh nothing, repositioning me in front of him on all fours.

"Give me this ass, Lucciolina," he growls. "I need to fuck you hard."

My cock twitches. "Fuck," I groan. "Yes. Do it."

"Knees together. Ass out," he commands.

I obey instantly, and he slides back in with a low, guttural moan.

This angle—Jesus. I see stars. My forehead drops to the pillow, my spine arching as he pounds into me like a man possessed.

Each thrust slams pleasure into me so deep I forget where I end, and he begins. My hands scrabble for purchase. His grip bruises my hips.

It's the fuck of my life.

But he's not done.

He pulls me upright again, settling me back against his chest, his cock never slipping free. His thighs bracket mine—thick and solid. His rhythm changes—deeper now, more controlled.

One arm wraps around my waist, his fist closing around my cock, stroking in time with his thrusts. The other hand rolls over my nipple, pinching, teasing—then moves up to my throat.

"Fuck, Grant," he pants. "Kiss me. I need to taste you."

I twist my head, meeting his mouth with mine—messy, desperate, perfect.

He moans into my lips, cock slamming up into me as he murmurs, "Arch that back for me, baby. I want to be so deep inside you."

I do.

"Watch how good I fuck you, bug," he groans, voice thick. "How we're made to fit together."

And we do.

Our bodies move in sync, thrust for thrust, stroke for stroke—a dance made only for us. We come together again, trembling in each other's arms, breathless and wrecked and whole.

But we don't stop right away.

We slow.

Our bodies continue to move in easy, perfect time. His cock still nestled deep inside me, his hands mapping every inch of my skin like he's committing it to memory.

We kiss—slow and reverent—as his fingers trace my ribs, my belly, my thighs.

I've never felt so full.

So safe.

So fucking loved.

And for the first time in my life, I don't feel like I'm performing.

I feel like myself.

"Now, *amore mio*."

He slowly slides out of me, his large, warm hand pushing me onto my hands and knees. He rubs my ass cheeks with reverence.

"Bear down."

He kisses one cheek, then spanks the other, pulling a surprised grunt from me that turns into a moan. He palms my ass, spreading me apart and blowing a cooling breath where he just destroyed me so fucking perfectly.

"Bear down and let me watch my cum drip from your slut ass."

MONDAY MORNING.

The office hums softly around us—phones ringing, footsteps muffled on polished floors. Outside, sunlight filters through the wide windows, golden and calm. It doesn't feel like a storm just passed. Doesn't feel like the kind of week that rewired my entire life.

But I know better.

Inside the conference room, it's just the three of us now —me, Dante, and Eve.

I stand near the window, sleeves rolled, coffee cooling on the table beside me. Dante lounges in one of the chairs, legs wide, toothpick dancing in the corner of his mouth and one arm slung along the backrest like he owns the room.

God, he looks fucking delicious.

And Eve—Eve stands at the head of the table like a goddamn general who already won the war. Cool. Composed. Dressed in Ledger red like blood never stains her.

"Contract's complete," she says. "Two weeks. Two clients. Results delivered."

There's a note of smug satisfaction in her voice—the kind she doesn't need to flaunt. She's already known the ending since the beginning.

"And murderer in custody." Dante adds.

"That is a freebie, baby." Eve winks.

Dante tips his head. "You make all your clients this happy?"

Eve doesn't blink. "Only the ones I care about."

He grins. I huff a quiet laugh.

But I can't stop thinking about it—how she figured Corrine out. How she found the thread that unraveled everything.

"How'd you know?" I ask. "How'd you figure her out?"

She walks to the sideboard, unhurried as always, and pours herself a glass of water like this is any other Monday.

"Corrine's last name at birth was Lachlan," she says. "After her father was murdered—and her mother almost was—she got adopted by some distant relatives upstate after she killed your mother."

She takes a sip.

"That's when she became Ashwood. New name, new records, new life."

I blink. "You found all that?"

"Once I had the right last name?" She shrugs. "A lot of doors opened."

She turns toward me, casual as sin. "Plus, I broke into her house and stole some things. Not to incriminate myself or anything."

Dante lets out a quiet laugh, shaking his head.

Eve continues, unfazed. "The newspaper clippings she kept weren't about you, by the way. They were about your father."

My stomach knots—slow and cold.

"Obsessively so," she adds. "Timelines. Quotes. Photos. She was still fixated on him. Even after all these years."

"And the rest was Jaxon," she says. "The drives were almost completely corrupted, but he worked a miracle— pulled just enough metadata to recover an old digital diary, partial surveillance files. It painted a full enough picture."

Once Eve told us everything, Dante was insistent on scanning the camera's of the office. He wanted to know what she had been up to these two weeks while we were trying to save our ass.

And it was nothing less than shocking.

The poisoned bottle she brought for me Friday. She was going to kill me. Get the last Harrow out of the way so she could be with my father.

That was her one true goal. Everything to get back to him.

"Well," I say, breaking some tension by glancing out at the city for a beat, "at least she won't be able to torment her mother anymore. If we can count one good thing coming out of this."

I exhale—long and slow. My pulse roars in my ears, but it's not panic. It's release.

"There's more than one good thing, in my book," she says.

I turn toward Eve, not sure what to say. There's no repayment for what she's done. What she gave us back.

"I don't think we could ever repay you," I murmur. "For any of it."

Eve smirks, still holding her water. "Don't worry," she says smoothly. "He paid me handsomely."

She winks at Dante.

I raise a brow just as she reaches into her bag and slides something across the table to me. A matte-black card. I pick it up and it's heavy in my palm.

Embossed in gold:

The Masquerade

Welcome to the Devil's Playground

I turn it over, but it's blank. "What is this?"

"Oh, no shit." Dante's grin grows wicked, looking at the card with a knowing gleam in his rich espresso eyes. "I'll tell you later, bug."

Why do I have a feeling this is something both terrifying and likely highly orgasmic?

Eve gathers her things and smooths her red mini. She looks between us like she's inspecting a job well done.

"You built something worth saving," she says. "Now don't fucking waste it."

She turns to Dante, leans down, and kisses his cheek. His hand slides up her thigh, and they smile at each other like devils who understand each other too well. She kisses him on the lips—brief, affectionate, gratuitous, almost.

"Take care of him," she says quietly.

"Forever," Dante replies—and his answer makes my stomach somersault.

"I better get an invitation to the wedding."

She makes her way to me, arms wrapping around my neck. I hold her tightly, nose pressed to her throat, inhaling her perfume like it's the last chapter of this chaos.

It kind of is.

"Will we see you again?" I murmur.

She pulls back, grinning. "I'm always for hire."

Then she kisses me. Open-mouthed. A little tongue. Just enough to say goodbye.

"I'll give you a discount," she whispers, "if you get this pretty mouth back on my pussy."

I laugh through my nose, heat crawling up my neck.

She reaches around, gives my ass a playful pinch, and heads for the door.

"I'm off, boys," she calls over her shoulder. "I've got a date with a sugar mama who wants to spoil me on her yacht for a month."

"Sounds tragic," Dante drawls.

Eve flips her hair and smirks. "Think of me in my time of misery as I drown in pussy and champagne."

The door closes behind her—soft. Final.

Silence returns, low and golden and warm.

I drop into the seat across from Dante. He hasn't moved, but his eyes are on me—rich, dark, gleaming with something that feels like a promise.

His arm still draped, his tempting body still sprawled. One brow arches, just a touch.

"So," I say, voice steady. "What's next?"

He smiles, and it feels like the last crack in my broken soul is healed by him.

"Whatever the fuck we want."

Welcome to
The Black Ledger

Where every desire has a price...
and every contract is final.

*Love The Rival's Obsession? Don't stop now.
The next Black Ledger book awaits...*

The Black Ledger
Billionaires

Check Out www.RebekahSinclairWrites.com for more!